Daytime was  nighttime

The wail of a siren jerked Dean out of a deep sleep. Cedar Wells had been so quiet, they might have been camping a hundred miles away from the nearest other humans, instead of sleeping in a motel at the edge of a town. In contrast, the blaring siren was almost deafening.

"That's not good," Sam said. He slipped out of his bed and started dressing.

"A siren is pretty much always bad news for someone," Dean agreed.

By the time they made it to the Impala—a gift from Dad, 1967, midnight black, newly rebuilt—the siren had faded into the distance. But they knew its direction of travel, through town and toward the Grand Canyon. Another couple of minutes later they could see flashing roof lights flickering through the trees up ahead.

Dean and Sam got out of the Impala and hurried to a driveway that led to a big white barn. A pickup truck was parked in the driveway, and beside it was the body of what must have been a man, probably not too long ago. The truck's driver's side door hung open. Blood had spattered up the side of the truck and onto the driver's seat, and the man's arm was hooked up over the step, but his throat was gone, along with the bottom half of his face, and something had opened his chest cavity. It looked like whatever had done that had been hunting for tender morsels, but Dean didn't spend a lot of time counting organs. He glanced long enough to estimate the damage, then looked away, sickened by the sight.

You could see a lot of carnage without ever growing to like it.

SUPERNATURAL Books
From HarperEntertainment

WITCH'S CANYON

NEVERMORE

THE SUPERNATURAL BOOK OF MONSTERS,
SPIRITS, DEMONS, AND GHOULS

ATTENTION: ORGANIZATIONS AND CORPORATIONS
Most HarperEntertainment paperbacks are available at special
quantity discounts for bulk purchases for sales promotions,
premiums, or fund raising. For information, please call or write:

**Special Markets Department, HarperCollins Publishers,
10 East 53rd Street, New York, New York 10022-5299.
Telephone: (212) 207-7528.   Fax: (212) 207-7222.**

SUPERNATURAL™
WITCH'S CANYON

Jeff Mariotte

Based on the hit CW series SUPERNATURAL
created by Eric Kripke

HarperEntertainment
An Imprint of HarperCollinsPublishers

This is a work of fiction. Names, characters, places, and incidents are products of the author's imagination or are used fictitiously and are not to be construed as real. Any resemblance to actual events, locales, organizations, or persons, living or dead, is entirely coincidental.

HARPERENTERTAINMENT
An Imprint of HarperCollins*Publishers*
195 Broadway,
New York, NY 10007.

ISBN: 978-0-06-137091-5
ISBN-10: 0-06-137091-6

First HarperEntertainment paperback printing: November 2007

Printed in the United States of America

Visit HarperEntertainment on the World Wide Web at
www.harpercollins.com

13

This novel is dedicated to Major John Wesley Powell, Clarence Dutton, Ed Abbey, Katie Lee, and everyone else who has gone into the Grand Canyon and Colorado Plateau country and described it for the rest of us. The river flows, the earth abides.

Acknowledgments

Without Eric Kripke, of course, all of the pages after this one would be blank.

Jared Padalecki, Jensen Ackles, and the rest of the massively talented cast and crew make the series one of the most entertaining on TV, and I'm honored to have been invited into their sandbox.

Great thanks go out to my family, to John Morgan and John Nee, to Howard Morhaim and Katie Menick, and to Cindy Chapman.

PROLOGUE

Cedar Wells, Arizona
December 5, 1966

From various houses along the block, Mike Tyler could hear the opening theme to *The Monkees* TV show. Its insistent notes made him hurry his step. He'd been at the Cedar Wells library doing research for an eighth-grade history report, and consumed by the books, had lost all track of time.

Now he had to rush home, and he'd still miss at least half of the program. It wasn't his favorite show—that particular honor fell to *Batman*—but it was his favorite show on Monday nights. His mom complained that he watched too much TV these days, but he didn't understand what that even meant. How could someone watch too much TV when great shows like *Star Trek*, *Green Acres*, *Lost in Space*, *Combat!*, and *The Rat Patrol* were on every night?

Not to mention the cool spy shows, like *Get Smart* and *Mission: Impossible* and *The F.B.I.* What bothered him was when his favorites were stacked up against each other, like *The Green Hornet* and *The Time Tunnel* on ABC Friday nights, while *Tarzan* and *The Man From U.N.C.L.E.* were on at the same time on NBC. He tried to flip back and forth sometimes, but his mom complained that he'd wear out the dial on their big Zenith. If he could figure out a way to watch one channel and then another, maybe Mom would have a legitimate complaint.

The Monkees was definitely catching on with Mike and his buddies at school. They could tell him at school tomorrow what the story was about, but he didn't want to miss the songs. When it ended, he'd leave the set on NBC for *I Dream of Jeannie*, then switch over to *The Rat Patrol* for a little army action before getting ready for bed.

He would have been home already if he'd taken his bike, but the streets had been a little icy, and he wasn't sure how many books he might end up checking out. As it happened, he had done more of his reading at the library than he expected, and he could have managed the books in his bike's basket.

He only had another two blocks to cover. He'd be home in time for the second song, if not the first. If his little sister Becky had claimed the set for *Gilligan's Island*, he would have to come up with a way to bribe or threaten her. He could almost see the house from here—would be able to, except for the Johnsons' Christmas decorations, which created a glow around their house from Thanksgiving night until the Saturday after New Year's, obstructing his view of everything beyond it on their side of the street.

He was about to step off the curb to cross the last street before home when he saw—almost sensed—a blur of movement out of the corner of his eye. Something near the back of Mrs. Izzi's house. The guys at school usually called her the creepy old lady, because she wore lots of black, sometimes with a shawl over her head, like she was in mourning. One rumor was that she'd had a son who was killed in Vietnam, but if so, it happened before she had moved onto Mike's street, and he'd never had a conversation with her to find out if it was true. Neither had his mom, who wasn't a widow but was divorced from his dad, and he lived in Virginia now so it was practically the same thing.

Mike turned to see what had caught his eye. It was just a guy, not much older than him. A teenager, maybe, dressed like he was coming home from a costume party. He had on a military-style coat. The street lamp didn't reach quite far enough, but it looked like the coat was dark blue, with gold braids on it. A gold stripe ran down the outside seam of his pants, which were tucked into high boots. On his head was a cowboy-type hat that looked to be the same dark blue. A saber hung from his belt, and he carried a rifle.

If it was a costume, it was a heck of a good one. The thing was, he was headed toward Mrs. Izzi's back door, and no one lived with Mrs. Izzi. That much Mike did know about her.

The other thing—and this made him let out a little gasp, against his will, because so far he didn't think the soldier had seen him—was that the guy was there one instant and then he kind of flickered, like when Becky messed with the rabbit ears during one of his programs. Then he was there again, and then he vanished into the shadows behind Mrs. Izzi's house.

Should I go to the front door and tell her there's someone in her backyard? he wondered. *Should I call the sheriff?*

Cops never listened to kids, though. Mike had been growing his hair out over the summer, and the last time he'd seen Sheriff Tait, at the swimming pool, the sheriff told him to get a haircut or wear a bathing cap. He'd laughed when he said it, but Mike could tell he meant it.

He decided to run home and let Mom make the call. He started to sprint, but he was barely across the street when he heard the first scream from Mrs. Izzi's.

Mike Taylor didn't know it, but what some would come to call the "forty-year" had already begun.

Again . . .

ONE

"That's a big hole."

"A big hole," Sam repeated.

"That's what I said. It's a big freakin' hole. And somehow that river got stuck inside it."

Sam shook his head sadly. His brother leaned casually on a railing, peering into the canyon. Across the way, the lowering sun's rays slanted in from the west, dripping gold paint across horizontal layers of pale rose, buff, and salmon strata of shale, limestone, and sandstone. Sometimes Sam had to wonder if Dad had destroyed Dean's soul altogether. "Dean, nature worked miracles for millions of years to create the Grand Canyon—the Colorado River's the reason it's there."

Dean turned slowly, fixing Sam with a steady

glare. From the way his mouth curled into a mischievous grin, Sam knew he'd been had. "Just because I didn't go to Stanford doesn't mean I'm an idiot, college boy," Dean said.

"I didn't say . . ." Sam paused, stuck. Dean loved to give him crap about having attended Stanford—and almost graduating prelaw—while Dean carried on the family business.

"Look, Sam, I know what made the Grand Canyon. I know about erosion. I even get why you wanted to stop here while we—"

"We were just passing so close."

"What did I just say? Dude, are you even listening to me?"

When Dean got in this kind of mood, there was no winning. After his years at college, away from his big brother, Sam had to learn Dean's habits and quirks all over again. These last months, riding around the country in Dean's precious Impala, he believed he had reacquainted himself with most of those traits, good and bad.

Didn't stop him from stepping right into it from time to time.

"It is pretty spectacular," Sam said, hoping to change the subject. Another glance at the opposite wall showed that in just minutes shifting light and shadow had altered the view as surely as if the Winchester brothers had moved to a different vantage point. Hints of pine and sage tickled Sam's nose on a whispered breeze from below; the same wind *shushed* through the branches of the firs and the gnarled junipers surrounding the overlook. "I'm glad we made the side trip."

"Me too," Dean said. He scratched his head, mussing his short brown hair. His leather jacket was zipped against the cold; the snow around his boots was hard-packed, a week old or more. "It's kinda cool."

"For a big hole."

"Am I wrong?"

"More like . . . incomplete," Sam said.

"You can give me detention. Oh, wait, that's right . . . you aren't the boss of me. So I guess you can just bite me."

"That's not happening," Sam said. "Maybe we should get on into town." Even as he said it, he recognized that Dean might take it as giving orders again. That was something he and Dean struggled with. Dean was older, and had stayed on the road with their dad while Sam turned his back on the family—at least, that was Dean's take on it. Sam's was that, having announced his intention to go to college, Dad had thrown him out, essentially disowning him. Dad's words, "Don't come back," had seemed plenty specific.

But now that Sam had rejoined the family business— and the brothers were left to run it themselves since their father's death—there had been friction between the two of them. Dean loved his little brother, and vice versa. But he didn't like being dictated to, and he had made that abundantly clear.

Which didn't mean it was easy for Sam to knock it

off. He had been on his own for a long time, and he was used to doing things his own way. Dean, having worked with Dad longer, was used to taking orders. More than that, he seemed to thrive on it, as if Dad had crushed the independent spirit he'd been born with. What was left behind was a Dean who Sam bossed around whether he meant to or not. Maybe it wasn't the natural order of things, but sometimes it felt that way to him.

Dean shot him a dark glance but didn't say anything. He pushed off the railing. "Let's hit it."

When they arrived, one other car had been parked on the gravel semicircle at the trailhead, but they hadn't seen its occupant anywhere. As they hiked back toward the parking area, not talking, Sam thought he heard something out of place. He stopped short, put a hand out to halt Dean. "Shh!"

"What?" Dean whispered.

"Listen." Not just wind through the pine needles, Sam was certain. "Someone's crying."

"Let's get out of here, then," Dean said. "That's not going to be any of our business."

"We don't know that."

"Yes we do," Dean argued. "We came here to go to Cedar Wells and stop people from getting killed. There aren't many things in life I am *more* positive about. I'm sorry for whoever's crying, but it's not what we're here for."

"What if it's a kid? Someone who got lost? How long can it take to check out?"

Dean rolled his eyes. In that instant, Sam could

still see Dean as he'd been at twelve, when that had been his response to almost every situation. He hadn't caught up to his older brother in height then—that hadn't come until Sam's sixteenth year—but he'd been closing in even then. Still, he had looked up to Dean, practically worshipping him, and Dean could cut him deep with one of those eye rolls. "Famous last words."

Without comment, Dean pointed at the PLEASE STAY ON PATH sign that Sam had stepped over. The crying was full-throated sobs now, as if the person— *a woman,* Sam thought, *no child weeps like that*— had stopped trying to hold back and decided to let it all go. It was coming from through the trees, not on the path, and Sam was only following the sound.

A couple of minutes later he stepped around a bushy fir and saw her. She sat on a flat rock in a small clearing—only her tracks showing on the snow-covered floor—her face buried in her hands, her back and slender shoulders hitching with every sob. Long dark hair cascaded in thick curls past her hands, falling like heavy smoke. She wore a red parka, jeans, and furry Ugg boots. Behind her, the sun's last rays streaked the far canyon wall.

"Miss?" Sam said, suddenly not at all sure this had been a good idea. The woman was an adult. She didn't look like a lost hiker. She just looked sad. "Are you okay?"

For a moment he wasn't sure she had heard. He was about to suggest to Dean that they turn around and head back to the car—his brother, a couple of paces back, hadn't even broken through to the clearing yet—when she lowered her hands, slowly, and tilted her face toward him.

Her eyes were huge and brown, ringed with red; her strong nose was equally red; and she sat with her lips slightly parted, breathing through her mouth. Her face made a triangle, wide at the eyes, tapering to a chin with a bit of a point. "Sorry," she said, and she fished a tissue from the cuff of her left sleeve and used it to blow her nose loudly. "I . . . yes, thank you. I didn't realize how loud I was."

"That's no problem," Dean said, shouldering ahead of Sam. Sam didn't blame him—she looked like she'd be pretty when she wasn't weeping inconsolably. "We just wanted to make sure you weren't hurt or lost or something."

"I . . ." Sam thought she was debating how much she wanted to tell two strangers who had just come at her out of the woods. "This used to be my husband's favorite spot," she said. Apparently, the Winchester brothers looked trustworthy. She waved a hand toward the view, which had mostly disappeared into darkness. The shadowy bulk of a condor passed, black slipping through the indigo sky, silent as oil through water. "He loved it here, and we used to come here to . . . well, never mind." A slight reddening of her cheeks told Sam all he needed to know about what they did in this secluded spot. "Anyway, when Ross died, I scattered his ashes from here—did you know they want you to pay to do that? Now I come here on his birthday. This is the second one since he passed, and I—" Her breath caught and she shook her head, casting her gaze toward the ground.

"We're sorry for your loss," Dean said.

Sam had been worried—you never really knew what might come out of Dean's mouth, and he might as easily have told her that they were undercover park rangers, out to bust people who illicitly scattered ashes.

"Thank you."

"I'm Dean," his brother went on. No last name, but at least he didn't lie or use an alias, which was rare for him. Maybe the fact that she was a widow had given Dean hope. Not for a relationship, Dean didn't tend to do those, but at least for a fling. "This is my brother Sam. Little brother," he added.

"I'm Juliet," the woman said. She dabbed at her cheeks and nose with the tissue and offered a tentative smile. "Juliet Monroe."

"Pleased to meet you, Juliet," Sam said.

"We're on our way to Cedar Wells," Dean said. "Do you live in the area?"

Juliet nodded. "Not far from there, really. We have a little ranch, just outside of town. Or I do, I guess. It was really Ross's dream, but I bought into it too. It's so beautiful around here. I was always a city girl, but Ross convinced me that it was a good move for us. Now I'm trying to sell the place—it's too lonely out there by myself—but I'm not getting a lot of offers." She tried on a surer smile, and it looked like it belonged on her face, brightening her eyes, swelling her cheeks. "You guys wouldn't be in the market, would you? I'll throw in the livestock for free."

"Us?" Dean tossed a private smirk at Sam. "No, no, we're kind of . . . we're on the road. A lot."

"I didn't really think you were the types," she said. "A ranch can really tie you down."

"I'm sure," Sam said. "Anyway, we'd better get back on the road, before all the good hotel rooms in Cedar Wells are taken."

Juliet laughed at that.

"What?" Sam asked.

"It's just . . . *good* hotel rooms in Cedar Wells is a funny concept. Kind of like saying you want to rustle up some good road kill before dinner."

"Not the most happening burg?" Dean asked.

"Not even close. Unless your idea of happening is Friday night bingo at the church and the occasional loose bull on Main Street."

"By which you mean a real bull," Sam guessed. "And not the kind of loose bull you find around politicians and actors."

"Or actors who become politicians," Juliet said. "But yes, the bull around here is the real kind, so watch where you step when you go looking for those hotel rooms."

"Is there anyplace to stay in town?" Dean asked.

"Sure," Juliet replied. "It was just your choice of adjectives I was commenting on. There's the Bide-A-Wee Motel—"

"Sounds adorable," Sam said.

"Some of the roaches there are bigger than my cattle," she said. "Or that's what I've heard."

"Anyplace else?"

"I'd probably stay at the Trail's End, if I had to stay somewhere."

"Trail's End. We'll look for it."

"You can't miss it," she assured them. "You can't miss anything in Cedar Wells, unless you blink. It's all on Main, and Main isn't that long."

"There really is a Main Street?" Sam asked.

"You bet. And Grand Avenue too. It's paved for three blocks, then dirt."

"And this place isn't paradise on Earth for you? I'm shocked."

"Like I said, I'm a city girl. It was fine when I had Ross—he loved it all so much, I enjoyed just seeing it through his eyes. But when you have to drive into Flagstaff for a decent half-caf mochaccino or a conversation that doesn't begin and end with the weather . . ." She sighed. "It gets a little old."

"I bet," Dean said. "We'll get out of your hair, Juliet. Thanks for the warning about the giant cockroaches."

"Thank you for checking on me," she said. "If you're in town long, maybe I'll see you at the Wagon Wheel."

"The Wagon Wheel?" Sam echoed.

"You'll see it."

* * *

"She was nice," Sam said when they reached the black Impala and were safely out of her range of hearing.

"She was hot."

"Sure, I guess."

"Don't tell me you didn't see it."

"More your type than mine, I guess."

"She was hot," Dean reiterated. "Trust me."

"So it's good that we investigated."

"Took a few minutes away from our real business," Dean said. "But I'm okay with that."

Sam hoped those few minutes hadn't cost anyone's life. They were going to Cedar Wells to look into a periodic killing spree that Marina McBain, a police detective in New York, had told them about. According to the article she gave them, every forty years the area became the scene of a rash of unexplained deaths. Twenty-nine killings, the last time. And the town had grown since then, the whole region becoming far more populous as the state of Arizona boomed.

According to their best calculations, December fifth would be the beginning of the next forty-year cycle. Today was the fourth. If their calculations had been off, and the time they spent at the Grand Canyon had meant death instead of life for anyone, they wouldn't feel so good about their side trip.

Sam and Dean Winchester both followed in their father's footsteps, and their father—since the horrifying death of his wife, their mother—had been a hunter.

Not of animals, or birds. John Winchester hunted monsters, ghosts, demons—the creatures most people only believed in deep down, in their 3:00 A.M. hearts, and that they laughed off when the sun was bright and their spirits high.

Even then, in the light of day, they talked about spirits.

They just didn't really understand what they were talking about.

Dean shoved the key into the ignition, gave it a crank, and the car's engine roared to satisfying life.

Ticking the vehicle into reverse, he glanced at Sam.

"It *is* a big hole," he said. "I was right about that."

"You were right, Dean. That canyon is one big freaking hole."

TWO

Ralph McCaig had been born over in Dolan Springs, to a father who had worked at the Tennessee Schuylkill Mine and a mother who mostly drank and complained, especially after the old man died in a mining accident and the pension checks never quite made it to the end of the month. Except for a hitch in the army during the Gulf War, in which the closest he had been to action was a street brawl outside a bar in Frankfurt, Germany, he'd always lived in Arizona's high country, land of canyons and plateaus, evergreen trees, mule deer, and tourists.

On the back bumper of his Chevy pickup, which had been new before that war but old by the time he bought it in 1998, he had a sticker that said, IF IT'S TOURIST SEASON, WHY CAN'T WE SHOOT 'EM? A gun rack over the rear window held a twelve-gauge and a 30.06, and he had actually used the ought-six once to fire at a BMW that whipped around a blind curve at eighty or more, startling him so much as he relieved himself beside the road that he'd peed on his Justin work boots. By the time he zipped up, scrambled to the truck, and yanked down the gun, though, the Beemer had been nothing but a pair of distant taillights, and he didn't think he came anywhere near hitting it.

Didn't mean he wouldn't try again in a similar circumstance. He made his living with a small salvage logging operation, so unlike some of his neighbors, his paycheck didn't depend on the tourist trade. At the moment, he was between contracts, but that wouldn't last long. The people who hired him were the ones who had to deal with environmental impact studies and logging permits and all the bureaucratic paperwork; all he had to do when they gave the word was gather a crew and go into the woods and take out the downed trees and the slash, or the skinny striplings that would never gain purchase there. Land managers liked neat, clean forests these days, big trees with plenty of space around them.

Ralph had some money in the bank, the fish were biting at Smoot Lake, and there was enough snow on the ground so he could stick a six-pack in it and every bottle would be as cold as the last, so he was a happy man.

Maybe a little too happy. As he negotiated the turn off the highway onto Lookout Trail—the dirt track that led past his place to a lookout tower that fire spotters hadn't used for a decade or more—he almost lost control of the truck. The rear end caught an icy patch and fishtailed and he barely got it back in line before it smacked into the stump of an oak he had cut down—illegally, since it wasn't on his land—because its branches had blocked his view of the highway.

But he did get it under control, and then it was just half a mile to his place. He could do that stretch with his eyes closed.

The close call had put him on edge, shaken a little of the buzz away. That was unfortunate, since the day had been just about perfect so far. He had been thinking, in fact, that the only thing that would make it more perfect would be if Doris Callender came over for dinner—better, *with* dinner—followed by a little of what his old man had called "knockin' boots." He'd give her a ring when he got inside, see if she wasn't free. Most nights, she was.

By the time Ralph came to a stop outside the old barn he used as a garage, the shakes from his near-accident had faded. It wasn't that he had been too concerned about crunching the truck, he thought, as much as it was the implication that he'd driven all the way back from Smoot Lake impaired. If six beers threw him off this much, did it mean he was getting old? Forty was closing in fast, after all. If the day came that he couldn't handle a chain saw or an ax, he really would have to worry.

He left the motor running and climbed down to open the barn door. The night air had turned cold, and he blew on his hands to warm them. He tripped over a root in the driveway but managed to keep his balance. "Jeez," he said out loud. "Six beers?" *Maybe I'm getting sick*, he added silently. *Catching a cold. Sure, that's probably it, no way six brews would hit me so hard otherwise.*

He had almost reached the barn door, where he knew the rusty hasp would give him problems because it always did, when he heard a strange sound. He froze. The woods around here were full of animals, deer and mountain lions and snakes, rabbits and chipmunks, various birds. Black bears too, sometimes, and at first he thought that's what had made the noise. He hadn't had a lot of close encounters with bears, he was glad to say, so he didn't know for sure if they made sounds like that. It had been a kind of irregular chuffing noise, like something that climbed a steep hill and hadn't caught its breath yet. But liquid, moist. Hearing it made Ralph envision something with loose, floppy jowls and big teeth and strings of saliva dangling from its open mouth, and he shivered, not because of the cool night air.

The noise came again, louder this time.

Closer.

He tried to gauge his distances. To the barn was closer, but there, he'd have to wrestle with that damn hasp, which gave him fits under the best of circumstances. Once he got it unlatched he would have to tug open the heavy barn door, on hinges he hadn't greased in he didn't know how long, then pull it closed behind him. And once he got in there, if it was something like a rabid bear, who knew how long it might wait around outside?

No, the truck was a better bet. Farther away, but if he needed to he could drive into Cedar Wells. And his guns were there.

Again, the noise. This time it was accompanied by something that sounded like smacking lips. Through the trees on the far side of the drive he saw a shape, vague and dark. But big.

Ralph dashed for the truck. Hit the root again, and this time it caught his foot, but good, sprawling him on his belly in the dirt. A shard of glass from a broken bottle sliced open his palm. He rose to a half kneel and yanked the glass out, and blood washed over his hand. At the same moment, a stench enveloped him, as if someone had draped a five-day-dead animal across his nose and mouth.

It had to be the bear, or whatever was out there. If he could smell it, that meant it was even closer. He could feel its hot breath on his neck—or was that his imagination? He didn't want to turn around and look.

Instead he gained his feet and charged for his truck. His bloody hand grabbed the door handle but slipped off before he could get it open. He clawed at it again, steel tacky with his blood this time, and it came easily, the door swinging open on its hinges.

Then the creature was on him, all thick dark fur and gnashing fangs. It swiped at him with a massive paw, knocking him to the ground. He gripped the truck's step with his left arm, like it was a life preserver that could hold him above the doom that would otherwise surely swallow him, and now for the first time he really saw it, except he couldn't be seeing it right because it changed, shifted, phased in and out of visibility—now a black bear, now a bear that had been dead for months, decomposed, bones showing through rotted flesh, now altogether invisible but still, horribly, breathing on his face, fat drops of drool splattering against his chin and neck—and it shoved its muzzle right against his throat, fur tickling his nostrils, the stink gigantic, and its huge razor teeth tore through skin, broke arteries and bones.

Ralph's last thought was that it would have been good to have knocked boots with old Doris one last time but it was probably for the best that he hadn't invited her over tonight.

Forty years before, the first victim had been hunting, alone, deep in the forest. He had fallen easily, and his body was never found; animals scattered the bones, the flesh eaten by worms and insects and scavengers and rot and in one form or another returned to the earth.

Forty years had passed since the instant of his death.

The cycle had come around again.

The killings had begun.

THREE

Main Street proved to be everything Juliet Monroe had promised. *Which,* Dean acknowledged, *wasn't much.* The buildings were mostly wooden fronted, with pitched roofs laden with snow and covered walkways in front. A few were made of brick, and they drove past a bank constructed from big blocks of gray stone. Christmas decorations already showed in many of the shop windows, and the lampposts had been wrapped with red ribbon. Sam pointed out the Wagon Wheel Café, which had a wagon wheel missing two spokes right at the one o'clock position, spotlighted next to a painted wooden sign. It looked to be a standard small town diner, like many the brothers had been in—and occasionally thrown out of—in the last year or so. He hoped they did see Juliet there—he definitely wanted to run into her again.

Two doors down only a neon OPEN sign glowing

in a blacked-out window gave any indication that the Plugged Bucket Saloon was occupied, but Dean guessed that there were a handful of drinkers at the bar, maybe a couple making eyes at each other in a dark booth, and a jukebox well stocked with country music hits that were at least two years old. He imagined he could hear Shania Twain singing "Man, I Feel Like a Woman" from here, although with a Rush cassette pounding from the Impala's stereo, he wouldn't have been able to hear her if she was standing on the sidewalk with her full band.

He reached out and cranked the volume knob to the left. "Any sign of the motel?"

"We passed the Bide-A-Wee on the way in," Sam said. "On my side. I didn't say anything because I thought we'd decided not to share a room with giant insects. Present company excluded."

"What about that other one Juliet mentioned?"

"The Trail's End? Not yet."

Dean scanned the street. A couple of trucks were parked along the sidewalks, but no people were in evidence. "Have you seen a single human being?"

"Not a one."

"You don't think . . ."

"What, we're too late? Something's already slaughtered the whole town? If that was the case, I think we'd see bodies, blood in the streets. I think it's just a small mountain town and people go home early."

"Okay," Dean said. "I like that better."

Up ahead, light spilled from a storefront that was set back from the road, with a parking area in front.

Swanson's High Country Market. Here there were people, including a woman with two kids, pushing a shopping cart toward a green Jeep. "See?" Sam said. "Nothing sinister. And if we don't like the Wagon Wheel, we can stock up there."

"Let's hope it stays quiet," Dean said. "I wouldn't mind if we were wrong for once and there was nothing strange going on at all. It'd be a decent place for a vacation if we didn't have to worry about people being murdered."

"That's what I like about you, Dean," Sam said. "Your eternal optimism. Always looking on the sunny side."

Dean glanced at his brother. He could see the family resemblance, particularly in the shape and sharpness of the nose, but Sam's face was rounder, softer somehow. His brother's eyes were brown, while Dean's were green. Longer hair, covering Sam's ears, curled over his collar and accentuated his youthful looks. Sam was four years younger, though, and had spent that time away at college. Dean supposed that by the time Sam reached twenty-seven—his age—those dimples and soft lines might harden, become deep crags, from the stress of fighting the denizens of the dark.

If, of course, they both survived that long.

He didn't like to think about the alternative. But they were soldiers, had been trained since childhood—almost from birth, in Sam's case—as soldiers, in a war that didn't seem to have an end. Soldiers needed to be prepared for death so they could take the necessary steps to avoid it. Still, they put themselves in harm's way, and he, Sam, and their father had done that almost every day since a demon killed their mother when Dean was four, until finally their father died too, a soldier's death, in battle as he would have wanted. His sons carried on the tradition without him. He wouldn't have had it any other way.

The image of their mother's death haunted him still—Mom, pinned to the ceiling over Sam's crib, her body consumed by spectral fire. Dad had ordered Dean to carry baby Sammy to safety outside. From the yard, Dean had watched the flames spread, engulfing the whole house in minutes. Dad had escaped, but alone.

Sam had been too young to remember it, too young, really, to know Mom at all. Her death came six months after his birth, to the day. But the same fate had claimed his girlfriend, Jessica Moore, after Sam abandoned Stanford to rejoin the battle at Dean's side. That one Sam had witnessed.

Sam felt incredible guilt over Jessica's death, because he had dreamed it during the days before it happened and hadn't warned her. He couldn't have known, of course, that the dreams were anything but that. And no warning he could have given would have prevented an attack by a demon they had not identified or defeated at that time.

Dean believed that his own guilt had a more solid basis. Their dad had gone missing, and Dean had essentially bullied Sam into leaving Jessica and Stanford to go looking for him. Bringing Sam back into the game like that, he thought afterward, might have stirred up the demon in some way, and the demon had responded by attacking the woman Sam loved, just as it had attacked their mother.

Dean finally decided there was plenty of blame to go around. The only way to live with it, to go on in spite of the lives they hadn't been able to save, was to keep up the fight, to save as many as they could and to kick as much supernatural ass as possible.

"There it is!" Sam said, yanking Dean from his memories. "Trail's End. Your side."

Dean saw the sign now too. One of the spotlights that were supposed to illuminate it had burned out, but he could still make out the monument sign beside the road, with the name painted on in Old West style lettering above a reproduction of that famous painting of a weary Indian sitting on an equally weary horse. A pink neon VACANCY sign sputtered just beneath the horse's tail. That Indian always made him sleepy, which he supposed was the whole point here. He bit back a yawn and turned into the driveway.

The motel consisted of a dozen or so adobe cottages arrayed in a U shape around the paved drive. Lights glowed in the office, a pink cottage closest to the street on the left. The other cottages were a natural tan color, with dark doors which had numbers affixed to the walls beside them. An empty pool surrounded by a tall fence dominated the center of the driveway, and a few scraggly plants stood beside the fence. Inside it, weeds broke through the sidewalk, almost to the pool's edge.

"Think it's too fancy for us?" he asked. "We can always go back to the roach motel."

"I didn't bring a tux," Sam said. "But I think they'll let us in."

Dean brought the car to a stop outside the office. "Best behavior now," he warned. "Don't embarrass me."

Inside, he had to bang on a countertop bell twice before anyone showed up. A door behind the check-in desk finally opened, and a man who had probably been old during the Eisenhower presidency hobbled in, using an aluminum cane. "Help you boys?" he asked. His hair had long since fled, and the crevasses in his face looked as deep as the canyon the brothers had so recently left.

Dean put a fake ID card on the counter—one of dozens he kept in the Impala's glove compartment. "I'm Dean Osbourne," he said. Giving fake names had become second nature. He identified himself as Dean Winchester so seldom that sometimes he had to ponder for a moment to remember his real name. "*National Geographic* magazine. We're doing an article on the communities around the outside of the national park, focusing on Cedar Wells. Sam Butler here takes the pictures. Got a room we can have for a few days? We're not sure how long it'll take, but at least that."

"*National Geographic*, eh?" the old man said. He showed them something that might have been a smile, or maybe a leer. Either way, it was terrifying. "Used to read that when I was a boy. Showed boobies."

"There's an Internet for that now," Dean said. "We're more interested in local history, legends, and of course the people who make up the community today. You probably know some stories."

The man nodded his oversized, liver-spotted cranium. Dean hoped he didn't unbalance himself and fall over. "Stories? Oh, I know some stories, all right. Got some good ones too."

"We'll definitely get you on tape, then," Dean promised. He jerked a thumb toward his brother. "And Sam here will take your picture. He might want you to show your chest, though, so watch out for him."

The clerk shoved a piece of paper at Dean, with X's where he was supposed to sign. "Room 9," he said. "Two beds. TV's busted, but it has one of those little refrigerators."

"Sounds perfect," Sam said, ignoring Dean's crack about the old man's chest. He snatched the key as soon as the guy put it on the counter. "Thanks."

Outside, Dean headed for the car, but Sam started across the frozen parking lot, going directly toward the room. "This time, I get first dibs on the beds!" he called over his shoulder. His tone was as icy as the blacktop. Driving over, Dean clicked off the Rush tape. He had Sabbath's *Paranoid* stuck in his head now, and he hoped there was nothing to that except the names he had given inside the office.

The wail of a siren jerked Dean out of a deep sleep. Cedar Wells had been so quiet, they might have been camping a hundred miles away from the nearest other humans, instead of sleeping in a motel at the edge of a town. In contrast, the blaring siren was almost deafening.

Dean sat up in bed, rubbing his eyes.

"That's not good," Sam said. He slipped out of his bed and started dressing.

"A siren is pretty much always bad news for someone," Dean agreed. "But we don't know that it has anything to do with why we're here."

"We won't find out sitting in this room," Sam reminded him.

"Yeah," Dean said. He liked his sleep. He especially liked to sleep at night. But that was when the bad things generally came out, so he spent more nights than he liked to think about awake and alert. Daytimes were for investigation, nighttimes for battle. He had gone to bed hoping this night's sleep would be without interruption.

Wishful thinking, that's all. He threw back the covers and tugged on his jeans.

By the time they made it to the Impala—a gift from Dad, 1967, midnight black, newly rebuilt—the siren had faded into the distance. But they knew the direction it had taken, back the way they'd come, through town and toward the Grand Canyon. A full moon had risen late and now hung low and golden over the treetops behind them.

Dean floored it, and within five minutes they could hear the siren again, outside of town. Another couple of minutes later they could see flashing roof lights flickering through the trees up ahead. Dean almost missed the turn onto a narrow dirt track, but he braked, reversed, and pulled in behind a white SUV with COCONINO COUNTY SHERIFF emblazoned on the side. Two similar SUVs clogged the road ahead of it, with a white and blue paramedics' van ahead of those. Trees curtained the sides of the road.

Dean and Sam got out of the Impala and hurried to a driveway that led to a big white barn. Fifty feet away stood a small house, a single-story cottage with three wooden steps leading to the front door, peeling paint, and a roof that looked like it might cave in at any moment. Cops milled about with big flashlights, beaming them every which way.

A pickup truck was parked in the driveway, and beside it was the body of what must have been a man, probably not too long ago. The driver's side door of the truck hung open. Blood had spattered up the side of the truck and onto the driver's seat, and the man's arm was hooked up over the step, but his throat was gone, along with the bottom half of his face, and something had opened his chest cavity. It looked like whatever had done that had been hunting for tender morsels, but Dean didn't spend a lot of time counting organs. He glanced long enough to estimate the damage, then looked away, sickened by the sight.

You could see a lot of carnage without ever growing to like it. He had. He was afraid that someday it *wouldn't* bother him, that he would be desensitized to it. He didn't want that to happen, because the sight filled him with rage, and that rage spurred him on, kept him in the fight.

"You need something?"

A man had stopped in front of them. He wore a white cowboy hat and a sheepskin coat, open, over a tan shirt with a badge on it. Around his waist was a black leather gun belt, and black stripes ran down the legs of his pants. He held a Maglite with its beam pointed at the ground. Cowboy boots and a thick brown mustache almost dwarfed by a generous nose and hard, inquisitive eyes told Dean everything he needed to know. This guy was in charge.

"We—" he began.

"You the boys from the *Geographic*?" Dean realized he must have looked surprised when the man with the badge added, "Don't look so shocked, son. Word travels in a small town. Delroy called us as soon as you checked in. Might have called the Bucket first, might have saved the news until he could go over there in person and let people bribe it out of him with free drinks. Either way, you're almost celebrities, and this ain't exactly tourist season." He toed a clump of snow on the drive, kicked it into trees. "Not tourist season at all. Which is just fine with me. Last thing we need's tourists hearing about this sort of thing."

"You're right, Sheriff," Sam said. He stuck out his hand. "Sam Butler. This is Dean Osbourne. Sorry for the circumstances, but it's a pleasure to meet you."

"I'm Jim Beckett," the man said, shaking Sam's hand, then Dean's. He held on like a vise grip. "Sheriff, spokesperson, and sometimes scapegoat, all rolled into one. We don't have a big department up here, so we have to combine duties." He eyed Dean, and for a bad few seconds Dean was afraid the sheriff had recognized him from a Wanted notice, since a shapeshifter in St. Louis had framed him for murder. "There's two t's in Beckett, son."

"I'll, uh, make a note of that," Dean said. "Can you tell us what happened here?"

"Something killed poor Ralph McCaig," Beckett said, eyeing the body. "That's about all I can tell you right this minute. About all I got. Animal, I'd say, but beyond that it's all guesswork. Maybe wolf, maybe bear, maybe . . . hell, I don't know. Bigfoot." He caught Dean's gaze again. "I see that in the magazine, I'll hunt you down."

"No problem," Dean said.

"No pictures either," he told Sam. "Not of this mess."

"I don't want to look at it, much less focus a camera on it," Sam assured him.

"That's good. My guys'll take some shots of it, and of the crime scene, if it's a crime. But like I said, looks like animal attack to me. Makes it an accidental death."

"Doesn't look like much of an accident," Sam said.

"Not on the animal's part, I guess, but it sure was on Ralph's. It's either accidental or death by misadventure, and I don't want to saddle Ralphie with that."

"I'd go accidental," Dean offered.

Beckett nodded. "Accidental it is."

"Have there been any other . . . accidents, lately?"

Beckett put a finger on his lips. "No . . . I mean, nothing like this. Nothing fatal. Construction worker fell off a ladder, over at the new mall, couple days ago. He broke a wrist, but he'll be fine."

"New mall?" Dean asked.

"Yeah. You haven't heard about that?"

"No," Dean said.

"Canyon Regional Mall," Beckett said. "It's inside the Cedar Wells town limits, but away from everything else—you must have come in from the park direction, otherwise you'd have seen it."

"We did," Sam said.

"Well, if you had kept driving another five, seven minutes from the Trail's End, you'd have gone right past it. Opens up on Saturday. Two department stores, three restaurants, plus a food court, movie theaters, the works. There's even a damn Baby Gap in there. Just like downtown. Not Cedar Wells's downtown, but you know what I mean."

"A real mall," Dean said. "All the way out here?"

"Population's growing," Beckett explained. "Arizona's one of the fastest growing states in the country, and not everybody's staying in Phoenix. We got a lot of small towns around here, but all those towns are getting a little bigger all the time. Out past the mall there are a couple of new housing developments. The developers of the mall think people will even come over from Nevada and southern Utah for it."

"That's . . . that's fascinating," Dean said. "We'll let you get back to what you're doing, but we'll definitely want to talk to you more later on."

"I'm easy to find," Beckett said.

Dean and Sam walked back to the car. Dean couldn't shake the image of the dead man, opened up like a present on Christmas morning.

"A mall," Sam said as they walked. "That's bad."

"Why's it bad? People need a place to shop."

"It's bad because if there are enough people for a mall, there are way more potential targets than we can possibly keep an eye on," Sam said. "Forty years ago there was hardly anyone living here, and what, ten percent of them were killed? If this killing cycle takes the same percentage of people in the area, we could be looking at hundreds of deaths."

Dean opened the driver's door and stopped there, looking across the roof at his brother. "Then we better figure out what's going on here, and fast."

FOUR

"Run! Run! Run! Go go go!"

There were times that the ex-Marine in John Winchester showed up as a wannabe drill sergeant. He had worked his boys hard, pretty much from the time he figured out what had killed their mother and decided to go up against it.

On this particular occasion, he was running them through an obstacle course he had built—Dean thought it might have been on a farm he'd rented in West Virginia, but they'd moved around so often that his memory of where most things had taken place was jumbled and uncertain. The objective was to scramble up an uneven wooden ramp slanted at about a sixty-five degree angle. At the top they were supposed to turn and shoot a target behind them with a .45 pistol, then jump into open space. On the other side they had to tuck their heads, land, roll, and come up shooting at another target.

Dean had made it on his third try. But he was twelve, and Sam was only eight. At that age, Dean recalled, Dad didn't allow Sam to handle real firearms, and for the purposes of this drill all Sam had to do was point his finger and shout "Bang!" Still, Sam didn't seem to have the strength in his skinny legs to propel him up the ramp, and the spaces between logs were far for him to stretch.

"You get up there, Sam!" Dad had screamed. Sam wiped snot from his nose, glared at Dad through tear-filled eyes, and tried again. He took a running start, his right hand balled into a fist, index finger extended, hit the log ramp at top speed and launched himself. About two-thirds of the way up there was a gap between logs, then a big log that stuck out past the rest. Sam slammed his knee against that one and let out a yelp of pain, dropping back to the ground.

"Get up!" Dad shouted. His voice was hoarse and angry. *Scary angry*, Dean thought. The more Sam couldn't make it, the more Dad seemed to get upset, like he thought Sam was intentionally failing. Dean raced to Sam's side as he sat in the dirt, rubbing his knee. He'd split the skin, Dean saw, and was smearing blood across his filthy kneecap. Tears cut pale traces down his smudged cheeks.

"You can do this," Dean said quietly.

"I can't. I can't get past that one log."

"I know it's hard, Sammy. But if you do it I'll buy you a candy bar next time we're at a store. You like Snickers, right? I'll buy you a Snickers."

Sam eyed him suspiciously. "How are you gonna buy me a Snickers bar? You don't have any money."

"Don't worry about that," Dean said. "I'll get you one."

Although Dad hadn't said anything outright, Dean already knew back then that the mission their father had set for himself—and for his sons—set them apart from regular people and their rules. They ate and had a home—a succession of them—and a truck, but John Winchester didn't have a job like other dads. Still, there was always money for his guns and bullets, knives and other weapons. They had clothing, of course, but also camouflage outfits and steel-toed boots, which couldn't have been cheap. Dad had decided that what he was about was more important than strict adherence to the laws of state and country.

Following that example, Dean knew he could acquire a Snickers bar for his brother without too much trouble.

"Okay," Sam said finally. "I'll try again."

"What's taking so long?" Dad demanded. "Your life might depend on this one day, Sam!"

That was always Dad's line when explaining anything he forced them to do. Dean couldn't actually foresee an occasion that would require them to dash up a crudely constructed wooden ramp, turn at the top and shoot a target, then land hard on the ground and shoot again, but Dad knew better than he did. He gave Sammy's bony shoulder a squeeze and got out of the way. "Kill it!" he said.

Sam nodded, backed up a dozen steps, then took another run at the ramp. This time his legs pushed off at the right moment and he flew over the jutting log. Above it, nearing the top, he slowed a little. Dean thought he was turning too soon, thought he would unbalance himself and come back down, this time from higher up with his arm dangerously extended and a pretend pistol in his hand. The number of ways this could be bad was too high to count.

But although Sam wavered, he kept his balance. A little slower than Dean had, but apparently fast enough to satisfy drill sergeant Dad, Sam aimed his finger and gave a shout, then hurled himself into space, landing on the far side of the gap, tucking his arms in and rolling. He came out of the roll a little unsteadily but on his feet, and pretended to shoot the next target.

Dean gave a whoop and ran to meet his brother on the other side. He expected to hear congratulations from Dad too, but instead the man stood with his arms folded over his chest, looking at them solemnly. "What are you waiting for?" he asked. He ticked his head toward the next station on the obstacle course, a series of low-strung strands of barbed wire they were supposed to slither under. Easy enough, and beneath the wire strands was slick, goopy mud, so, *bonus*.

"Look at this, Dean." Sam pushed a book—an old journal, in fact, kept in longhand in a spiral-bound notebook—across the scarred library table toward him. Before letting his mind drift into his own distant past, Dean had been studying accounts, preserved on microfiche, of the 1966 attacks from the *Canyon County Gazette,* a small local newspaper that went out of business in the 1980s. But Mrs. Frankel, the librarian, dug a little deeper to find the journals Sam was now reading, which had never been scanned or otherwise duplicated. The Cedar Wells Public Library was in an old wood-shingled building on Grand Avenue, and at ten-thirty in the morning it was empty except for the Winchesters and Mrs. Frankel.

"Summarize it for me," Dean said. He was in the middle of a story and didn't want to confuse details of the two by trying to read both at once.

"According to this," Sam said, "in 1966 there might have been an attack before December fifth."

"Might have been?"

"The woman who kept this journal had an uncle who disappeared on the second. He went out on a hunting trip and never came back. This was long before things like cell phones and GPS technology, of course, so when someone went on a hunting trip he was out of touch until he came home. This guy never came home, and they never found out what happened to him."

"So it's not necessarily part of the pattern," Dean pointed out. "Maybe he'd just had enough and moved to Ohio."

"Sure, that's a possibility. I can't imagine voluntarily moving to Ohio from here, but that's just me."

"Or maybe the pattern's right, and the cycle doesn't start until the fifth," Dean said. "Maybe Ralph McCaig wasn't part of it at all."

"So what got him, a werewolf?" Sam asked. Just in case, they had already checked lunar cycle history for 1966 and 1926, and the full moon hadn't been a factor on those occasions.

"Could be," Dean said. "The moon was definitely full last night. I admit it'd be a bizarre coincidence to have a werewolf attack occur in Cedar Wells so close to the beginning of the next killing cycle. But we've seen coincidences before."

"Shhh!" Mrs. Frankel, a woman in her sixties with a rigid spine, silver hair, and a habit of peering over the tops of her reading glasses—a librarian straight out of Central Casting, Dean had thought when they met her—was giving them the over-the-top glare now.

"Sorry," Dean whispered. He turned back to Sam and said, in a lower voice, "Anyway, you could be right. I'd like to try to confirm it, though."

"What the hell?" Sam asked. "We're the only ones in here."

Watching them whisper to each other, Mrs. Frankel burst into loud guffaws. "I was just funning you boys," she said. "The place is empty—you can hoot and holler all you want."

"That shouldn't be necessary, ma'am," Sam said, shooting her a completely artificial friendly grin.

Most people wouldn't have spotted its manufactured quality, but Dean knew the real thing when he saw it, and that wasn't it.

"Anyway," Sam continued, a little softer than before, but probably just because he was afraid Mrs. Frankel might be listening, "the problem is that we don't have a big enough sample size. We think the start date is December fifth because that's when it seems to have begun in 1966 and 1926, but two occasions isn't enough to really give us firm data. If even one of them is off—if this hunter guy really did disappear because he was the first victim—then our start date could be off by a few days. Which means that Ralph McCaig might have been part of the cycle, and there could even be other deaths that we haven't heard about yet."

"We should focus on figuring out what's doing it, then," Dean said. "If we assume that it's started, then even if we're wrong we'll still have a head start when it does."

"You have any good guesses yet?"

Dean shook his head. He should have been focusing on the articles, or running through the information in his head looking for patterns, not recalling ancient history. But even that was not as significant as the training sessions with Dad. The old man had been right, his lessons had saved their lives many times over. And they had saved more lives than could be counted, by taking out one paranormal killer after another.

Sometimes he just wanted something in front of

him to punch or stab or strangle, and instead he found himself stuck inside a library, reading badly written news reports on aging microfiche.

"I got nothing, Sammy."

Sam closed the notebook he'd been working through. "Same here," he said. "Big fat zero."

FIVE

Juliet Monroe watched Stu Hansen from her kitchen window, where she had been washing lunch dishes. He looked . . . well, she didn't know what he looked. Sad? Worried? Definitely an unusual state for Stu, who was about the steadiest guy she had ever known. He worked on the Bar M, as Ross had named their small spread, as their only full-time ranch hand. He'd come with the ranch, in fact, having worked for the previous owners too. She had seen him attending the birth of calves—even once carrying a calf for half a mile on his shoulders through a near blizzard—mending barbed-wire fences in hundred-plus degree heat, on his back beneath a truck for hours, hauling hay and shoveling out the stables, and he never complained, most always smiled, even whistled sometimes. Ranching was in Stu's blood, and he seemed to love every aspect of it.

As he approached the house, though, his shoulders were slumped, his creased, tanned face sagged, and his big hands hung loosely at his sides, looking strangely naked without a tool or an animal in them.

She hurried to the refrigerator and poured some lemonade into a tall glass, then dropped a couple of ice cubes in it. Rain or shine, hot or cold, Stu loved his lemonade. By the time his boots sounded on the back steps, she had the glass sitting on the kitchen table, waiting for him.

When he came inside, he seemed to bring a miasma of worry with him; like the cloud of dust that followed Pigpen everywhere in those *Peanuts* comics. She saw his gaze take in the lemonade, then settle on her.

"I fixed that for you, Stu," she said.

"Not just now, thanks, ma'am." He almost always called her that, in spite of her efforts since she and Ross bought the place to convince him to call her Juliet.

"What is it, Stu? What's the matter?"

"It's strange," he said. "I was just out in the pasture." He tugged a chair out from under the kitchen table, spun it around on one leg, and straddled it. He wore a straw cowboy hat, a denim work shirt with snap closures, dirty jeans, and scarred leather work boots. "And what I saw there . . ."

"What was it, Stu?"

"Some of the cattle, ma'am. Six of 'em, near as I could tell."

Juliet didn't like the sound of that. What could make them hard to count? "What about them?"

"They've been . . . well, slaughtered. Right there in the pasture. I thought maybe wolves, but I've seen predation by wolves before and it don't look like that."

"Something's gone after the cows?" She couldn't quite grasp what he was trying to tell her. He wouldn't look at her, but kept his gaze trained on the floor, the refrigerator, anything else. The ranch house had been built sixty years ago, and Ross had put some physical effort and money into restoring it to look like it might have then, with rustic, western furnishings and accessories.

"Yes, ma'am. Something strong enough and mean enough to tear 'em to pieces. There's—" His voice caught, and he cleared his throat. "I'm sorry, ma'am. It was just awful. There's blood all over the place back there, and bits of those animals. I startled what must've been a dozen buzzards and ravens helpin' themselves to the parts."

"But . . . what would do something like that?"

Stu shook his head sadly. "I wish I knew. Like I said, I've never seen wolves act that way. Bears, maybe. Seems like it'd have to be something at least that big and strong. Still not something I've ever come across. Something I'd be glad never to see again, I can tell you that."

Juliet had refused to name any of the ranch's cattle, although she was pretty sure that Ross and Stu had named some, because she didn't want them to have identities or personalities if they were destined for slaughter. This was worse, though—the animals Stu was describing wouldn't even go to feed people. They were essentially wasted, not good for anything *except* the scavengers. The waste shocked her, and the longer she thought about it the worse she felt.

"God," she said, gripping the counter because her knees had suddenly turned rubbery. "I . . . I don't know what to say, Stu."

"Ain't much to say. I figured you should know because it's money out of your pocket. I'll clean up what I can, but a lot of it's just too small to do anything about."

"Maybe we should just keep the cattle out of that pasture for a while," she suggested. "And let the scavengers take care of the rest."

"That'd work too," Stu said. "It'll take some time, and then there'll still be the bones to get rid of."

"I think that's still our best bet."

"That's what I'll do, then." When he had a specific idea for something he wanted to do, he let her know it, albeit in a roundabout way because he didn't want her to feel like he was dictating to her. Since he didn't press her on this, Juliet got the sense that her suggestion was in line with how he'd wanted to handle it all along. He rose, meeting her gaze for just a moment, his own brown eyes shaded by the brim of his big straw hat, replaced the chair, and left the kitchen without another word. His lemonade remained, untouched, on the kitchen table.

Juliet thought she might just down it herself, and wondered what kind of alcohol would taste the least nasty mixed with it. She was not ordinarily a heavy drinker, but maybe the time had come to reevaluate that position.

She sat down heavily in the chair that Stu had just vacated. There had been many days since Ross's death when she wished she could sell the ranch, or had never agreed to buy it, or could simply walk away from it.

So far she hadn't been able to bring herself to walk away, though, and selling the ranch required finding a buyer. She had advertised it all over the place, in specialty magazines, on the Web, in local papers, and elsewhere. A few potential buyers had come around, but not many, and although she had reduced the price below market value, she didn't have any takers. Too bad those guys she met at the South Rim yesterday, Dean and Sam, weren't in the market. She was so surprised to see them, she hadn't even thought to ask why they were going to a backwater town like Cedar Wells in the first place.

She was starting to get up from the chair when a stray thought struck her and she froze, her intestines turning to liquid. Could Dean and Sam be the ones who had attacked her livestock? They were strangers in town, she knew nothing about them, and she'd probably confided far too much—including her name and the fact that her husband was dead. How stupid was that?

Stu had thought animals were responsible, though,

and he knew more about such things than she did. She decided to ask him if he thought the sheriff should be notified, and if he said yes, then she would tell him about the strangers.

Until then she'd have to be a little more careful. She went to the kitchen door and locked it, then walked around the house locking the others. Through a bedroom window she spotted Stu chugging out on an ATV to move the herd.

Part of her was glad that Ross wasn't around to see this. He had loved the ranch and everything about it. The pointless slaughter of his stock would have broken his heart.

But mostly it was one more reason to get herself gone, and as fast as she possibly could.

SIX

Sam and Dean found Canyon Regional Mall just where they'd been told it would be, a couple of miles from the center of town, to the east—the direction they hadn't been yet. While driving out, they began to wonder if they'd taken the wrong road—not that there were a lot of choices—because the forest seemed to grow thicker for a time, evergreens growing so closely together that Sam got the sense of a wall of green out the passenger window. The rich tang of pine trees filled the car.

Suddenly, they rounded a curve and the trees were gone. In their place stood a massive structure surrounded by a vast, pristine parking lot. A few cars and trucks crowded the building, most of them obviously belonging to construction workers, painters, and landscapers. Sam found it disturbingly ironic that they had taken a stretch of beautiful, practically virgin forest and razed it, and now hired hands were hard at work planting saplings and grooming stretches of freshly laid sod.

The building itself had been built in a giant T shape, jutting forward toward the road and spreading out in back. Huge national department stores bulged the ends of the T's crossbar. The exterior was mostly surfaced in native stone, with display windows and electric signs breaking up the facade.

"Looks about ready to open," Dean said as he pulled into the lot.

"Let's hope that's not a huge mistake."

"It's our job to make sure it's not."

Sam recognized the sentiment. It was a habit Dean had picked up from Dad—referring to what they did as a "job." To Sam it was more of a mission, even a calling. He'd picked up the job terminology too— having been raised by John Winchester, it was second nature—but to him a job was something one was hired to do, and no one had hired them for this. Mom's murder had driven them to it, and Dad's obsession had fueled Dean's. Life had tugged Sam in a different direction, but Jess's death pushed him back onto the path.

Dean circled the mall once, drawing suspicious stares from a uniformed security guard walking outside. "What do you think?" he asked, bringing the Impala to a stop.

"I think it wouldn't hurt to get the lay of the land," Sam said. "Place like this, especially if it draws a big crowd, might turn into a battleground. I'd be more comfortable scoping it out without the crowd in our way."

"Ditto," Dean said. "I don't want some *Dawn of the Dead* scenario going down and us not knowing our way around." He opened his door and got out.

Sam followed, but before they even reached the building the guard had set an interception course for them. "Here we go," Dean muttered under his breath.

"The mall's not open yet," the security guard said as he approached. He had bushy dark hair curling out from underneath a police-style cap, and more poking up from beneath his ill-fitting uniform shirt. He fixed a dark-eyed gaze on them and let his hand rest on the handle of his heavy steel flashlight. "Not till this weekend."

"We know," Sam said quickly, before Dean could give him a response like *No kidding, Einstein*. Sometimes Sam could sense those remarks building up in Dean, like an electrical charge. "We're not shopping. We're reporters."

"Mall won't be open until the weekend," the security guard told them again. Sam was starting to get the idea that he was not the shiniest bullet in the ammo belt.

"We get that," Dean said. "But when they do open, they might want some people to have heard of them. That's where publicity comes in."

The guard looked at them blankly, as if now that he had delivered his message he couldn't understand why they hadn't left.

"Can we talk to the mall manager?" Sam asked.

The guard seemed to consider his request for a moment, although the possibility existed that he was just remembering a sports score or worrying about his boxers creeping. "I guess," he said after what seemed a very long pause. Having said that, he remained standing in their path.

"I guess we'll find him inside," Dean said, stepping around the guard.

"Her. It's a her. Ms. Krug."

"We'll track her down," Sam said. "Thanks."

The guard stayed where he was, as if there might be other people hiding behind the two of them. Sam didn't think he turned around until they were pulling open the huge glass and steel front doors and walking in.

The interior still smelled like paint and glue and exhaust from the forklifts and cranes working inside. Scaffolding stood in front of some of the shops, and men and women in hard hats and T-shirts and jeans and heavy boots were everywhere. At first glance it looked like the mall had a tool sale going on.

They approached one of the painters, a bearded guy in his forties, adding gold trim to the doorway of a lingerie shop. Through a gap in the paper covering the window, Sam could see young women arranging display racks and wall fixtures. As at the Grand Canyon, he admired the view.

"You know where the management office is?" Dean asked.

The guy didn't look away from his painting, but

kept moving his brush in precise, careful strokes. "Second floor, east wing, between the Gap and Kaybee. Look for the restrooms and you can't miss it."

No one challenged them as they made their way to the office. As the painter had promised, it was easy to find, down a hallway that also contained restrooms, a security office, and an entrance to the utility corridor that ran behind the stores. The door to the management office was mostly glass, but with miniblinds behind it blocking the view inside. The door was ajar, so Dean pushed it open, tapping on it as he went in. "Hello?"

A woman in a crisp green business suit over a gold blouse emerged from a back office into a reception area that was mostly office supply boxes waiting to be unpacked, and an empty desk. She looked professional but harried, with a few strands of honey-gold hair escaping from a clip and dangling around her face. With the business suit, Sam noted, she wore pink-trimmed white Reeboks. "Can I do something for you?"

"We're looking for the mall manager," Dean said.

"You've found her. I'm Carla Krug. Excuse the mess in here, we're a little chaotic at the moment."

"Understood," Sam said. "We don't want to take up much of your time."

"We're with the *National Geographic*," Dean said, extending that lie. "I'm Dean, and that's Sam. We're here working on a piece about the region outside the park, and thought that the opening of a big shopping center here should be part of the story."

"It's a little unexpected," Sam said, picking up the thread. "I don't think of the area as being populous enough to support a major mall."

"It all depends on how wide an area you can draw from," Carla said. She tucked one of the stray locks behind her ear. "There really is nothing on our scale north of Phoenix, so we have a potential customer base of hundreds of miles in every direction. We expect to draw from Nevada and Utah as well as Arizona."

She settled back against the receptionist's desk. "Look at it this way. One of those huge chain stores could have moved in here selling a few brands of clothing and shoes, appliances and housewares, even groceries. Most of it made in China, and all the proceeds would go to Arkansas or someplace instead of staying in the community. They still might come into the area, for all we know. But if they do, they'll find that we're ready for them, with dozens of shops offering hundreds of brand names they couldn't hope to carry. We'll have national chains and locally owned businesses. We're creating six hundred jobs that didn't exist here—ongoing permanent jobs, not counting all the local construction workers we employed to get the center built. Many of those jobs are management positions that build leadership skills, benefiting the whole region."

No one had asked for the sales pitch, but she had given it anyway, fast and concise. Now that it was done, Carla took a deep breath and smiled at them. "I've been doing a lot of interviews lately. I guess that just comes out naturally now."

"I think you're probably right," Sam said. "A place like this is bound to be good for the area economically. That's just the kind of detail we need for our piece."

"I heard you were around," she said. "I wondered if you'd come by."

"Can we look around the mall?" Dean asked. "I'd like to see, you know, what stores are here. And maybe the behind-the-scenes stuff our readers love, like the security office and the back hallways."

"I don't see why not. I can take you next door to Security, but after that I'll have to leave you on your own. I have a million things to do."

"Of course," Sam said. "That would be great."

"Let's go," Carla said. She was too busy to waste time looking at their phony ID cards or to interrogate them in any detail, which worked for Sam. She squeezed between them and led the way out into the hall, then opened the door to the security office and held it for them.

"Thanks," Sam said as he went past her. The security office was darker than hers, with two banks of TV monitors showing scenes from around the property. Three uniformed guards were in the room, two men watching the monitors and the third, a woman, doing paperwork at a desk in the corner. The guy from the parking lot wasn't there. The office smelled like stale coffee, and the mall hadn't even opened yet.

"Here's the nerve center," Carla announced. "Lady and gentlemen, these two fellows are with the press.

They'll be poking around for a while, so don't arrest them unless you have to."

The guards chuckled at that, and the woman at the desk shot them a friendly grin. "My guys haven't had a chance to shoot anybody yet, so if you really misbehave, maybe we can use you as an object lesson."

"We'll be good," Dean assured her. "What kind of security problems are you anticipating? The usual shoplifters?"

"Definitely that," the female guard said. She had short black hair and olive skin, and her uniform was snug on her thick form. "And beyond that, who knows? Pretty much anything that can happen will happen at a place like this."

"And with those monitors you can keep track of the whole place?"

"There are some blind spots," one of the male guards answered. "And we don't have cameras inside the shops, or in the bathrooms. But common areas, and the exterior . . . yeah, we got those covered."

Sam leaned closer to the monitors. The images were black and white, but clearer and sharper than most surveillance camera footage he'd seen. The advantage of using brand-new equipment, he guessed. He didn't want to sound overly interested in their security force, but if whatever was coming to Cedar Wells targeted the mall, he wanted to know their capabilities. He hadn't seen any guns, but hoped the female guard wasn't kidding about being able to shoot.

Not at him and Dean. Just in general.

"Good pictures," he said.

"At the right angle," the male guard said, "I can read a license plate."

"Wow."

"What's that?" Dean asked. He was pointing at one of the other monitors, which no one had been watching because they were all watching Sam.

"What?" the male guard asked.

"It was just on this screen," Dean said. He indicated the lower right corner. "It walked off this way."

"A person?" the guard asked. "Or what?"

"That's what I couldn't tell," Dean said.

The guard punched some keys and the image changed. "We have more cameras than we do screens," he said. "I'll bring up a wider angle."

The monitor flickered and the picture changed. Sam could see a stretch of parking lot, with a slab in the foreground that had to be the mall's exterior wall.

Walking—*more of a stagger*, Sam thought, *as if he's been injured*—across the vacant parking lot was what looked like a man in a cavalry uniform.

But a uniform from a hundred years ago.

SEVEN

"Is he wearing a costume?" Carla Krug asked.

Before anyone could respond—although the answer almost certainly had to be yes—the image flickered and the man faded out.

No, Sam corrected himself mentally. *The image didn't flicker. Just the* guy *flickered within the image.* The parking lot and the wall stayed on the screen, but the man was gone.

Then he was back, but farther from the camera. Almost to the edge of the frame. Then gone again.

He didn't return. The guard at the keyboard brought up a couple of different cameras, showing varying views of the lot, but the guy in the old soldier's outfit was nowhere.

"What the hell . . . ?" the guard asked.

"If there's something wrong with this system, we need to know about it right now," Carla said. "And we need to get it fixed."

"I don't think it was the system," the female guard said. "The cameras are working fine. I've never heard of a camera losing just part of an image and keeping the rest of it."

"Like you said, Lynnette, anything that can happen will happen here."

"I know, but I didn't mean things that are physically impossible." She returned to her desk, grabbed a microphone and thumbed its button. "Anyone in the northwest section of the parking lot, or with a visual of it?"

"I can be there in a minute," a voice came back, staticky but distinct.

"Go, then," Lynnette said. "You're looking for a guy in some kind of military costume. Like a Civil War soldier or something."

More like the Indian Wars, Sam thought, but he kept his mouth shut.

"On the way," the voice said.

"I guess you guys didn't anticipate something like this happening while you were here," Carla said to Sam and Dean while they waited for the guard's report.

"You never know," Dean said. "We see some pretty strange things."

The radio speakers crackled. "I'm here. Don't see anybody in a uniform, though."

The guard sitting at the console brought up a view that showed the guard Sam and Dean had met in the parking lot striking out across the lot, toward the fringe of forest surrounding it. All the screen showed was his form against a background of black pavement marked with white lines.

But as Sam watched, the image flickered again. One moment the guard was alone in the lot, and the next the soldier had appeared behind him.

And he was drawing his saber from its scabbard.

"Johnny!" Lynnette shrieked into the radio. "Johnny, he's right behind you! Do you see him?"

Johnny started to turn, his face as blank as it had been earlier. He tucked his chin toward his chest, and Sam understood that he was talking into a microphone mounted at his collar. "I don't see—oh!"

"Johnny, be careful!" Lynnette cried.

Johnny said something else, but they couldn't hear him now, only see his mouth moving, in miniature, on the monitor in the dark, silent room where the smell of overheated coffee filled the air. The old soldier still flickered a little, as if he couldn't come entirely into view. The sword in his right hand looked long and deadly.

"Oh, God," Carla said softly. "This can't be happening."

You'd be amazed at what can happen, Sam thought. He slapped Dean's back. "Let's get out there."

"Right behind you," Dean said.

"Everyone report to the northwest parking lot!" Lynnette called into her radio. "Now! Suspect is armed and extremely dangerous!"

Sam and Dean burst through the security office door and out into the mall. Once they got there, Sam realized they still didn't know their way around well enough to pick the fastest route to the back parking area. They held back a moment and let the two male guards who had been watching the monitors go first, just long enough to lead them to a door that opened onto that lot.

Once they spotted the door, the Winchesters poured on the speed, passing the guards easily. They wanted to be first on the scene.

Not that it would help Johnny.

The last thing Sam had seen on the monitor, before racing out of the office, was the old soldier thrusting his sword through Johnny's gut, and the security guard—his eyes wide with fright, as he had at last seen his attacker—falling to his knees on the pavement.

Sheriff Jim Beckett wore the same sheepskin coat and white hat he had at the McCaig death scene. The paramedics arrived in what might have been the same van, roof lights flashing bright against low, leaden clouds. As far as Sam could tell, the only new player was the mayor of Cedar Wells, Donald Milner. He had a knee-length black coat on over a plaid blazer in maroon, white, and black, for which he might have mugged a real estate agent. His pants were sharply creased khakis and his loafers had tassels on them.

They all stood around a bloody patch of blacktop, from which the paramedics had removed the body of the guard named Johnny. By the time Sam and Dean had reached him, the soldier was long gone—or simply invisible again. Out of sight, in any case.

"You boys aren't going to say anything about this before the opening, are you?" Mayor Milner asked, fixing Dean and Sam with an anxious glare. "I mean, you're not with the local press, right?"

"We have a long lead time," Dean said. "Don't worry about us."

"There isn't anyone else here from the media, is there, Jim?"

The sheriff glanced around. "Don't appear to be."

"If I were you, though," Sam said, "I'd give serious thought to delaying the opening."

Carla Krug blanched. Mayor Milner scowled and bunched his right hand into a fist, like he might start throwing punches. "We're not delaying the damn opening!" he declared. "This mall opens tomorrow no matter what. There's too much at stake not to. Not to mention all the advertising that's already been done."

"But if this, and the killing last night, are part of the forty-year murder cycle," Sam objected, "then it's not—"

The mayor cut him off angrily. "There is no forty-year murder cycle! That's nothing but an urban legend. Preposterous claptrap!"

Sam glanced about them. Except for the mall, nothing but deep woods in any direction. About as far from "urban" as one could get.

Dean turned toward Sam. "Great," he muttered. "Instead of *Dawn of the Dead*, we wind up in *Jaws*."

"Shark?" Sam replied. "I don't see any shark."

"Cedar Wells is perfectly safe," Milner went on. "Isn't it, Jim? You've got an APB or whatever out on that maniac, right?"

Beckett rubbed the side of his substantial nose. "My people are out there combing the woods. We're keeping an eye on the roads too. If there's some nut in a military uniform around, we'll pick him up, don't you worry about that." Sam was more worried about the fact that they were all standing around on the crime scene, which had been photographed from a couple of angles but hadn't been given the precise search that might have led to the discovery of an actual clue or two.

"What if he's changed clothes?" Dean challenged.

"We'll find him, son," Beckett said. "Somewhere in these parts there's a lunatic with a bloody sword. Can't be that hard to track him down. You fellows are lucky you have the best alibi there is, because with two deaths since you came to town, you'd be my number one suspect. Numbers one and two, I guess."

"So you don't think the killer's a local?"

"Lynnette knows just about everyone in town, and she didn't recognize him."

"He's not from around here," Lynnette added. "I know that for a fact."

"So you've got someone who traveled here, presumably in a car, with an antique military uniform and a cavalry saber," Sam said. "Have you checked the motels?"

"You don't need to worry about how we do our

jobs," Beckett said. "We may look like ignorant hicks to you, but we're professionals."

"I didn't mean to imply that you weren't," Sam said.

"Sammy really likes cops," Dean said. "If he didn't have any talents he might have become one."

Sheriff Beckett shot Sam a curious look, like he wasn't quite sure how to take that. Sam knew that his brother had a habit of getting on the wrong side of the law, although it wasn't always his fault.

Beckett apparently decided to let it slide. "Anyhow, we're on the case, Mayor."

"There you go," Milner said. "This mall opens on schedule, and there won't be any more discussion of that." His tone indicated that he meant it, that the matter was settled once and for all.

Maybe he was right.

Then again, if history was any guide, the murders were just beginning . . .

EIGHT

"If Mayor McCheese there has his way," Dean groused, "the whole town could end up shish-kabobbed, and as long as the mall opens on time he'll be happy."

"It's kind of his job to be a booster," Sam said.

"But not a moron. And I'm not sure Barney Fife is much smarter." Dean was back behind the wheel, tooling toward downtown Cedar Wells again. "So what do you think that was? Spirit?"

"That'd be my guess," Sam said. "Especially with the phasing in and out of visibility, and the old clothes."

"Yeah," Dean agreed. "Which means we have to figure out why it keeps coming back at these forty-year intervals, and how to make it stop. Looks like we've got some bones to dig up and burn."

"If we can find out whose bones. There was nothing promising in the library that I saw."

"There's got to be someone around here with a long memory. Or a diary that hasn't been scrubbed."

"What are we going to do?" Sam asked. "Knock on random doors until we find one?"

Dean shot Sam an angry glare. Sometimes the old resentments cropped up—the resentments that Dad had encouraged, it seemed, after Sam decided to go to college—and he suspected Sam of being a quitter, willing to stay in the fight as long as the going got easy but ready to bail when things were tough.

In fact, he knew that wasn't true. There had been plenty of tough times since their reunion, plenty of chances for Sam to take off if he wanted to. The fact that Sam was still in the passenger seat, thumbing through his cassette tapes, meant that he was in this for the long haul. That certainty softened Dean's expression and his response. "If that's what we have to do," he said. "I'd rather find a more immediate solution, since I don't think the sheriff has much experience hunting spirits."

Any death from supernatural assault was too many, but Dean especially hated for victims to fall while he was in the area and on the case.

Two had already happened while they'd been in Cedar Wells. If they didn't get a handle on the situation soon, who knew how bad it could get?

Brittany Gardner loved the snow. Not all the time, not every day, but a few good snowfalls a year made her feel like she was part of the world. All day, the sky had been thick with clouds, blocking out the sun and threatening (promising!) precipitation. The air had a crisp, cold, still quality, suggesting that if the clouds did open up, the snow would fall steadily for a good long while. She had moved to Arizona's high country from the Phoenix area because she wanted to feel snow on her face more than once every decade or so, and today she kept looking out the living room window of her small cottage hoping to see the flakes coming down. She worked at home, editing technical manuals on a freelance basis, but today the work paled in comparison to the snow she wished for, and she had barely made it through three pages in the last hour.

Beside her computer—far enough away that if she dumped it, the mess would flow elsewhere—she kept a cup of Lapsang Souchong tea. Every now and then she carried it into the kitchen to refill it or heat it up in the microwave. A jazz station played softly on her satellite radio, and the cottage was warm and cozy. A perfect morning—or it would have been if the white stuff would fall.

Brittany tried to work for twenty minutes straight. After thirteen minutes she gave up and went back to the window. The day had darkened, as more layers of cloud, she supposed, passed in front of the sun. Still nothing falling, but she was more convinced than ever that it would.

Turning to go back to her computer, movement attracted her attention. Someone passing through the trees across the street. She knew the people who lived in the little house over there, the Sawyers, an elderly couple who rarely ventured outside. The person in the trees was neither of them, but he seemed to be skulking toward their house. Brittany backed away from the window a bit, pulling the sheer curtain between herself and the man. He looked like an old guy, grizzled and stooped. His coat was leather, she thought, and he wore tall boots pulled up over his pants, and on his head he had one of those hunting caps with the earflaps you could pull down.

As she watched, he closed in on one of the Sawyers' windows. He looked old for a Peeping Tom, but then again she wasn't sure if there was a particular age range for that kind of thing. Either way, she didn't like the looks of him.

Then he turned a little and something in his right hand swung into sight. He was carrying a rifle!

Brittany released the curtain and dashed to her phone, beside her computer. She dialed 911. A moment later a dispatcher came on the line.

"There's an old man across the street, in the woods, and he has a gun," she said quickly. "By the Sawyers' house."

"Do you know the address, ma'am?" the voice asked.

"He's across the street, not here. I don't know their address offhand."

"I understand, ma'am. I have your address, and I'm dispatching a sheriff's officer out there right away. Has the man seen you?"

"I don't think so, no."

"Stay indoors, ma'am. Officers will knock on your door and identify themselves, but don't let anyone in until they do."

"Okay," Brittany said. "Don't worry, I won't."

"Do you want me to stay on the line?"

"That's okay," Brittany said. "I don't think that's necessary." Hands shaking, she put the phone down and cautiously returned to the window. When she got close, she lowered herself to her knees and crept the rest of the way, peering out with only her eyes and forehead exposed.

Snow had started to fall, big white flakes of it drifting slowly earthward.

It wasn't fair. She had been waiting for this moment, for the first falling snow, to go outside and revel in it.

Across the way, she couldn't see the man with the gun anymore. She hoped he wasn't already inside the Sawyers' house, terrorizing those nice old people. In the distance, she could hear an approaching siren. The sheriff's car, already on the way. She allowed herself a smile. They'd be here soon enough, and the whole thing would be over, a strange adventure, and she could go out and luxuriate in the day, more alive then ever.

A noise from behind startled her. Brittany spun around, rocking on her knees, barely able to keep her balance. Had he come into her place?

But no—there was someone inside her living room, but it wasn't the old man. The intruder looked like something out of a movie, an Indian, but old-fashioned, wearing leather leggings, bare-chested, with bands around his arms and legs and a red cloth wrapped around his head. He glowered at her through small, dark eyes.

The most disturbing part was not his fierce gaze or even the tomahawk clutched in his fist, but the gaping wound in his broad chest, as if he'd been cleaved open by his own weapon. The sides of the wound were pale, not red, as if the wound was old. No blood ran from it, although she could see what must have been bone and muscle inside.

A scream caught in her throat, and only the faintest squeak emerged. She could hear the sirens now, just outside. She had dropped to one knee, with one hand on the ground for support and the other clamped over her mouth, and she was frozen to the spot. The Indian walked toward her, stumbling a little, head lolling to the side. For an instant he seemed to change, to shift into something the same shape but made of glowing black light, then into a bone-and-muscle version of himself, but when she blinked he looked as he had at first. Brittany had the sense that he was already dead, that his wound was fatal, but he hadn't figured out that it was time to lie down.

"What do you . . . are you . . . ?" She couldn't figure out what to ask him, and her voice sounded distant, barely audible through the blood rushing in her ears. If he heard her, he gave no indication of it.

She could hear wind whistling in and out of his chest wound as he breathed.

When he reached for her, Brittany finally thawed, trying to break and run. He surprised her with his quickness, though, and got a fistful of her curly red hair. He yanked on it. Her feet went out from under her and she sprawled on the hardwood floor of her living room, breathing fast now, working toward a really good scream, the kind that would raise the rafters of this old place and bring the police running. Either they'd shoot the Indian or tell her that she had gone insane, and at the moment that seemed the likeliest prospect, because only madness could explain what she faced.

The knee against her belly felt real enough, pressing her down against the floor, and the smell of the man, sour, like meat left too long in the sun, that was real too, and when he brought the tomahawk down against her chest, in the same place where his wound was, for just the briefest instant that felt staggeringly real too.

"This is a mess," Jim Beckett said. "A godawful mess, no two ways about it."

Deputy Trace Johannsen nodded soberly. "You're not kidding about that."

Beckett looked at Brittany Gardner's body again. She had suffered a massive chest wound, as if an unskilled doctor had cracked her open to perform emergency heart surgery but hadn't bothered to close her up again. Until her heart had stopped beating, it had pumped blood out through the gaping wound, soaking her sweatshirt and pooling on the floor.

Three bodies in less than twenty-four hours. He liked Cedar Wells because it was a quiet town, close to good hunting and fishing. The Grand Canyon was a bonus, although he rarely visited it; simply knowing it was there was good enough.

Suddenly it wasn't so quiet. Instead it looked like Detroit during its worst days, or Washington, or maybe L.A. when the Bloods and Crips went at it with knives and guns. Beckett was old enough to remember the good old days when youth gangs armed themselves with little switchblades and bicycle chains. Not that this looked like a gangster killing, but there was a principle involved, and the principle was that people in his town shouldn't kill each other. Nor should strangers kill the locals, not near a national park that drew somewhere around five million visitors a year. He just wanted his old town back, the one where people rarely died violently.

"Dispatch said she reported a prowler across the street," Trace explained. He had already gone through the story once, but seemed compelled to tell it again, and listening to him was easier than thinking. "An old geezer carrying a gun. I checked over there, but the Sawyers hadn't seen anyone. I knocked over here to ask her about it, and she didn't answer. I knew she had been home just a few minutes before, so I looked in her window and saw her here."

"But no sign of an intruder?" Beckett asked. "No old man with a gun?"

"Nothing like that. Anyway, if he had a gun, why would he open her up like that? Why not just shoot her?"

"I wish I knew the answer to that. Did you find any footprints or anything, either here or by the Sawyer place?"

"Some over there, across the street. Good one right outside one of their windows, like someone raising up on tiptoes to look in."

"Figure that's our geezer?"

"That's my guess."

"I had a call on my way over," Beckett said. "Another sighting of the old man, less than a block away from here. I drove around for a couple minutes, didn't see anything, and I don't have enough bodies available for a full-on search."

"You think he's looking for another victim?"

"At this point, I don't necessarily like him for the murder at all. Like you said, he's got a gun. This lady wasn't shot. I don't know what opened her up, but that's no bullet hole."

Trace fell silent. That was okay with Beckett. He didn't want to have to think, but sometimes there was just no avoiding it. Mayor Milner didn't want anything getting in the way of the mall opening, and he understood Milner's position.

But a man didn't live for a long time in Cedar Wells without hearing whispers of a murder cycle, as that young reporter had called it. Especially when he made his living in law enforcement. People talked about it after a few drinks over at the Plugged Bucket, or at backyard barbecues in the summer when the beer came out of ice-filled coolers and the smoke was thick and nobody listened to anyone else's conversation. And sometimes a sheriff could just be walking down the street and one of the town's oldsters would call him over, summon him with that imperious attitude the truly ancient sometimes assumed when dealing with whippersnappers who were merely in their forties or fifties, and whisper to him that it was this year, wasn't it? Come summer, or spring, or whenever they got it in their head the fortieth anniversary was, people would start to die again. That, finally, was what had convinced him that it was all a local legend—the fact that none of the people who had been adults here forty years before seemed to agree on when it was supposed to happen.

If he was wrong, though—if it was real, and the forty years was up, and it was all beginning again— then he would be in for a bad week or two, however long it would last. And opening a mall during that time would be a heroically bad idea. Bad enough when there were a few victims spread around the area. How much worse might it be if there were several thousand inside the mall, and whoever or whatever was behind the murder spree decided to try some kind of terrorist stunt? A bomb, a small plane flown into the mall, something like that. The death count could easily rise into the hundreds in a matter of minutes.

The thing was, could he convince the mayor and the mall management to call it off?

Not without more evidence than he had so far.

He had to find that old man. Or the soldier from the mall parking lot. Or whatever had torn up Ralph McCaig. Ideally, they were all the same guy. Jailing one man was a lot easier than jailing a figment or a legend.

NINE

Mrs. Frankel, the silver-coiffed librarian, wore perfume just musky enough to make Dean wonder if she had a secret life. He and Sam had returned to the library after their mall visit, with a different goal in mind than last time. Before, they had been in search of information about the previous episodes of unexplained murders, in 1926 and 1966. This time they wanted to find out if the old soldier was the spirit of someone who bore a grudge against the town.

The fact that neither of them were familiar enough with military uniforms to know precisely when the soldier might have lived would, they realized, make the quest somewhat difficult. Hence the up-close-and-personal conversation with Mrs. Frankel.

"I'm surprised the *Geographic* is so interested in the minutiae of our history," she said when Dean explained what they needed.

"Our readers are an inquisitive bunch," Sam said.

"The more interesting details we can provide, the more they like it."

"Well, here in Cedar Wells and Coconino County, we certainly have our share of 'interesting detail,'" she said. "Lots of kooks, I guess you'd say, have settled here or at least passed through. I can't think of any off the top of my head who might have a grudge like you're describing, though."

"Maybe the grudge would never have revealed itself," Dean suggested. "Maybe he was just someone who felt like he'd been badly mistreated."

"That sort of thing happens all the time, of course," Mrs. Frankel said. She twisted a thin gold necklace around her left index finger. Dean noted that there was no wedding ring on her ring finger, although she had definitely introduced herself as *Mrs.* Frankel. "People feel like local government singles them out for maltreatment, or like it has let them down in some way because their particular case or cause isn't its top priority. And some, of course, have legitimate grievances. I can think of half a dozen of those, but those are all just in the last few years. Going back to the old days . . . well, that would be a matter of going through the newspapers, I guess. As far back as they go."

"How far is that?" Sam asked. "The soldier we're looking for might have been here late in the nineteenth century."

Mrs. Frankel released her knot of necklace and tapped her fingertips against her chin. "Oh, I don't think the papers go that far back. The *Canyon*

County Gazette didn't start publishing until 1920 or thereabouts. Well after the national park was established. Before that, there just weren't enough people in the area to make a newspaper worthwhile."

"How can we get information on people who might have been here before that?" Dean asked.

She glanced toward a series of wooden filing cabinets shoved up against one wall. "There are some records from Camp Hualpai, a local military post from the late 1860s to early 1870s. It didn't exist for long, but you're certainly welcome to see what's there."

Dean caught Sam's eye. That sounded like a lot of hard, boring work. He didn't necessarily have a problem with hard, boring work that had a reasonable chance of success. The problem here was that they were hunting for the proverbial needle in the haystack—complicated further by the fact that they didn't even know in which farmer's field the right haystack could be found. Sam gave a minute shrug.

"Maybe a little later," Dean said. "We'll definitely keep that in mind."

Outside, Sam grabbed his arm before they even made it to the car. "I could tell you didn't want to sit in there and read those old files, but do you have any better ideas? We're kind of running out of time here."

"Of course I have an idea," Dean said. Sam released him and stood on the sidewalk, waiting to hear it. The snow, which started out falling lightly, had intensified, as if the clouds themselves had shredded and spun to the ground as confetti. Since Dean didn't actually have an idea, he watched the sky for a moment, hoping one would come to him. "Only not so much, at the moment."

"Yeah, that's what I thought. Fortunately, I have one."

"Why didn't you say so? What is it?"

"We're looking for a soldier, right? Someone who died in the area, which is why his spirit is still here. So let's check the local cemeteries. We can scan them for electromagnetic frequency activity. If nothing else, sometimes military graves are marked, and if we can find one that's out of the ordinary in some way, maybe we can kill two birds with one stone and dig it up right away."

Dean smiled. *Little brother comes through again.* "That's good, Sammy. That's good. Can't be too many cemeteries around here, can there?"

As it turned out, there were three.

The first one didn't have any graves older than 1954, which it took twenty minutes of wandering, bending over, sometimes scraping off snow that had started to accumulate on headstones, to determine.

The second one was behind a Catholic church. A priest looked at them from inside, so they tried their best to appear solemn and respectful as they perused the graves. It was cold enough that Sam pulled up the hood of the sweatshirt he wore under a canvas jacket. Dean had a leather coat on, no hat, but in the pockets were gloves that he tugged onto his hands.

Some of the graves here were older. They found a

few from the 1890s, but none that could be identified as belonging to military people, and none that suggested unquiet rest, either visually or on their EMF reader.

"One more to go," Sam said when they were back in the car.

"Yeah, this was a great freakin' idea," Dean complained. "Freezin' our asses off out there in the snow. I see dead people."

"We're *looking* for a dead guy!"

"I know. I just . . . I don't like the snow, okay? I mean, snow's cool and all, but I like it better when I'm inside with a hot toddy and a roaring fire."

"I don't think I've ever had a hot toddy," Sam said. "I don't even think I know what's in it."

"I don't, either," Dean said. "But I like the idea of it more than I like the idea of losing a toe to frostbite."

"We're not going to lose any toes, Dean."

The route to the third cemetery took them through what passed for a residential neighborhood in Cedar Wells, a couple of blocks off Main Street. The houses were old, mostly wood and brick, with snow covering their slanted roofs and fenced yards. Smoke wafted from a few chimneys, scenting the air and sending gray curls skyward. Snow gathered on the road, except where tires had carved through it, making black streaks that looked like miniature roads themselves, viewed from the clouds.

Dean slowed, fighting the Impala's desire to fishtail into a parked truck. "You'd think a town like this would have snowplows."

"They probably have a snowplow," Sam said.

"And they're probably using it to keep Main Street clear. And maybe Grand Avenue."

"All three blocks of it."

"Hey, it's a small town."

"Which is gonna get a lot smaller if we don't find this spirit." The more time that passed, the more possibility that other people were dying. Dean hated that possibility, and while he didn't want to snap at his brother, anger pushed itself to the surface.

Besides, what good was having a brother if you couldn't snap at him once in a while?

"Dean!" Sam grabbed Dean's sleeve, startling him. He twisted the wheel to his right, started to slide on wet slushy pavement, corrected to the left. The Impala shuddered but maintained course.

"Don't do that, Sam."

"Dean, look!"

Sam pointed to a house up the street, about a quarter of a block away. From the road they could see a screened-in porch in front of the door, three stairs up from the street.

Emerging from the door was a big, dark bulk. The wrong shape to be a person. "What the hell . . . ?" Dean stopped in the middle of the lane, watching.

A black bear nosed out the screen door as if sniffing the air. Apparently finding it to his liking, he pawed it out of the way and dropped to all fours to descend the stairs. Rump swaying, he crossed the snowy yard and headed for the woods behind the house. The screen door, on a spring, slammed closed behind him.

"A bear just came out of that house," Dean said.

"Maybe he lives there."

"Like what? A circus bear? I don't think—"

"I'm kidding. Come on, we'd better check the place out."

"Gee, you think?" Dean pulled the car awkwardly toward the curb and got out. Sam was out his door before the vehicle stopped moving. Dean caught up to him as they reached the steps. The air smelled like bear—or like animal, anyway, since Dean wasn't too sure what a bear actually smelled like in person. Muskier than Mrs. Frankel, but not as manurelike as a zoo.

They climbed the steps. Sam opened the screen door, and they went through; the bear had left the front door open. "Was he raised in a barn?" Dean asked.

Sam ignored him. Dean didn't blame him a bit. Sam paused and leaned inside the open doorway, holding onto the jamb with both hands. "Hello! Is anyone here?"

No one answered. He released the jamb and stepped inside, Dean following close behind him.

The bear had not been as tidy as he might have. In the front room, a couch was overturned, its cushions spilling onto the carpet. A small table had stood in front of it, but it was splintered now, with only one leg remaining whole. Mud and claw marks marred the off-white carpeting.

"Why do I feel like Goldilocks?" Sam asked.

Turnabout being fair play, Dean ignored him. "Anyone home?" he called.

Still no answer. They walked through the house, which had the taut, tentative feeling of a home that was still occupied. An empty house had its own stillness, but this place felt unsettled.

In the kitchen they found out why.

She was probably fifty, still fit, and when the bear caught up with her, she had been wearing a green terry-cloth bathrobe and fuzzy pink slippers. Her hair was blond and damp, maybe from a shower.

The animal had mauled her. It probably swiped her only once with its giant forepaw, but that caught her at the collarbone and tore her head and neck almost completely off her body. A few bits of skin stretched between her neck and shoulders and the remainder of her torso. Blood pooled around her, with shards of bone and cartilage standing in it like islands in a sea of red.

Dean regarded her for a long moment, finally deciding she wasn't going to tell him anything he didn't already know. "Sammy," he said, his voice suddenly hoarse. "I think we need to talk to that bear."

TEN

In order to let Ross realize his ranching dream, Juliet Monroe had given up a middle management job at a big industrial design firm back in Chicago. The job had paid well, but provided few of what she called "spiritual benefits," a classic case of having been promoted out of what drew her to it in the first place—the challenge and creativity of rethinking the form and function of toothbrushes and toilet plungers, lamp shades and lasagna dishes. Instead she found herself in a world where only numbers mattered, how many plungers could be moved through Target, Kmart, and Costco, how a few pennies might be shaved from manufacturing costs or freight charges. Given that scenario, she was happy to leave it behind.

Money was not yet a problem, but looking down the pike she could see where it would become one, especially without Ross and his nearly infallible stock-trading instincts. It was like standing on the shore and watching an oncoming tidal wave, knowing it was big enough to swamp her but not quite able to determine how to escape it. There were no industrial design firms here in the wilderness, or many jobs at all outside of low-wage service or retail positions. If it became necessary, she would hunt for one of those, but until then she had focused her ambition on selling the ranch and returning to the city.

And one other project. Juliet had read studies showing that people married later and later these days, and that single people were too busy with careers and social lives to take the necessary steps to eat well. She included widows and widowers in this category, because although finding the time wasn't a problem for her, sometimes finding the motivation was.

But living on the ranch, she had learned the pleasures of truly fresh foods. Grass-fed beef that hadn't traveled any farther than the processing house in Williams. Organically grown vegetables and potatoes from her own place or a neighbor's. Eggs fresh from the chickens. Not only was it all healthy, it was environmentally friendlier than supermarket food because it hadn't required long-distance travel.

The single people she had in mind, however, lived mostly in urban areas. Her idea was to create farm-fresh meals for one, that could be prepared and then flash-frozen or even delivered fresh, ready to be warmed for a few minutes in an oven or microwave.

To pull it off would mean creating a network of farms and ranches near major cities, establishing the kitchens that would do the food prep, the methods of delivery, the retail channels. It was a huge undertaking.

Juliet thought it could be done, though, and had been devoting most of her time these last few months to working on it, one step at a time. While doing all the planning and calling and long-distance networking, she had also been working in her own kitchen on recipes that would be nutritious and tasty but could provide meals in bulk.

Tonight she had been planning on trying a dish of chicken parts on a bed of potatoes, garlic, onion, and vegetables. But Stu's story about the massacred cows made her uninterested in meat of any kind. Instead, she figured she would put a couple of frozen mini-pizzas in the oven—proving her point about single people and their quick meals—and save the chicken parts for another day.

It was just after four o'clock when she heard Stu's boots clomping up the steps outside. She wondered if he was ready for some lemonade. He lived in town, a twenty-five minute drive away, and sometimes stayed for dinner. Juliet was happy to feed him, most times. She liked having a man who smelled of sweat and hard work in her kitchen as she cooked.

When she saw his face, though, she didn't think he looked like a man who wanted lemonade. "I think we ought to call the sheriff, Juliet," he said, his voice tight with emotion.

"What is it? Stu, what's—"

"Time I got back out there, after I talked to you before, there were more of the cows butchered."

Her stomach churned at the news. "Who's doing it?"

"What's doing it, more like, and I just can't tell you. Whatever it is, it's fast and quiet." He sat down at the kitchen table without being asked, pulled his hat off, and rubbed his head briskly. "And one more thing, ma'am. It's just plain mean."

"How . . . ?"

"It just tears those animals up for no good reason. It's not eatin' 'em. It's . . . well, it's just murder."

Juliet had a cordless phone on the kitchen counter. Although the counter was a plain wooden butcher-block type, and dominated by an old steel watering can that usually held freshly cut flowers during the spring and summer, the appliances on it were modern. On unsteady legs, she crossed to it, picked it up, and pressed Talk. She held it to her ear, expecting to hear a dial tone.

Instead she heard dull silence.

She punched End and Talk again, but nothing changed. The display showed that the battery power was strong. "It's dead," she said. "Wait here, I'll try another one."

Leaving Stu in the kitchen, she rushed to the bedroom. The phone there was an old-fashioned corded one, which she had always kept on a nightstand beside her bed—even though long experience had taught her that the only calls she got late at night were wrong numbers, or her brothers back in Illinois calling with some kind of trouble, as when her mother had died suddenly a few years back. She lifted the handset. No tone.

"It must be the line!" she called. As she hurried back into the kitchen, she added, "This storm must have—"

"Ain't the storm." Stu's certainty unnerved her.

"Are you sure? Sometimes the lines here go—"

"There's something out there, Juliet. I don't like even thinkin' like this, much less saying it, but when I was out there in the pasture, movin' the stock, I had this sense. Pricked up the hairs on my arms and neck. It was . . . hell, I'm no philosopher or anything, I'm just a ranch hand. But I'd swear it felt like I was walking through a soup made of pure evil."

The metaphor brought a smile to Juliet's face, even as she recognized the inappropriateness of that particular response. She caught her expression midway and erased it. "That's . . . I don't know, Stu."

"It sounds crazy as hell," Stu said. "I can barely believe I said it. I'm just telling you what I felt."

"And you think that has something to do with the phones being down?"

"Couldn't tell you why. But yes, I do think that."

Cell phones didn't work out here in the middle of nowhere—the ranch was located in a canyon that blocked the signals. Ross had talked about getting a satellite phone for emergencies but had never done it. Even her Internet access was on dial-up, so without phones the ranch was completely disconnected. "I guess we can drive into town," she suggested. Stu drove back and forth from home in an old pickup that the ranch owned, and she had her Pathfinder as well.

"I guess we got to," Stu agreed. "You have a gun here?"

"A gun?" Neighbors had told them to get a rifle when they moved in, for mountain lions or snakes or wolves, none of which she or Ross could have imagined shooting. They wanted the ranch to make money, but the reason they had come to this part of the world was to feel closer to nature. They were transplanted urban liberals. Shooting animals was not in their makeup. People had told her to get a dog, too, but since the death of their collie Rusty they hadn't been willing to get another pet. And wasn't she surrounded by death these last few years? What was with that? "No, no gun."

"What I thought," Stu said. He glanced about the kitchen as if somebody might have left one lying around. "Let's go, then."

He tugged keys from his jeans pocket and screwed his hat back onto his head. Juliet hadn't been outside nor planning to go, so it took her a couple of minutes to gather herself, pulling on a sweater and a heavy coat, leather gloves and a knit cap, against the snow-storm that gathered strength out there. Finally she grabbed her purse. "Okay," she said. "Let's get the sheriff."

They went to the truck. Stu opened the passenger door for her, demonstrating old-fashioned male politeness, and she climbed up into the cab. He got in behind the wheel, closed and locked his door, and pushed the key into the ignition. Turned it.

Nothing happened.

He tried it a second time, with the same result.

"Damn it," he said. "Got me here this morning with no trouble."

"You think the battery's dead?"

"I don't see why it would be."

"Let's take the Pathfinder, then."

Stu hesitated with his hand on the door handle, peering through the snow outside as if trying to see what might be waiting out there, between where the truck was parked in the drive and the SUV's haven under a covered carport. "Let's hurry," he said.

They both swung their doors open at the same time, dropped to the gravel driveway, and dashed through falling snow to the carport. On the way she yanked her right glove off with her teeth and dug for her keys in her purse.

When they reached the carport, she stopped short.

All four tires on the Pathfinder had been shredded. Bits of rubber were strewn all over the concrete floor and out into the driveway. "Oh," she said. Nothing else came to her, not even a curse. Just that single, inadequate word, barely more than an exhalation given a little bit of voice.

"This ain't good, Juliet."

She swallowed and found her voice again. "No. No, it's not. I mean, we can drive out on rims if we have to. But—"

"It's been here. It's trying to keep us here."

"It looks like it's succeeding."

"Try the engine," Stu suggested. Then he bent down, glanced under the hood. Even from a standing position, Juliet could see pools of liquid on the concrete, with bits of wire and tubing in it. "No, don't bother. It got to this one, too."

Juliet felt the chill that Stu had described, and it had nothing to do with snow blowing down her collar. She hadn't seen the cows, and ranch cattle were destined for eventual slaughter anyway, and that whole thing had seemed a little abstract to her.

Seeing the vehicles disabled, though, and the phone lines . . . these things indicated some sort of malevolent intelligence that seemed to have it in for them. It wanted to keep them on the ranch, and that couldn't be for any good reason.

How had he put it? A soup of evil?

It hadn't made sense at the time.

Now it did. And it was perfect.

Perfect, and horrible.

ELEVEN

The bear had loped around the house, headed for the forest behind it. Sam and Dean made a breakneck tour of the house to verify that there were no other victims, then dashed outside. Tracks in the snow confirmed the animal's direction, and that it hadn't changed course. Beyond the backyard, as far as they could see, were trees. Nothing but trees.

And somewhere among them, a killer bear.

Sam flung his left arm out, blocking Dean before he could tear off into the woods after it. "What?" Dean said.

"That thing was huge," Sam said. "We're going to need some firepower."

"Right." They both reversed course, headed for the Impala. Or as Sam sometimes thought of it, the mobile armory. He'd have been happiest with a bazooka, but he settled for a sawed-off, double-barreled, twelve-gauge shotgun with a pistol grip. He cracked it open, fed in two shells of buckshot, and pocketed a dozen more. Dean chose a .45 automatic handgun, a Smith & Wesson that was just like—possibly even the same one, given its scarred grip—the one Dad had trained them with. Sam noted that he put a couple of extra magazines in his pockets.

"Loaded for bear," Dean said.

The silence in the forest was almost eerie. The snow on the ground muffled their footfalls. The stuff coming down seemed to Sam like it should have made some kind of sound—rain did, after all, and so did falling leaves. Shouldn't there be little puffing sounds or something? But no, not a peep. If there were birds around, they were still and quiet, no doubt trying to stay out of the weather.

Fortunately, the snow wasn't falling fast enough to fill in the bear's tracks. They were deep, five-toed, with the rear feet showing more pad than the front. Sam was surprised they couldn't hear it crashing through trees and brush up ahead, but apparently the bear knew its way around the forest.

"How long are we going to track this thing?" he asked after about twenty minutes. The sun was invisible behind pewter clouds, but it would be setting before too much longer.

"Till we find it. You want to quit, you know where the car is."

"I'm not saying I want to quit, Dean. I'm only saying we didn't really come prepared for a long hunt. If that thing's moving fast, it could take us all night to catch up to it. We're not equipped for spending the night out here. Won't do anyone any good if we freeze to death."

"Then I guess we should go faster." Dean picked up the pace even as he spoke, stepping over a low shrub and around another.

Sam knew his brother well enough to recognize what was going on. Nothing pissed Dean off like failure. They had been taught from childhood that when they failed, people could die. Dean took it a step further, believing that if he was even a little slow in succeeding, people would definitely die.

Dad had wanted to make soldiers of his boys. In Dean's case, he had clearly succeeded. Almost everything about Dean said soldier, from the short hair to the solid build, the straight shoulders, the easy familiarity with weapons and combat of all kinds.

It was internal, too, even more than external. Dean had no sense of romance, of wonder. They dealt on a daily basis with things most people only imagined in nightmares, they saw things that would qualify as miraculous. But the creatures they battled weren't mysteries or marvels to Dean, they were simply enemies. To him, everything was the mission, the hunt.

Here in Cedar Wells, Sam had to admit, Dean's concern had definitely materialized. Which meant that he didn't blame Dean for taking this personally. He did, too. He just kept enough emotional separation so he could tell when they were in danger of making things worse by killing themselves. Sometimes he thought Dean wouldn't mind dying if he could go out in a blaze of glory, as the saying went.

In moments of fairness, Sam knew that wasn't true. Dean didn't care about the glory; he cared about making a difference.

Sam had to step lively to keep up.

"When we catch up to it," he said a few minutes later, slightly out of breath from the pace, "what are we going to do? Interrogate it?"

"We're gonna kill it, Sammy."

"But . . ."

"But what? You want to make friends with it? That's not Gentle Ben. Or . . . or Yogi."

"I know that. It's just that, well, this changes things."

"Changes them how?"

"We're not looking for the spirit of some old soldier anymore. Not if this bear is involved, too. We're back to square one."

Dean paused, mid-stride, and caught his eye. "Good point," he said, and continued after the bear.

"I mean it, Dean," Sam continued. "We thought we were dealing with one dead guy. But now we've got, what, animal spirits?" In his haste he had only brought buckshot shells, not rock salt ones. If it was a spirit bear, he'd be sorry for that oversight.

"Animal spirits working in collusion with human ones," Dean muttered. "That could happen. Or maybe it's a werebear."

"In broad daylight?"

"Yeah, another good point."

"I'm full of 'em."

"Full of something, anyway."

"Dean, I'm all for killing as many unnatural creatures as we can. But right now we have to decide what's a higher priority, finding this bear or figuring out what's behind the murder cycle here. I vote for the murder cycle."

"I've always been bad at prioritizing," Dean said. "I'm better at the whole killing thing." He came to a sudden halt. Sam could tell by his body language that something was wrong. Dean stood awkwardly at the edge of a small clearing in the trees, his hands splayed out, staring at the ground.

"What is it?" Sam asked, fearing the worst.

"You tell me."

Sam shouldered in beside Dean, his right arm brushing snow from low-hanging pine branches. The bear tracks led into the clearing, plain in the fresh snow.

But then they stopped, halfway across it.

From the last tracks, it would have taken an Olympic long jumper to reach any spot outside the clearing. There were no trees close enough for the bear to have climbed up. The tracks just ended, and the bear was gone.

"Where'd he—"

"I wish I knew."

From a branch about twenty feet up one of the nearest trees, a raven *cawed*. It sounded disturbingly like it was laughing at them.

"That thing must have weighed five hundred pounds," Sam said. "It can't just up and vanish."

"Don't tell me," Dean said. "Tell it."

The raven gave another double *caw*. Sam could have sworn it was looking right at them, its head cocked, a sinister grin on its bill. Then it spread its wings, pure black, like midnight shadows stretching out, and took flight. Voicing its amusement, it circled over them twice, inscribing the perimeter of the clearing. Dean raised his .45 like he might shoot it down on the wing. "Thing bothers me," he said.

"Me, too." The raven swept its wings against the air and flew out of sight.

"You don't think . . ." Sam began.

"What? That raven was the bear? Some kind of animal shapeshifter?"

"That's what I was thinking. The bear transformed into a bird, and that's why the footprints stopped."

Dean shot him a frustrated glance. "Why didn't you say something? Maybe I should have shot it."

"Maybe so," Sam agreed. "I didn't think of it until it was too late."

"Next time, think faster."

"I'll try, Dean."

"Good."

"And Dean?"

"What?"

"What the hell are we dealing with here?"

Dean considered this for a moment. "You figure that out, college boy, you let me know."

TWELVE

Since the mall's food court wasn't open yet, Sam and Dean had skipped lunch. On the way back into town, having called the sheriff's office about the bear's victim from the victim's own house, Dean slowed outside the Wagon Wheel Café. Sam realized that hunger pangs had started eating his stomach from the inside out. "Sure," he said. "I could eat. And maybe we can find something out from the locals."

"The ones who are still alive, you mean." Dean pulled over at the curb. "I can always eat, but I'm pretty hungry now, too."

Inside, the Wagon Wheel carried out its theme visually, with wagon wheels printed on the menu and antique ones hung on the walls like works of art. A waitress with a knot of thick straw-blond hair on her head, an apron around her waist, and a frenzied air ticked her head toward the tables, most of which were empty. "Sit anywhere you like," she said. "I'll be there in a jif."

"A jif," Dean said as they sat down. "Don't hear that often enough these days."

"Place is quiet," Sam observed.

"It's early for dinner," Dean said. "And it looks like it's busy enough for her."

Of the four occupied tables, three had what looked like families gathered around them, one of which spanned the generations from very elderly grandparents to an infant in a high chair. When Sam saw families like that, he sometimes felt a pang of regret—that was a storybook life, as far as he was concerned, something that real people did sometimes but that he could never be part of. He had hoped for a time that he might have it with Jess, even though he hadn't grown up in that kind of setting. But it was hard to overcome one's early life, he guessed. Kids who are homeless are more likely to become homeless as adults than kids who have always had a roof over their heads. Children in dysfunctional families often re-created them when they grew up. His chances at a "normal" family life had ended on November 2, 1983, when his mother was slaughtered against the ceiling of his nursery, and he hadn't accepted that until Dean took him away from Stanford the weekend before his law school interview.

Since then, events had convinced him that his hopes of normalcy with Jessica would have been doomed anyway. He was simply not a normal guy. He had been chosen for something—it was no accident that

Mom had died above his crib and not Dean's bed, or her own. Sam had been targeted.

But knowing that didn't mean it hurt any less to look at what might have been.

He noticed Dean gazing around the big room, studying the people at the tables. After a moment he realized why. "Looking for that widow? Juliet?"

"I wouldn't mind seeing her again."

"I bet you wouldn't."

Dean was about to say something else when the waitress stopped beside their table, having delivered an armload of dishes to the big family. "What can I get you? Coffee to start?"

"Sure," Dean said. "That'd be good."

Sam thought it over for a second. The snow was still falling outside, and there was no telling when they'd be in for the night—if at all. "Sure, coffee works."

"Ready to order?"

Dean ordered a hamburger, Sam a hot open-faced turkey sandwich with mashed potatoes. The menu was heavy on all-American dishes and comfort foods, light on anything trendy or even remotely healthy. Sam hoped the gravy didn't come with extra artery blockers already mixed in.

The brothers were quiet while they waited for the food, unwinding from the tension of the bear chase and the two dead bodies they'd already seen that day—three if you counted the fact that they hadn't made it to Ralph McCaig's place until after midnight. When the waitress came back with their orders, Dean flashed a smile at her. "You from around here?"

"Sure thing. Bred and born."

She looked to be in her mid to late thirties, so wouldn't remember the last murder cycle firsthand. "We're just visiting," Dean said. "But it sounds like we picked a bad time."

She brushed a stray hair off her cheek. "Bad how? The snow?"

"No, I don't mind that. But people seem to be dying around here this week."

She moved her shoulders up and down, turning her head, like she was trying to work out a sore muscle. "I guess that's true."

"Have you heard about it?"

"You know how it is, place like this. People talk. I hear things. I don't always credit what they have to say."

"Way we hear it is, three since last night," Dean said.

"Ralph was a good man," the waitress said. Color flooded into her cheeks. "I didn't really know Johnny that well. But poor Brittany Gardner—she worked here for a time, when she first moved to town."

"Was she in her fifties or so, gray hair?" Sam asked.

"Oh, no. Brittany is—was—younger than me."

"Then it's four," Sam said.

"It's four." The new speaker was a man sitting alone at a nearby table with a folded newspaper and a cup of coffee in front of him. He had brown hair turning gray at the temples, a big head with enormous ears that looked like they would flap in a high wind, and a somber expression. "Four, and it's just begun."

"Now, Cal," the waitress said. "Don't go filling these boys' heads."

Cal ignored her. His lower lip jutted out far enough for fighter jets to land on. "You can still get out of town," he said. "If you're just passing through, you must have someplace better you can go." He nodded toward the waitress. "Eileen and I, we don't know anything other than Cedar Wells. We'll stick it out, like my family did last time, and most probably be fine. But there's no reason for you to put yourselves at risk."

"Well, I wasn't born yet, if there really was a last time," Eileen said. "But I think it's a lot of crazy talk."

"You just said it yourself, you wasn't born," Cal said dismissively. "I was. I was fourteen. And let me tell you, it was a scary time. My pa locked us kids up in an inside bedroom and sat out on the porch with three rifles, day and night. When he had to sleep, my uncle spelled him, on account of he didn't have a family of his own. Time betimes, they thought it was safe, and Uncle Jute went back to his place. Pa let us all out of the house. That night, Uncle Jute took an arrow through the throat. They said it killed him instantly and he didn't suffer, but I have my doubts about that part."

"An arrow?" Sam asked.

"That's right. The killings happen in all sorts of ways. Guns, knives, arrows, everything."

"What about animal attacks?"

"That, too," Cal said.

"Cal, honestly, I don't think—" Eileen began.

"Don't tell me, Eileen. I was there. Forty years ago, it was, and now it's happening again. It don't do no good to pretend it's not."

"But nobody knows why?" Dean asked. "Or who's behind it?"

"I heard the sheriffs had a suspect today," Cal said. "Or—what did Trace call him when he was in here, Eileen?"

"A person of interest," Eileen said.

"That's right, a person of interest. Witnesses saw some old codger with a long gun near one of the scenes."

"An old man?" Sam asked. "Was he dressed in a military uniform?"

"No. I heard about that, too, over at the shopping center. Jim Beckett don't think the two are the same man. For one thing, the attacks happened too close together, timewise, but far apart in distance. Unless the old guy had a truck or something, which nobody saw, he couldn't have got to Brittany Gardner's place that fast."

Sam wasn't so sure about that. The old soldier hadn't seemed particularly spry, but he hadn't been particularly substantial, either. The way he phased in and out of visibility made him a spirit, most likely, and spirits weren't bound by the same laws of physics as human beings. The only part that didn't add up was losing the uniform and gaining a rifle.

"Boys, your food's getting cold while you listen to Cal here," Eileen said. "And I can tell you from personal experience that Cal can talk all night if you let him."

Sam looked down at his plate. The gravy had started to congeal on his untouched meal. *And I was so hungry.*

But Cal was the first person who seemed willing to discuss the murder cycle openly, instead of pretending it wasn't happening.

Cal regarded the Winchesters for a long moment, gave one somber nod, then drained his cup, put some bills on the table, and picked up his newspaper. "I'll be going, then," he said. "You boys be careful. And if you heed my advice, you'll get yourselves gone, quicker instead of slower."

"Thanks, Cal," Dean said. "We'll keep that in mind."

Cal sauntered out of the café, Eileen watching him leave before scooping up the cash. "He means well," she said. "He's just a little on the excitable side."

He didn't look that excitable to me, Sam thought, finally digging into his dinner. *Excitable like a judge, maybe.*

Or an undertaker.

Cal Pohlens lived three blocks from the Wagon Wheel, with his wife Lorene and a half-blind house cat who was too mean to die, or too dumb—he hadn't decided which. The feline was mostly Lorene's, but since she had taken sick and spent most of her days in a wheelchair and most of her nights hooked up to a ventilator, he wasn't sure who really took care of who. She didn't eat much these days, so he'd taken to getting more and more of his meals at the Wheel. It helped him to get away from the house, to take some fresh air, and to see other people now and again.

He was halfway home when something caught his eye.

A dark shape had passed just beyond the half-circle glow thrown by a motion light above the Richardsons' door. The motion had been furtive, like someone, or something, ducking into the shadows before he or it could be seen. Cal slipped a hand into the pocket of his Carhartt barn coat and gripped the .38 revolver he carried there. He took a few steps forward, until he could see into the shadows at the side of the Richardson house.

The figure was still on the move. This time it passed through a stray slice of moonlight cutting through the trees of the property next door, and he saw an old man in a heavy coat and a hunting cap, the kind with flaps that tied up on top or could be let down over your ears. He carried a rifle at port arms. When he saw Cal looking at him, he darted from the light, vanishing into the black shadows behind the Richardsons' place.

"You there!" Cal shouted. "Come back here!"

The old man didn't answer. Any other time, any other year, Cal might have thought he had imagined it, or he might rightly have believed that he'd had one too many at the Plugged Bucket. But he hadn't had a drink since the first of December. He wanted his hands steady and his mind sharp. Leaving Lorene alone except for that damn cat wasn't the best idea, maybe, but he needed some time to himself, and he needed to eat. Most hours of the day and night he was right there with her, and anything that wanted to kill her would have to face him first.

In his other coat pocket, Cal had a cell phone. He drew out both hands at once, .38 in his right, phone in his left, and started down the Richardsons' driveway. With his left hand he flipped the phone open and punched 911, and in a moment Susannah Brighton, the night dispatcher, answered.

"It's Cal Pohlens, Susannah," he said. "I'm outside Lew and Billie Richardsons' place on School, and I just saw some old bastard with a rifle sneaking around the back."

"An old man?" Susannah asked.

"Twice my age if he's a day," Cal replied. "I'm surprised he don't need a walker, but he can move pretty good."

"I'll dispatch some officers right away, Cal," she said. "You just stay back and point them in the right direction when they get there. And be careful."

"Yes'm," he said, and ended his call. He dropped the phone back into his pocket but kept the pistol out. "Screw that," he mumbled to himself. Lew Richardson wasn't exactly his friend—man had borrowed a chain saw ten years ago, and gave it back two years later with the chain about rusted through and the engine fouled. But Lew was a neighbor, and he'd be damned if he would just stand around with his thumb up his ass while the old man killed Lew and Billie.

Alert for anything, finger resting lightly on the trigger, Cal headed down the driveway. He kept his tread soft, checking the ground every couple of steps to make sure he didn't step on anything that might make noise. If he did, the snow quieted it.

When he reached the back corner of the house, he squeezed in close to the wall and came around slowly. The old man was still back there, about ten feet from the kitchen door, hunkered down behind a bush just out of the light that spilled from the windows. He studied the house something fierce, and that old gun—was it an old Henry rifle?—was pointed right at it.

Cal didn't want the guy to get off a shot at Billie or Lew. He showed himself, leveling his .38 at the man's torso. "Drop that antique and come out of there," he demanded. "Right now, before I lose patience and just shoot—"

His command was interrupted by the kitchen door swinging open with a bang and a shape launching out of it. Cal tore his gaze from the old man and caught the briefest glimpse of someone who looked like a rancher—not a modern rancher, but one from a century past, wearing cotton dungarees and a plaid shirt and plain, heavy boots, carrying a big bowie-type knife—just before the man slammed into him and bulled him to the ground. Cal heard two shots ring out, one his own, which went wild, and one that must have been from the old guy with the Henry rifle. That one struck the rancher—Cal saw the impact as the bullet hit him in the temple and saw his head swing from the force, saw tissue and bone fly from an exit wound on the other side.

What it didn't do was stop him or seem to slow him down at all. The rancher landed astride Cal, and he took the thick-bladed, heavy bowie, grabbed Cal's hair with his left hand, and commenced sawing at Cal's scalp. Cal screamed and screamed, thought maybe he heard one more shot, thought maybe he saw a puff of dust from a bullet that might have passed through the rancher's plaid shirt, but he couldn't be sure about any of that because his own screams drowned everything out and his own blood was splashing into his eyes.

A third shot sounded, and this time Cal was pretty sure he heard it. Blinking away the stinging blood, he saw the old man, not six feet from the guy who was scalping him alive. The rancher's face showed pain this time, his mouth dropping open, his head tilting toward Cal. For the first time, Cal saw that the rancher had lost his own scalp; the top of his head was shorn down to the bone in spots, although no blood showed there.

The rancher slumped forward, sliding off Cal and falling to the ground beside him. Cal tried to move, to gain his feet, to run away or shoot or do anything, but he was too weak. Cold and weak. Lying in the snow, the scalped rancher just inches away, he watched the man blink in and out like a flashlight with a drained battery. He was there and then he wasn't and then he was, and then he was gone. Cal didn't think he was coming back, but by then everything had grown dark, so he wasn't at all sure.

THIRTEEN

A siren pierced the quiet of Main Street.

"Let's go," Sam said.

Dean threw money on the table. Eileen caught his gaze as he shrugged into his coat. "Thanks, guys," she called.

"Food was great," Sam assured her. He had eaten about half his dinner, Dean guessed. Dean had wolfed down a little more, but he'd been eating as Cal was talking, while Sam had been listening.

They rushed outside, ran for the car. Dean got his door open while Sam was still running around to the passenger side, and he had the engine roaring by the time Sam sat down. Checking the rearview, he lurched out into the road. Sam was thrown back into the seat, still wrestling with the seat belt.

By the time they were under way, the siren had stopped.

"That's not far away," Dean said.

"Not at all." Sam pointed to the left. "I think it went down there, maybe to the street that parallels this one."

Dean turned left at the corner. When they reached the next street—School Street, the sign said, and another sign warned of a 15 MPH SPEED LIMIT WHEN SCHOOL IS IN SESSION—he could see the sheriff's SUV, roof lights flashing, less than a block away. He pulled up across the street from the SUV, and they were just climbing out of the Impala when another siren sounded. They stayed where they were, out of the way, while another sheriff's office vehicle raced in and Sheriff Jim Beckett jumped out. He had a grim look on his face, and the two younger deputies who came around the house to meet him looked like they were seasick, hung over, or both.

"Come on," Dean said. He started across the street. The deputies and Beckett had gathered in the driveway of a two-story house with a deep yard. Every light in the house seemed to be blazing. The same was true of the house on the other side of the drive, where the residents and people who must have been neighbors had gathered on a porch.

A deputy blocking off the driveway with crime scene tape stopped Dean and Sam when they approached. "This is a crime scene," he said. "No spectators."

"We're press," Dean told him.

"No press, either."

"Could you ask Sheriff Beckett?" Sam pressed. "He knows us."

"Sheriff knows everyone," the deputy replied. "Sorry."

Dean saw more people coming up the street and climbing up onto the neighbors' porch. "Let's try up there," he said quietly.

Sam followed his gaze. "Worth a shot."

They moved next door and up the stairs, almost in the wake of the last couple of people. "Anybody clear on what happened over there?" Dean asked no one in particular. He hoped that on the darkened porch, people wouldn't realize that they didn't know him.

"I've only heard bits and pieces," a woman said. "But what I heard sounds pretty awful."

"What's that?"

"A couple of the sheriffs used the word 'scalped.' And I saw one of them lose his dinner in the back-yard, over there near where Cal is."

"Cal's the victim?" Sam asked, a note of horror in his voice.

"*One* of the victims," a man said, picking up the story. "Sounds like it's Lew and Billie Richardson inside, and Cal outside."

"And they were all scalped?" Dean asked.

"I heard gunshots, too, but we're still not clear on who got shot."

"And I heard Sheriff Beckett asking about some old man with a gun," the woman added. "But I'm not sure who he's talking about."

That old man again.

"Do we know if they're dead?" Sam wondered.

"They were *scalped*," someone else said.

"But you can be scalped without being killed. It's all a matter of how careful the scalper is."

"From what I've heard," the first man said, "there wasn't a whole lot of finesse practiced here." Dean wished he could see the speakers, but everyone was backlit from inside the house. Besides, if he could see them, they'd be able to see him, and that might prove awkward.

Seven victims, then. That we know of.

So far.

And two of them inside a house. Like the bear they had encountered earlier, the killer seemed able to get through doors.

They had to find that old man. That much remained clear, even if not much else did. Soldiers and bears and Bigfoot and whatever else aside, he was the only common element to any two killings so far. Three, if he was indeed the soldier.

"Anybody see where the old man went?" he asked.

"I went to the window as soon as I heard the shots," the first man said. "But it was all over by then. I could see poor Cal on the ground, even though I didn't know it was him at the time. That's it, though. We could hear sirens on the way, so we stayed inside until the first sheriff's car came."

"That's probably wise," someone else said.

"That's what we thought."

Sam nudged Dean's shoulder. "We're not going to get anything else here," he said. "Let's go."

Dean nodded and followed him down the stairs and back to the car. "I wouldn't mind talking to the sheriff again," he said as they got in. "But there's a point of diminishing returns, and I think we're reaching it. Nobody knows as much about what's going on as we do . . . and we don't know jack."

Sam laughed. "Sounds impressive when you put it that way. Good thing the professionals are on the case."

"The difference is that when we do figure it out, we'll be able to do something," Dean pointed out. "If Sheriff Beckett figures it out, he'll assume that he's crazy and ignore the evidence even if it bites him on the ass."

"Whatever's going on, I don't think it's possible anymore for them to pretend that it's not happening."

"I don't know, that mayor seems pretty divorced from reality. The rest of the town is probably coming around fast, though."

"You think that'll slow it down? If people stay inside and keep their doors locked?"

"We don't know if these last people had their doors locked," Dean said. "It can't hurt, but there's no sign that it'll help."

"Let's cruise around a little," Sam suggested. "If the old man's still in the neighborhood, maybe we'll spot him."

Having no better ideas, Dean started the car.

Jim Beckett looked at the bloody scene in the Richardson living room and felt a weight in his gut as if he had swallowed a bowling ball. He had known Lew and Billie half his life. Now they were empty shells with most of the tops of their heads torn off—not even taken away, just scraped off and tossed to the floor like used tissues. Outside, Cal Pohlens was in basically the same shape, except his scalp had only been peeled away but not completely removed. He had known Cal his whole life, pretty much. Since sixth grade, anyway.

The resources of his forensics team were being stretched to the limit. His was a small department, and seven murders in less than twenty-four hours were more than his people could cope with. Maybe more than he could cope with. He took these deaths personally, and so many at once wore heavily on his heart.

They also, quite frankly, scared him. If the forty-year murder cycle was real, there were a lot more deaths to come. And if it was real, what did it mean? Who could be behind killings that had started eighty years ago? Yes, Brittany Gardner and Cal had both reported an old man near the scenes of their murders, but he would have had to be at least in his teens in 1926, which would make him over ninety now. From what he had seen of the brutal killings, they had taken a good deal of strength.

And then there were the two that seemed to have been committed by animals. That added a whole new, even more bizarre dimension to the whole thing.

He had a bad feeling he was going to need to call in help. State troopers from Arizona's Department of Public Safety, the FBI, even the National Guard. He wouldn't give in to that impulse quite yet, though.

Mayor Milner was right about the mall. If he asked for help from any of those agencies, the press would get wind of it—out-of-town press that he couldn't control. Something like this could not only destroy Cedar Wells in the short term, but even threaten the tourist-traffic to the Grand Canyon. Losing that trade would choke off the whole county. Sheriff Beckett didn't want to lose any more lives, but neither did he want to lose the whole region.

Talk about your rocks and your hard places, he thought. *No wonder my chest feels like it's being squeezed in a vise.*

FOURTEEN

Juliet and Stu were still standing in the carport, debating whether Stu should walk the six miles to the nearest neighbor's house, when they heard something on the roof. Stu froze in place, an anxious look etched on his face.

Not knowing what he had seen or heard, Juliet followed his lead, going still and silent. A moment later she heard it. A gentle thud, then something that sounded like claws scraping the roof.

When Stu spoke, his tone was soft but urgent. "Get in the house and lock the door, and stay there no matter what happens," he said. The next part was shouted, an anxious command. "Do it now!"

Juliet ran for the door. She hadn't put away the key ring, but she fumbled with it briefly, trying to find the right key for the knob, sorry she had turned the thumb latch before walking out. Stu came close behind her. Behind him—she knew because she heard his exhaled curse, not its landing—was something *else*. She didn't want to see what it was—knowing it was there and that it was frightening enough to make Stu run into her in his haste was bad enough.

She finally opened the door and fell inside. Stu was still behind, but she was sprawled out on the floor, and he paused, ever so briefly, maybe deciding if he should walk right on her or try to leap over. He was still standing there when something snatched him out the door again, hurling him into the yard.

"Lock the door!" he screamed.

She forced herself to slide out of the way enough to shove it closed with her feet. When she heard it latch, she pulled herself up on the knob, setting the thumb latch again, then the dead bolt. She leaned against the solid wooden door for a few moments, catching her breath.

But outside, Stu struggled with whatever had attacked them. She heard his shouts of terror and anguish, and deep, throaty animal roars. Once again she wished she had taken the advice of her neighbors and bought a gun.

Rushing to the window, she peeked out.

What she saw filled her with a kind of horror she had never imagined.

Stu had fallen to the snow-covered lawn—the snow had stopped falling; the sky was the color the edge of her hand got when she drew with a soft pencil for too long. He flailed with his arms and legs against a beast, a silvery canine with black markings. *A rabid dog?* she wondered.

Then it came to her. Not a dog.

Stu fought a wolf.

She remembered hearing reports of occasional wolf sightings locally. Wolves, virtually wiped out in the late nineteenth century, were being reintroduced to wild places around the West. Some farmers and ranchers objected, but the wolf-recovery forces usually seemed to win out.

The canine was huge and muscular, far larger than any wolf she had ever seen a picture of, and it snarled and snapped and pawed at Stu, who was on the ground, screaming and trying to fight but growing weaker even as Juliet watched.

Helpless.

If she'd had a gun she might have been able to hit it. Its broad shoulders and big head provided reasonable targets. But the best weapon she could come up with was one of the carving knives from her kitchen. If she went out with that, all it would get her was killed.

Stu had told her to stay inside, no matter what happened.

Did he understand what he was asking? Did he know that it would mean she would have to stand here and watch him die, doing nothing because there was nothing she could do?

He couldn't have known the noises on the roof were a wolf, could he? He had dismissed that idea after seeing the cattle. But even if he'd thought so, he couldn't have known how big it was, or that it could climb so well, or that it would be fast enough, vicious enough, to yank him out an open door.

She watched Stu bat at it hopelessly. The canine had one massive paw on his chest, holding him down. When the wolf lowered its head toward Stu's throat, she cringed and squeezed her eyes shut. That lasted only an instant; by the time she opened them again, the wolf was lifting its head, its muzzle slick and red. Stu's screams had finally stopped.

Tears streamed down Juliet's cheeks. What had she been thinking earlier? That death surrounded her?

She hadn't known the half of it then.

Stu no longer moved. The animal lowered its head again, then whipped it from side to side. Tearing at something. Juliet saw stringy, bloody tissue clutched in its teeth. It chewed, swallowed. The snow around the wolf and Stu's lifeless shape was disturbed, lumpy, melting, and splattered with so much red that it looked spray-painted.

Then slowly, horribly, the wolf turned its head, looking past its left shoulder.

Right at her.

In its yellow eyes she saw a ferocious intelligence and a terrible hunger.

The cattle weren't enough for it. Neither was Stu.

That beast wanted *her.*

Juliet made sure that every door was locked. Where there were curtains open, she closed them. She turned on every light in the house. She tried the phones again, even carrying her cell phone upstairs and standing as close as she dared to all the windows, in case there was a stray signal that had seeped into the canyon. No luck.

Having done all that, she sat down on the couch in the living room and pulled a blanket around herself. She shivered, even though she had turned the thermostat up to eighty and the heater blasted away. She tried to empty her mind, to force herself to stop seeing the awful way the wolf had regarded her, to stop hearing Stu's screams and the wet ripping noises the animal made long after she had stopped watching. The last time she'd peeked from an upstairs window, bloody paw prints led away from the mangled remains of the man who had been her friend and her ranch hand.

She couldn't assume it had left, though. That's what it wanted her to think. It wanted her to believe that it had moved on, so she would go outside, make a run for the Bledsoe place down the road. Then it would come at her, like a cat chasing a mouse, toying with her until it got tired of the game and finished her off.

How long could she stay inside? She had enough food for a week, probably. The ranch had its own well and septic system, so water and sewage wouldn't be issues. Electricity, like phone service, came in on wires from the road, so if it had been clever enough to cut the phone lines, it could do the same to the power. A propane tank provided heat, but the furnace needed electricity to work. To operate the thermostat? She wasn't sure about that, although she thought not. So even if the canine shut off her lights, she wouldn't have to freeze.

Until the propane ran out.

Surely before that might happen she would be saved. Every now and then the mail carrier came to the door with a package too big for the mailbox at the end of the lane. Or a UPS driver. The mailman might even come to check when he saw her mail start to pile up inside the box. All she would need to do then was run from the house and get inside his Jeep, or the UPS truck, and slam the door and tell the driver to drive, drive away as fast as he could. One of her friends from town might even come out when a few days went by without her answering her phone.

Her thoughts brightened a little at that. There was a way out of this, after all. She would have to stay awake during the daytime, when it was likeliest that someone would drive close to the house. And weren't wolves nocturnal? So when the best opportunity presented itself, the canine would likely be sleeping somewhere.

She would leave this damned ranch and never return, never even look back. Let it go back to the land, let the house collapse with everything in it, she didn't care. Let the wolf have it all.

"You can have the ranch, but you won't get me," she said out loud. She meant for it to sound defiant, but instead it rang hollow, pitiful, to her ears. She wrapped the blanket tighter around herself and trembled.

FIFTEEN

As it had the night they first came in—just last night, Sam realized, although much had happened—the town seemed to close up early. Even the neon OPEN sign at the Plugged Bucket was turned off when they went past after leaving the Richardsons' house. The Wagon Wheel was dark and empty. It seemed word had spread, finally convincing enough people to drive them to their homes.

Where, Sam feared, they were no safer than they were at any other place. If it chose you, it chose you, whether it was an old man or a spirit or a shape-shifter, and there didn't seem to be a hell of a lot you could say about it.

They cruised dark and silent streets, searching for the old man. The snow had stopped falling, although now and then a breeze puffed some into the air. In fact, Main Street had been plowed, but nothing else had, and the Impala made a shushing noise as they drove. On the tape deck, Bob Seger sang "Turn the Page," about being on the cold and lonely road, and Sam empathized. Dean tapped his fingers quietly on the steering wheel, in time to the music.

"This is pointless," Dean said after twenty minutes or so. "There's nobody out, much less an old man with a gun."

"The killer might be out there somewhere," Sam said. "We're just not seeing him."

"Or it. And if it's a spirit, we might never see it. We've got to be on the scene when a killing happens, or right after. That's the only way we're going to run it to ground."

"Like we were on the scene with the bear."

"Yeah, except at the time we thought it was just a bear. Now we know better."

"Let's go back to our room," Sam suggested. "We can listen to the police band radio, maybe get online and see if there's something else we can learn. Something we've been missing."

"We're missing something, that's for sure," Dean said. He changed course, back to Main and toward the Trail's End.

They had stayed in so many motels during Sam's younger days that, growing up, he'd been surprised to learn that there actually were families like the ones he saw on TV, who lived in the same place day after day and didn't have to collect their mail, if they got any at all, from some desk clerk or other. Stanford was the only place he had ever felt close to settled in, and the apartment he shared with Jess was the only home he'd ever looked forward to getting back to at the end of the day. He wondered what it might be like to have bookshelves, family pictures and your own artwork on the walls, a pantry full of food that you liked and wanted to eat.

He might never find out. People in his line of work—not that there were many of them—probably didn't get the chance to retire peacefully.

The Trail's End was like most other motels. Inexpensive and anonymous. Most of the vehicles scattered around the parking lot when they pulled in hadn't been there in the morning, when they left. Their room was decorated with an over-the-top cowboy theme. It had two beds covered in western-print bedspreads, with the legs of the beds standing in old, worn-out, painted cowboy boots. The dresser on which the broken TV sat had cow-horn drawer pulls, while the single nightstand between the beds had miniature lassoes instead, along with phone books on an open shelf, a Bible and the *Book of Mormon* in the drawer, and a telephone and clock radio on top. The closet door was mirrored, and there were six hangers inside, the kind that fit into little hooks that the pole slid through, so people couldn't steal them to use at home. Boots and ropes and cattle danced around on the wallpaper.

The cowboy motif didn't carry through to the bathroom. There was a flat counter with a tissue box and what looked like an ashtray laden with little packets of shampoo and conditioner, along with a single bar of soap and a coffeepot. Behind the coffeepot, a bucket held sugar, creamer, and plastic stirring sticks. There were also a standard toilet and a tub with a plain white shower curtain.

All the comforts of home, if your home was a Super 8 or a Motel 6.

Sam's pretty much was. He guessed that motels had won their way into the hearts of Americans by offering low prices and a kind of sameness, so whether you were visiting Niagara Falls or the Rocky Mountains or Graceland, the view inside the room would be more or less the same, once you got past the regional differences in decor.

Unless you were a Winchester.

When they stayed in a motel, they kept the Do Not Disturb sign out at all times. The walls quickly became papered with news clippings and printouts from the Web, most dealing with unsavory topics that might frighten your average motel housekeeper. They traveled with a police band radio, guns and knives and other assorted weaponry, electromagnetic frequency readers and infrared thermal scanners, a laptop computer and a printer, and enough miscellaneous equipment to make the unschooled suspect terrorism or worse. Any room they occupied turned almost immediately into a command center for their spook-busting operation, and when every surface was covered, they started setting stuff up on the floor.

They had hardly spent any time in this room yet, so Sam could still see the walls and furniture when he walked in and clicked on the light. Most of the gear they would have set up in the room had been hauled in and left on the floor. Without discussion, they both went to work, as they had so many times before. Sam got the laptop booted up and online, with the printer connected and ready to go. Dean turned on the radio and found the frequency of the local sheriff's office. As the room filled with the buzz and crackle and unique shorthand of cop talk, he started cleaning and reloading some of their guns.

Sam plugged into the LexisNexis database, which gathered news items from newspapers, radio, TV, and the Internet, and ran a search for Cedar Wells. Most of what came up had to do with the Grand Canyon, although there were also some stories about a logging controversy when a nearby mill had been bought out and shut down. Beyond that, he found a small handful of stories about the killings, mostly breathless tabloid tales that made the whole thing less believable instead of more. If he'd seen some of those before coming out, he might have recommended not bothering to make the trip.

Scanning a few of them, however, he found references to someone named Peter Panolli, who claimed to have witnessed one of the murders, back in 1966. The article had been published in 2002. "Dean, check the phone book for me."

"Yes, boss," Dean said wryly. "What am I checking for?"

Sam spelled the last name. "Peter," he added. "See if he still lives in the area." He kept reading through the largely useless articles as Dean flipped pages in the background.

"Got him," Dean said a minute later. "Cedar Wells address. Peter Panolli, M.D."

"He's a doctor?"

"That's what it says."

Sam checked the digital readout on the clock radio: 9:30. A little late to be considered polite, but etiquette was far from his first priority at the moment. And doctors had to be used to getting calls at all hours, right?

He turned away from the laptop and snatched up the motel phone. "Read me the number." Dean did, and Sam punched the buttons.

The voice that answered didn't belong to the doctor. It was too young to have been around in 1966, and too female to be anyone named Peter. "Hello?"

"Hi," Sam said. "I'm sorry to call so late. I'm looking for Dr. Panolli."

"Hold on a sec," she said. He heard thumping noises, and then a muffled shout. "Dad!"

More thumping sounds, and a minute later an older, deeper voice came on the line. "This is Dr. Panolli."

"Peter Panolli?"

"That's right."

"This is going to sound strange, Doctor, but I just read that you were a witness to one of the killings in the last Cedar Wells murder cycle, back in 1966. Is that true?"

Panolli let a long pause elapse before he spoke. "What's your interest?"

Sam had known that question was coming, and

as usual, there was no easy answer for it. "I don't know if you've heard, but it's started again. Right on schedule." Honesty seemed like the best policy in this case, so he took a breath and continued. "My brother and I are trying to stop it, not just for now but forever. But we need to understand what we're dealing with. I wondered if you'd take a few minutes to tell us about your experience."

"Tonight?"

"People are dying, Dr. Panolli. Tonight would be good."

Another pause, but not as long this time. "Very well. Can you come around right away?"

"We're leaving right now," Sam said. "And thank you."

The Panollis lived in a large white house on the edge of town. A wrought-iron fence stood around the property, but the gate was open when they arrived. Driveway lights illuminated the way to the front door, which was made of some heavy, carved wood. A brass knocker hung on it, just below a huge fresh pine wreath, but before either of the brothers could grab it, the door swung wide.

Sam guessed that the girl who opened it was the one who had answered the phone. She was nineteen or twenty, he speculated, wearing a red cable-knit sweater with a white reindeer emblazoned on the front over faded jeans and thick purple socks. "I'm Heather," she said with a bright smile.

"I'm Sam. This is Dean."

"Your dad here?" Dean asked.

"I'll get him." Her pale blond hair was shoulder length and loose, and when she pivoted to fetch her father it whirled around her head like a hoop skirt on a square dancer.

"Cute," Sam muttered when she was gone.

"For a kid, I guess," Dean said.

Any reply Sam might have made was cut off by footsteps coming toward them from inside the big house. One set was Heather's soft shuffling, the other heavier, and with an added knocking sound. Sam saw why when Dr. Panolli came into view. He was a big man, tall and broad and with a gut of substantial mass preceding him into the room. He carried a wooden cane, and the cane's rubber tip tapped the floor with every step.

"You're Dean?" he said, approaching Sam and extending his right hand.

"No, Sam. This is Dean." Sam took the hand and gave it a quick shake.

The doctor turned to Dean, shook his as well, and said, "Delighted to meet you both. Welcome to my home. It's late for coffee, but if you'd like a cup of herbal tea? Or hot chocolate?"

"No thanks," Dean said. "We don't want to take much of your time."

"Let's at least make ourselves comfortable," Panolli said. He gestured toward a double doorway with a pocket door that was mostly tucked into its slot. "Shall we?"

Dean led the way, followed by Sam, Dr. Panolli,

and Heather. They went into a living room stuffed with antiques, in the way that some antique stores are stuffed. Threading a line between tables and lamps and tables that had lamps built into them, between a sailor's trunk and a huge copper urn, around a spindly chair that looked like a stiff wind would break it, much less the good doctor's bulk, Dean found a couch that looked like it could support some body weight and sat down on it. Sam joined him. Panolli chose a chair on the other side of a glass-topped coffee table—a big chair. Heather perched on the fragile looking one.

"I hope you haven't wasted a trip out here," Panolli began. He pressed on the sides of his head with both hands, as if trying to tame his mane of graying hair. His eyes were hooded, his jowls like a bulldog's, and his lips rubbery and moist. "I'm afraid there's very little I can tell you beyond what is commonly known and what has been reported in the press. I was about Heather's age. A little younger. This was 1966, right? You might not think it to look at me now, or at the town, but there were hippies in Cedar Wells, and I was one of them. I'm not certain we called ourselves hippies yet, that may have come a year later, after the Summer of Love. But I had hair longer than Heather's, and I wore ragged jeans and protested the war in Vietnam and listened to rock and roll and folk music. Bob Dylan's *Blonde on Blonde* had come out that year, and it was a revelation. That was also the year that he had the motorcycle accident that changed his life, and American music, forever."

He gazed past Sam and Dean, as if he was looking into his own history. But then his eyes clari-
fied and sparkled as he warmed to his subject. Most
people acted like this, Sam had found, if you let
them talk about themselves long enough. Dr. Panolli
hadn't needed any catalyst at all, just the opportunity. "What a year for music that was. The Beach
Boys released *Pet Sounds*, Brian Wilson's master-
piece. The Beatles put out *Revolver* and quit tour-
ing. The Byrds had *Turn! Turn! Turn!* An incredible
time. My friends and I had heard about drugs, of
course, psychedelics, but with music like that on the
record player, who needed them?"

"I'm sure the music was great," Dean said abruptly.
"More of a metal fan myself, but—"

Panolli laughed, making a wheezy sound that Sam
hoped didn't lead to a heart attack. "Now we see
who the impatient one is," he said when he could
manage. "I'm coming around to the point, Sam."

"He's Dean," Sam corrected. "I'm Sam."

"Sorry. For some reason, you just look more like
a Dean to me. At any rate, I'll move it along, Sam
and Dean. We lived in a house near town, what you
might call a commune today. Seven of us, boys and
girls." He met his daughter's gaze. "Don't get any
ideas, Heather. Those were different times."

"I know, Daddy," she said, with the tone of a teenager who had heard variations on this theme many
times before.

"Early that December—I suppose it must have
been forty years ago today, or perhaps yesterday—I

was upstairs in the house. No doubt listening to records, and probably reading something by Harlan Ellison or Roger Zelazny or Samuel Delany, the science fiction gods I worshipped at the time." He smoothed down his hair again, and Sam realized it was just a habitual motion. "Yes, now that I think about it, I believe it was Delany's *Babel 17*. But that's neither here nor there. Only a few of us were home, some had gone to Berkeley for a Quicksilver Messenger Service concert, and stayed over for a Grateful Dead show at Winterland. Or was it at The Matrix?

"At any rate, it was late afternoon, that time of day when the sun is going down and everything is bathed in a kind of golden light. I heard a scream, and went to the bedroom window with my book in my hand so I didn't lose my place, and when I looked out, I saw Janet, who we called Marsh Mellow because she was the most peaceful, mellow person any of us had ever met. She had taken some laundry out to hang on the line—I hate to admit it now, but yes, the girls did the laundry and most of the cooking at the house—and she was standing there with a sheet clutched to her bosom, and all I could think as I watched was that I was witnessing something out of history, out of the Old West, the homesteader's wife in peril."

"Why history?" Sam prompted.

"Because staring at Janet, across the backyard, was an Indian warrior, in full war paint and holding a bow and arrow. Now you might call him a Native American, or a First American, but we didn't know those phrases then. He was an Indian brave. As I watched, he drew back the string and shot it at her. The arrow must have hit her right in the heart—I learned later that it did, at any rate—because she went down immediately, not moving. The sheet across her chest began to redden, but then her heart must have stopped beating because the blood stopped spreading. I dropped the book, which incidentally I have not finished, to this day, and ran downstairs and outside. But she was dead by the time I reached her, or that's what I thought. The fact that I didn't know what to do, how to save her, is what inspired me to practice medicine."

"An Indian," Dean said flatly.

"That's what I told the police when they came, and the newspapers as well. Not that anyone ever believed me. But it's the gospel truth, then and now. An Indian killed Marsh Mellow with his bow and arrow."

SIXTEEN

"An Indian," Dean said. They were back in the car—Sam driving, this time—headed for the Trail's End. "This just gets worse and worse. Wouldn't somebody have mentioned if the old man we're looking for was an Indian?"

"That's what I was thinking, too," Sam said. It always made Dean nervous when he drove the Impala, so he kept his hands on the wheel and his eyes on the road as he spoke. "But in some ways it ties in. Native American magic makes frequent use of animal totems, right?"

Dean snapped his fingers. "Like that bear. And the raven. Or the bear-raven, whatever."

"The Chippewa bear walkers, the Navajo *yee naaldlooshi*, the Hopi ya ya ceremony . . . skin walkers and animal spirits are commonplace in many Native American cultures."

"So the reason we can't find this dude is that he

keeps changing into other forms," Dean said. He couldn't suppress a shudder. "I freakin' hate shape-shifters."

"I don't blame you."

"And what about those scalpings?" Dean said. "That could be an Indian, too."

"Or not," Sam countered. There were times his Stanford education proved helpful, after all. "Some historians say that scalping was a European practice adopted by the Native Americans, while others insist it was carried out on both sides of the Atlantic long before Columbus made his trip."

"Okay, whatever. Point is, if we're dealing with Indian shapeshifters, we've got to focus in a different direction, right? There's no point in looking for an old man if he's not going to stay one."

Sam pulled into the motel parking lot. "And it gives us another area to research. We're looking for a Native American, probably a shaman or medicine man, with a grudge against the town."

"That's just great," Dean said. "While people are dying, we get to start from scratch. Again."

"We're narrowing it down, Dean. We're doing the best we can."

Sam parked the car right in front of the room, and Dean got out, slamming his door. He winced, and Sam knew he regretted his action, as he did anything that might damage his baby. "I know. I just want to get my hands on someone whose ass I can kick. I don't care if it's an old man or an Indian or a troop of Girl Scouts at this point."

Sam slid his key card through the slot—even an older motel like this had graduated beyond metal keys—and opened the door. "I think we can safely rule out the Girl Scouts."

"I'm not ruling out anything," Dean said. "Not until we have something to go on better than one crazy old doctor's memory from forty years ago. He says he wasn't smoking pot, but I'm not sure I believe him."

Inside, Sam plopped onto one of the beds. "He also says he doesn't remember what happened to the Indian. And I just don't buy that."

"He said he was really shaken up by the attack on the girl."

"True, and I believe he was. But he remembers everything else. He remembers the book he was reading, and the way the sun looked. How could he forget if the Indian ran away, or vanished, or turned into a woodpecker and flew away? He acts like he's telling everything, but he's holding back."

"Why didn't you say something when we were there?"

Sam shrugged. "He's kept that secret for forty years, he's not going to tell two strangers off the street. He told us exactly what's already been in the press. A little more detail, but no new facts."

"So you already knew about the whole Indian angle?" Dean asked. He hated it when Sam kept things from him, and Sam could hear suspicion in his voice.

"I read it online. I wanted to hear it directly from him, to be sure."

Dean settled on the other bed. He had been cleaning a nickel-plated Colt .45 when Sam had interrupted him to look up Peter Panolli's number, and had brushes and rods on the bedspread, with the weapon open and a bottle of solvent on the nightstand. He'd capped the solvent but left the rest where it was. As if he had never left, Dean now picked up a bore brush and started swabbing out the magazine well. Dad always impressed upon them the necessity of taking care of their equipment, and Dean had taken the lesson to heart. "What now, then?"

Sam clicked on the police band, but it didn't sound like there had been any more incidents. A yawn took him by surprise. "Now we should probably get some rest, while we can. We won't do anybody any good if we're dead on our feet when we finally do catch up to one of these things."

"If."

"What?"

"If we catch up to one of them." Dean was ordinarily optimistic. So far they had caught and destroyed nearly every paranormal entity they'd set their sights on. This one seemed particularly elusive, though, and it was eating away at what little patience he had left.

Sam didn't like it either, but he was better about reining in his anger, unleashing it only when he thought it would be helpful. In most respects he was the emotional one, the impulsive one, while Dean kept his feelings in check. When it came to anger, however, Dean could let loose with the best of them.

"But I'm down with the rest idea," he said. "Little shut-eye will do us both good."

When someone knocked on the door—tentatively, as if in consideration of the hour, not demanding, the way cops knocked—Sam's gaze swept past the glowing numbers on the clock: 2:11. Just once, he wanted to sleep all night.

Dean was already sitting up, his .45—freshly cleaned and loaded—in his fist. "Got you covered," he whispered.

Sam went to the door, dressed only in boxer shorts, and pulled it open a couple of inches. The motel had a bar lock that kept it from opening any farther.

"Sam?"

It was Heather Panolli, with light from the fixture by the door turning her blond hair into a halo. "Heather? You shouldn't be out alone so late. It's not safe—"

"I know, I'm sorry. My dad doesn't always go to sleep that early, and I had to wait until I was sure before I snuck out."

Sam closed the door long enough to release the bar lock, then opened it again, suddenly very conscious of his near nudity.

"Told you," Dean said when she entered. He had insisted, before bed, that the only reason Heather had stayed in the room during her dad's story, which she'd clearly heard many times, was because she was sweet on Sam. "She's into you, Sammy," was the way he'd put it, smirking all the while.

"What are you doing here?" Sam asked her now, grabbing a pair of jeans off the floor and pulling them on.

"I had to—my dad," she stammered. "He's told that story so many times, he thinks it's the truth."

"It's not?"

Sam sat on his pillows and invited her to take the end of the bed, the only clear seating area in the room now. She unzipped a heavy down coat and shrugged it off her shoulders. She still had on the same sweater and jeans, but with leather boots that had what looked like rabbit fur trim. "Well, it is, I mean, as far as it goes. It just doesn't go far enough."

"What do you mean, Heather?"

"I've heard him tell other people. My mom, when she was around, and close friends. Usually after he's had a couple of drinks, to be honest. But there's more to the story, stuff he didn't tell you tonight. I could tell you were interested for a good reason—you said you're trying to stop the killing, and I believe you. So I thought you should hear the rest of it, in case it's important."

"So spill it," Dean said.

Heather swallowed hard and looked at her boots as if they had just been placed on her feet by an alien being. "It's . . . when he talks about those days, he makes it sound like they were all peace, love, and brotherhood, right? Listening to music, reading science fiction, protesting the war and weaving baskets."

"You saying they weren't?" Dean asked. Sam wondered where the basket weaving had come from.

Still looking everywhere except at them, Heather sucked in a deep breath. "Some of the people living in that house with Dad weren't the peaceful type," she said. "Maybe they liked the same music or whatever, but from the stories he tells privately, there were a couple of guys—one in particular, who later got involved in bank robbery—who were mostly there for the easy sex and cheap rent. At least one of them had a gun in the house."

She paused. She had pulled her legs in close to her chest and wrapped her arms around them. Sam wanted to encourage her to go on, but he didn't want to spook her, so he waited. At last she gathered her courage. "When he looked out that window and saw the Indian with the bow and arrow, the first thing he did was run to that other guy's room. The guy was one of the people who were out of town, but everyone knew where he kept his gun. Dad grabbed it and ran back to the window. He fired at the same time the Indian did, he says. The arrow hit his friend Janet, but he hit the Indian. Dad's father had always been a hunter, and he'd been hunting and shooting plenty of times before the whole nonviolence thing happened."

"So he shot the Indian and didn't want to tell anyone? Why not?"

"I guess because of what happened next. He said when his bullet hit, the Indian fell down. Then he . . . I know this sounds crazy, so you can see why he doesn't like to talk about it—not that the whole story's not pretty crazy, right? The Indian faded in and out, like Dad could see him and then he couldn't, a couple of times. But then he got up, and it was like he hadn't been hurt at all. He walked away, or just faded away, Dad says he's still not sure about that part. At the same time, his arrow vanished. So then Dad's friend was in the yard with a hole in her and no explanation, and Dad had fired a pistol into the yard. He didn't think he was crazy—he thinks something was going on that he still can't explain, and it was connected to the murders that happen every forty years. But he swears he didn't shoot her, he shot the disappearing Indian."

"Only it'd be hard to sell that story to the cops," Dean said.

"That's right. I guess they weren't all up on the CSI stuff like they are these days, right? Maybe if they had tested him they could have found that he had shot a gun, but he put it away and didn't mention it, and told the story the way you heard it. The sheriffs didn't like it, he says, but there were so many other killings around town that they had to just accept it the way he said."

"And he still tells it that way now," Sam said.

"No statute of limitations for murder," Dean pointed out. "If they wanted to charge him with shooting her, they might be able to make a case."

Heather chewed on her bottom lip, her eyes finally meeting Sam's. "You won't tell anyone, will you? I don't want to get him in trouble, I just wanted you to know what you're really dealing with."

"No, of course not," Sam said. "Dean and I, we're

pretty used to dealing with strange, inexplicable events. In our world the disappearing Indian is a lot more likely than someone like your dad having a psychotic episode and shooting a friend."

"Sounds like you live in a strange world."

"We do."

"I don't think I'd like it there."

"I'd be surprised if you did," Sam said. "It takes a lot of getting used to. And even then it can be pretty unpleasant."

She regarded them for a long few moments, not like she was into Sam, as Dean had speculated, but like she was curious about people who weren't like any she had ever met. When her gaze moved away from them, it roamed across the room, taking in the equipment and the weapons and the clippings taped to the wall. "I should probably be getting home," she said.

"Yeah. Let's go, Dean."

"Go where?"

"We're not letting her drive home alone. We're following you back, Heather. If Dean doesn't want to come then I'll go by myself."

"Oh, all right," Dean grumbled, finally throwing back the blankets covering him. "But maybe she should turn the other way while I get dressed. Wouldn't want to ruin her for other men."

SEVENTEEN

Heather had driven to the motel in a red compact pickup truck that she said she used when she commuted on Mondays, Wednesdays, and Fridays to college in Flagstaff. "Told you she's into you," Dean said as they followed along behind her through the dark and empty streets.

"She's not into me," Sam protested.

"She totally is. She couldn't stop looking at you."

"Are you high? She couldn't bring herself to look at either one of us most of the time. Then all she could look at was our stuff. She must have thought we were whack jobs."

Dean snorted a laugh. "I can think of about three nasty responses to that, but I'm not even going to bother."

"You sure?" Sam asked. "Seems a little late in life for you to develop manners. Or good taste."

"It's not that. It's just that sometimes you leave

yourself so wide open, it's like shooting monkeys in a barrel. It's so easy it's no fun."

"I think it's fish," Sam said.

Dean looked away from the road and the headlights ahead long enough to shoot his brother a puzzled glance. "Fish? The hell . . . ?"

"Shooting fish in a barrel."

"What fun is a barrel full of fish?"

Sam didn't answer. Dean liked to throw his own logic back in his face, and being able to shut his brother up was its own reward.

Anyway, he had something else preying on his mind.

"Can you see in the rearview without looking like a freak?" Dean asked.

Sam tried, but couldn't.

"Take my word for it, then. There's a pair of headlights back there that I'd swear has been there since we left the motel."

"Someone's following us?"

"That's what it looks like."

"I didn't think our spirits drove."

"Maybe they're in league with humans. Or doing the bidding of humans."

"Or humans are doing their bidding. Makes as much sense as anything else we've come up with," Sam admitted.

"Think I should try to lose 'em?"

"But that'll mean losing Heather," Sam said. "The whole point of this—"

"Yeah, I know," Dean said. "It just bothers me."

He drove on, dividing his attention between Heather's truck and the lights behind them. They stayed consistently a couple of blocks back. When Dean slowed, letting Heather get farther ahead, the vehicle behind them slowed.

When they were about half a mile from Heather's place, the car Dean had thought was following them made a left turn onto a side road. "Huh," he said. "So much for that."

"For what?"

"They peeled off."

"They're not following us after all?"

"Maybe not. I guess a town this small, there are only so many roads someone can be on, and we just happened to be taking the same ones they needed."

"Whatever," Sam said. "We're here."

Heather turned into the gated driveway. After she sat there for a couple of seconds, the gates swung open for her. Dean and Sam sat on the road outside until they closed again and she was on her way to the house. Dean started to put the Impala into gear when Sam said, "Let's give her a minute."

"She's home," Dean said.

"Let's just wait till she's inside."

Dean shrugged. They already knew that people weren't actually any safer in their homes than outside, but maybe Sam was into her.

Like she was into him.

Across Cedar Wells, the attacks began in earnest.

Dennis Gladstone was sound asleep in his bed,

dreaming of three women who were very friendly and very blond, when a smell in his room, a pungent mix of stale earth and sour air, woke him. He sat up and switched on a bedside light. The smell came from what looked like a cowboy. Air sucking in and out of a ragged lung wound made a wet whistling noise. Before Dennis could say anything to the intruder, the cowboy drew a gun and fired it once, piercing Dennis's lung.

Maria Lima hadn't been able to sleep. She'd finally given up and gone downstairs so she wouldn't risk waking up her husband or their baby girl. She sat on the living room couch with a pillow across her lap, watching a late movie with the sound turned low. Seemingly from nowhere—since the couch was pushed against the wall—hands reached around from behind her and closed on her throat, cutting off her air supply. She struggled, but the hands couldn't be pried away. Before she lost consciousness, she saw—and then didn't see, and then did, and then didn't again—a woman wearing a nightdress that looked like something pioneer women might have worn. The nightdress left her neck exposed, and Maria could see dark bruises ringing the woman's throat. Then she couldn't see anything at all.

Larry Gottschalk worked nights at the Stop-N-Gas on the eastern fringe of town. The only people who ever drove up after midnight were drunk, and they were usually coming in so they could stock up on more booze to continue their buzz. A couple of times people had been so drunk that they parked at the gas pumps, came inside and bought a twelve-pack or a box of wine, and then drove away again, all without remembering that they actually did need gas. Larry took a perverse pleasure in seeing them stumbling back twenty or thirty minutes later carrying empty gas cans.

But tonight the bell on the door rang and he looked up from the scandal rag in which he'd been reading about Paris Hilton's latest escapade, which would have humiliated anyone with common sense or a feeling of self-worth, and standing in the doorway was someone who was either a cavalry soldier from the time of the Indian Wars or someone who played one in a movie. If the latter, it was a gory movie with realistic makeup effects, because a chunk of the soldier's lower jaw was missing. He had skin halfway down his cheek, and then there was just exposed bone and upper teeth, and then nothing. Larry felt the frozen burrito he'd microwaved for dinner lurch in his stomach.

Maybe even stranger, the soldier carried what looked like an Indian spear, with feathers and hair dangling from it.

"Dude, you need a hospital—" Larry started to say.

The soldier raised the spear and hurled it. Larry tried to dodge but he had hooked his ankle around the crossbar of the stool he sat on, and when he moved suddenly, the stool tipped over and pinned his ankle there just long enough. He could tell the spear would hit him in the face, in the jaw, but he couldn't do anything to prevent it.

Gibson Brower, who went by the name Gib, was out in his garage installing a winch on his 1947 Jeep Willys. He liked working in the garage late at night with the door wide open, even in winter, with a space heater and a radio going and a work light hanging down. He found it peaceful. He never had to worry about neighbors dropping by or phone calls. He lived far enough from town that nobody would complain if power tools or engines made noise.

He was flat on his back, underneath the front end, when he heard a fluttering noise. He pulled his head out from under the Jeep, thinking that an owl must have flown into the garage. But when he spotted it, flapping around the ceiling, it was not an owl, but a red-tailed hawk. He couldn't remember ever having seen one of those about at night, and certainly had never heard of one going into a noisy, occupied garage.

"Get out of here!" he shouted. He pushed himself to a sitting position, intending to get up and wave it out the door. But it dropped at him before he had time, talons and sharp bill extended. The talons bit into the flesh of his neck and chest and the bill poked through his eyelid into his left eye, and as hard as he tried to grab it and hurl it away, he couldn't budge it before the strength ran out of him completely.

And so it went.

* * *

Jim Beckett was overwhelmed. Grief and shock and fury warred within him, and he tried to push them all back, to focus on the job at hand, but with each passing moment, each panicked call to 911, the job grew more and more impossible. Police work required a degree of detachment that he could no longer achieve. When Susannah, the dispatcher, handed him a piece of paper detailing the call from Ward Burrows, in which he said that his son Kyle had been attacked by unknown intruders and his skull split open, Jim buried his face in his hands and tried to fight back tears.

"I'm calling DPS," he said. "Hell, I'll call the President if I have to. We need help here."

The moment he admitted it, he was filled with regret that he had not done so earlier. Maybe lives could have been saved if he hadn't been so proud, or so concerned for the county's economic bottom line. He wasn't the mayor or a county supervisor, he was a cop, responsible for people's safety above all else. He had made the wrong decision and his neighbors had paid for it—were continuing to pay—with their lives.

Susannah just gazed at him for a moment. Her face looked like he felt—tired and heartsick, with dark bags under her eyes and frown lines etched, seemingly permanently, across her forehead and around her mouth. "Good luck," she said. The words fell out into the air, but they rang flat, without hope.

Beckett had looked at the phone number so many times in the past thirty hours or so that he had it committed to memory. He reached around a foam cup containing his millionth coffee of the day, its aroma bitter from sitting too long, hoisted the receiver to his ear—it felt like it weighed fifty pounds—and punched the buttons. Instead of ringing, though, he heard the phone company's standard "Don't bother trying" tone, and then a message telling him that his call could not be completed.

In case he had misdialed, he tried again, but with the same results. Thinking exhaustion might be playing tricks with him, he looked up the number again and discovered that he had indeed been dialing it correctly. He tried once more, fully aware of the definition of insanity as repeating the same action while expecting a different result. He didn't really expect anything different, though, because that would require too big a departure from the way the rest of his week had gone. His pessimism proved not unfounded. The same tone and message came again.

He tried another number and got the same thing. He flipped through his business card file and found the mobile phone number of a DPS detective he'd met at a state law enforcement function. Same thing. As a test, he went online and found the phone number for a pizza parlor in Phoenix and dialed that. Same thing.

"Can anyone get a long distance call through?" he shouted to no one in particular.

"I did about an hour ago," someone called back. "Haven't tried since then."

"Try," Beckett said. "I want to know if it's just my phone, or if I'm cursed, or what."

He heard phones being dialed throughout the station. Then he heard receivers clacking back into their holders. "No luck," someone said.

"Same here."

"Ditto."

This was just great. Having finally decided that he needed help, he couldn't make a phone call out of town. He decided to try another approach, and sent an e-mail to the DPS. Within seconds it bounced back as undeliverable. He tried a couple of test e-mails to other people, friends and family, and they did the same. Finally he sent one to himself, knowing that he was online and able to receive. Undeliverable.

Unbelievable.

EIGHTEEN

"We're completely cut off," Sheriff Beckett had said.

He'd taken Trace Johannsen outside, where they wouldn't be overheard. The night—early morning, Trace supposed, was more accurate—was frigid, and they zipped up their heavy coats and wore hats and moved about in close circles as they talked.

"The long distance, you mean?"

"Long distance, e-mail, shortwave radio. I even tried sending a fax, but of course that requires long distance service, too. I don't understand it." The sheriff's face looked pale and pinched. "There's a lot I don't understand right about now," he admitted.

Trace had felt more shaken by this admission than he would have expected. He looked up to Jim Beckett, who knew more about law enforcement than Trace believed he ever could, and who combined that knowledge with an understanding of people that let him apply his experience wisely and well. Maybe Jim was a country sheriff, but he was the best lawman Trace had ever known. All he had ever wanted was to be a cop, and much of that was because of the example that Jim had set. The idea that anything could trouble Jim was scary.

"What can we do?" Trace asked.

"What I want you to do is take one of the department Yukons and drive like hell," Beckett said. "Go all the way to Flagstaff if you have to. Use your cell phone, your radio, smoke signals if need be, but get hold of DPS and get some troopers here as fast as you can."

"You got it, boss."

"And you be careful out there, Trace. I don't want to put too much pressure on you, but there's a lot riding on this. We're completely overwhelmed here, and I have a feeling things are going to get worse before they get better. The number of attacks keeps climbing, we've all been on duty too long, we're tired and we're going to be losing our edge, making mistakes. We need reinforcements, and we need 'em bad. We'll keep trying to get through from here, but I have this bad feeling. Like we're not just dealing with the kinds of things we can understand, you know? Like somehow the rules have changed."

"I'm right there with you."

"Good. You're a good man, Trace, and you're destined for big things in this department. Now get on the road and find us some cops."

Trace took a minute to pour himself some of the

sludge that passed for coffee and to grab a couple of bottles of water. He made sure he had his cell phone, that the gas tank was full, and the shotgun was in the Yukon he checked out. Once he'd done that, he climbed up behind the wheel and pulled away from the station house, in the northeast corner of town. Highway 180 was nineteen miles from the station, and it would take him right into Flagstaff.

The first twelve miles passed quickly. The clouds had passed on and the night sky was clear, with stars and a half-moon shining down on the road. It wasn't fitting for a law officer to think it, but when he pulled this off, he knew, he would be some kind of hero. The day would be saved because of his desperate ride. He smiled at the thought, and wondered if he'd get a medal, maybe get his picture in the papers.

At mile thirteen the engine started to knock. Trace knew the department maintained their vehicles well, and so he figured it wouldn't be a problem. Anyway, given the urgency of his mission, he didn't want to turn around and check out another car. He pushed on.

In another mile or so the knocking got worse. The SUV started to actually shudder on the road during the worst of it. Trace swore silently. At this rate he wouldn't even make the highway, much less Flagstaff.

He pulled over to the side. He hadn't seen any other vehicles out, and the road was a remote forested two-lane, but he still wanted to be safely out of the traffic lanes just in case. Once he had stopped on the shoulder, he tried his mobile phone and his radio.

Neither one worked. No choice but to press onward, then.

He turned the wheel toward the road and pushed lightly on the accelerator. As the SUV started to inch forward, he saw clouds of insects in the double streams of the headlights. Bugs, in this weather? It didn't make any sense. Normally they wouldn't be out in quantity until spring, and especially on such a cold, snowy day—the temperature now couldn't be higher than twenty-five or so—he would not have expected to see as much as a single housefly.

They were out in force, though. Flies, bees, wasps, moths, mosquitoes, dragonflies, beetles . . . as many as he might see in a full summer's day outside. But these were swarming together, which never happened, and all gathered right around his vehicle. More seemed to be appearing every second, as if they were materializing in his headlight beams. That couldn't be—they had to be flying in from the surrounding woods, attracted by the light. Trace didn't like it, though, and he gunned the engine, pushing through the bugs and onto the road.

He thought he would leave them behind quickly, but he didn't. The insects stayed in the headlights, except for those that splatted against the windshield. He pressed on the gas, and the SUV knocked but lurched forward. Fifty, fifty-five, sixty. No way those bugs should be flitting around in his way at these speeds.

But they were.

More and more hit the windshield. Bug guts littered the glass. He flicked on the wipers and sprayed the windshield, but that just smeared them, turning them into an opaque film. And still more smacked into it every second. He'd have to stop soon, or risk driving off the road or into an oncoming vehicle.

Then he heard the buzzing of a bug inside the Yukon. It sounded like a bee, but could as easily have been a horse fly, or a wasp or something else. He couldn't see it in the dark and didn't dare take his eyes off what little he could make out of the road to look for it. It buzzed toward his head, then away, darted for him and swooped back again.

Within seconds the buzzing was joined by a high-pitched whine that could only have been a mosquito. As soon as Trace heard it, it bit him on the cheek. He slapped at it, smacked himself. This time he cursed out loud.

Another buzz chimed in. He had to stop, had to close the vents or whatever these pests were using to get inside, and had to kill them before they stung. A bee stinging him while he was driving, more than half blind anyway, could turn out to be fatal. Besides, he reasoned, if he had left the others behind—through the windshield he couldn't see them anymore—he could scrape the glass off and continue.

He braked suddenly and yanked the wheel to the right. The shoulder came faster than he'd expected, and he took a bounce that almost slammed his head into the roof. As it was, the seat belt bit painfully into his shoulder. As he brought the vehicle to a shuddering stop, one of the bees sank its stinger into the side of his neck, just below his right ear.

"Damn it!" he shouted, swiping his right hand across his neck. He thought it collided with the insect's body, but the damage was already done.

He clicked on the dome light. Time to find that other one and finish it off, too.

The vents were thick with insects, writhing through the slots. They dropped to the floor when they came through, pushed aside by the ones behind, or they took flight—most almost soundless, the fluttering of tiny wings drowned out by the roar of the big engine, but some adding their own buzzes and whines to the mix.

Trace reached to close the vents, but the action brought a dozen or more to his right hand, stinging and biting as if choreographed. He yanked his hand away, suddenly on fire. The bugs seemed encouraged by their small victory, and wriggled through the vents in greater numbers.

He took off his hat and swatted at them, but within a second several dozen lit on his scalp and started attacking. They were on his face, in his eyes. He opened his mouth to scream a wordless curse and felt them dive inside, stinging the insides of his cheeks, his gums, his tongue.

They would kill him if he stayed in the SUV's cab a second longer, he knew. Jim and the people of Cedar Wells were counting on him. He couldn't let a few insects stop him from getting help. And outside, he would be able to run.

He steeled himself and threw open his door. As he

did, he lost his balance, tumbling out to land in the snow and grass on the road's shoulder.

And they swarmed him. From the ground, the ants came, the cockroaches, the spiders, tarantulas, scorpions, centipedes, their bites and stings like liquid fire injected directly into Trace's veins. From the sky, the bees and yellowjackets and mosquitoes attacked. Moths flew up his nose, plugging his nasal passages. Clouds of gnats flew into his mouth, gagging him, choking him.

He tried to rise, but they weighted him down, and the poisons rushing through him weakened his muscles. He couldn't see anymore, his eyes long since swollen shut. He pawed uselessly, pointlessly, at the Beretta in his holster, as if he could shoot a million impossible insects with the bullets it carried.

His mind flitted to the people he had left behind, his parents, his big sister, Jim and everyone he worked with in the sheriff's department.

Being entrusted with a badge and a gun and a uniform had been the greatest thing that ever happened to Trace Johannsen. Living up to that, being the hero of the hour . . . that would have been so perfect.

Would have been . . .

NINETEEN

They were a couple of blocks from the motel, heading up Main, when a car darted out of a side road directly in front of them. Its driver slammed on the brakes and the car swerved, coming to a stop across both lanes.

Dean reacted, stomping on his own brakes. The Impala fishtailed, then caught a patch of black ice on the roadway and launched into an uncontrolled slide. He wrestled with the wheel, but it did no good. His precious car would end up where it ended up.

Which, at the moment, looked to Sam like it would be right on top of the car that had startled them both.

It was a station wagon, roughly a thousand years old, with fake wood paneling on the sides, rust growing around the wheel wells like lichen on rocks, and a ladder in the back along with some paint buckets and drop cloths. Sam could see all this in the headlights with perfect clarity as the Impala skated toward it.

He could also see its driver, a skinny young man wearing a baggy fatigue coat, with long greasy hair that flopped into his face as he rushed from the car. He didn't bother closing his door, possibly more worried about trying to keep his balance on the ice and not shoot himself in the leg with the cannon he carried.

Okay, not a cannon exactly, but when he raced around behind the wagon and propped his arm on its top and leveled the .358 at them, its muzzle looked like one.

"Dean—"

"I know!"

That was all they had time for. The Impala slid to a graceful stop about three feet away from the station wagon, side by side with it.

Which meant that when they got out, Sam's head would be about level with that big gun.

"We're not looking for a kid with a gun, right?" he asked. "Old man, right?"

"Old man, Indian, bear . . . we're looking for a lot of things," Dean replied. "But this is the first I've heard about a kid."

"Looks like maybe he's looking for us."

Dean opened his door and got out, using careful, measured motions. He showed the kid his empty hands. "Easy, pal," he said as he did so. "I think there's some kind of confusion here, but we can straighten it out."

With the kid's attention focused on Dean, Sam

risked getting out on his own side. He raised empty hands toward the kid, too. The kid's gaze snapped between the two of them, the gun's muzzle shifting along with it. "Let's talk about this," Sam said.

"I just want to know which one of you it is," the kid said. His voice quaked. He was scared, which worried Sam all the more. Scared people weren't exactly known for steady trigger fingers, or for careful consideration of their actions.

"Which one what is?" Dean snapped. "Dude, you got the gun, least you could do is be clear about what you're doing with it."

"Don't play dumb," the kid warned. "I saw you all."

"Saw what?" Sam asked.

"I saw Heather go to your hotel room, in the middle of the night." He twitched the gun at Sam. "I saw you open the door in your underwear and let her in. Don't tell me you're both doing her."

"You were following Heather?" Sam asked, bewildered. The station wagon, he realized, must have been the car Dean saw behind them earlier. When the kid knew for sure that Heather was going home, he turned off so he could be in place to lay this trap.

"She's my girlfriend," the kid said. "I was talking to her on the phone earlier, and she sounded weird. Plus we were supposed to go out tonight, but she canceled on me."

"She probably canceled because it's not safe to be out tonight," Sam said.

"I already thought she was cheating on me, but I

couldn't figure out with who. Now I know. You guys are all tall and buff and such."

"You only think you know, kid," Dean said. "But you're wrong, except for the tall and buff part. Put that peashooter down and let's talk. Preferably inside."

"I know what I saw."

"You saw Heather come to our room for something totally unrelated to sex," Sam said.

"Why don't you tell me why, then?"

"It's a little hard to explain," Dean said.

"Right."

"Look, it's freezing out here," Dean said, "so if you're going to shoot us, just go ahead and freaking do it! A hot bullet and a hospital bed would feel good right about now."

The kid's hands started trembling harder, the gun in them wagging dangerously now. Sam knew Dean didn't really want to get shot, and neither did he. But if they didn't get the kid disarmed soon, something disastrous would happen.

Just keep yakking at him, Dean, he thought as he began slowly working his way toward the rear of the wagon. It was a long way around the big car, and getting to the kid unnoticed would be almost impossible. But going over or under would surely result in a panicked shot fired. Unless he could be persuaded to put it down, slow and steady was the only way to reach the gun.

"You!" the kid shouted, swinging the gun around to keep it lined up on Sam's head. "Keep still!"

"Hit the dirt, Sammy!" Dean called.

When Dean said something like that, he usually had good reason, and Sam had learned to go along with him. He did so now, hurling himself to the ground, trying to keep the wagon's rear wheel between himself and the kid.

As he had suspected, the kid took the sudden move as an assault. He crouched and fired, but without aiming, and his first shot went into the ground. Before he could squeeze off a second, Dean was in motion, clomping onto the Impala's hood and launching himself from there onto the station wagon's. From there he dropped onto the kid like vengeance from above. By the time Sam scrambled to his feet and around the car, Dean was tucking the Magnum into his waistband and the kid was up against his station wagon, disheveled but apparently unharmed.

"I told you, bud, you've got it wrong," Dean said. "We have nothing to do with Heather. Not that way. You want to know anything more about it, though, you'll have to ask her."

"Yeah," the kid muttered. "And tell her I was following her."

"That's something you'll have to work out," Dean said. "Sooner the better, if you ask me. Trust is a pretty important part of a relationship."

"I know. That's why I don't want her to know that I didn't trust her."

"Do you?"

"You've seen her," the kid said. "Do you think

she'd be satisfied with a loser like me for long? She's probably met all kinds of guys at college."

"She probably has," Sam agreed. "And if she's still with you, it's because she wants to be with you. You might want to think about appreciating that instead of questioning it."

"I guess." He frowned at the road, looking sullen and petulant. But maybe, Sam hoped, having learned at least one lesson—don't pull a gun on two guys unless you intend to use it immediately.

"Can I have my gun back? It's my dad's."

"You tried to shoot my brother," Dean said.

"It is kind of dangerous around here, Dean," Sam pointed out. "Maybe you should let him keep it."

Dean studied the kid for a few seconds, then drew the gun from his waistband and emptied the bullets out. "Here you go," he said, handing over the empty weapon. "There's one in the chamber, in case you run into trouble on the way home. Like Sammy said, there are real dangers out tonight, so if you're attacked by an old soldier or a bear or an Indian, something like that, you might want to use it. Otherwise, you're best off giving it back to your dad and forgetting you ever took it."

The kid took the gun, weighed it in his hand for a couple of seconds. "Okay, thanks." He stood there like he thought there should be something else said, then shrugged again and opened the passenger-side door. He slid across the bench seat, leaving the gun beside him on the right, and started the car.

"Let's get back to the room," Dean said. "This sucks. Why'd I even let you talk me into going in the first place?"

Sam climbed back into the Impala. "I'm glad you came," he said. He barely got the sentence out when he started laughing.

"What? Something funny I'm not seeing?"

"Just thinking about you giving advice on relationships and trust," Sam said.

"Hey, I've had relationships!"

"Yeah. The longest lasted, what, a month? And how many of them started with you lying about who you are and what you do?"

"Case you haven't noticed, Sammy, women don't exactly flock around hunters. And you can't really blame 'em. We're not the most stable individuals around."

"No, we're not. We're bad bets for long-term things, but good investments on life insurance."

"There's a selling point I hadn't thought of." Dean started the engine and got the Impala back on the road, headed for the Trail's End. "Hook up with us and see a quick return on your premiums." He laughed. "I like it, Sammy. Think we can fit it on a bumper sticker?"

TWENTY

Juliet Monroe woke up with a nagging headache and the sense that the previous night's ordeal must have been some sort of terrible nightmare. Dawn's light filtered in through the living room blinds. She was still on her couch, though she'd slumped over onto her side and lost part of the blanket that had covered her. The house was warm and cozy, and it seemed impossible that life could look as hopeless, that survival could be as unlikely, as it had seemed before she'd gone to sleep.

She shook off the remaining blanket and forced herself to her feet. Her head throbbed with every move she made. The house was quiet. She started toward the TV set, thinking that maybe some chattering voices would help fill the silence, but halfway there she decided against it. If the big canine was still around, she wanted to be able to hear it.

Instead, she went to the window, poked a finger between the miniblinds—which needed dusting, she realized, and the windows could stand some Windex—and parted them just enough to look into the front yard.

Stu's body, red and mangled, hadn't budged. The snow right around it had melted but then had frozen again during the night. Crimson-splashed ice surrounded it now, holding it in a fierce grip.

Either it had snowed a little more during the few hours she slept or the wind had smoothed out the snow, but she couldn't see the wolf's tracks anymore. Again, a sense of unreality invaded her mind, like it hadn't actually been a wolf after all. Like Stu had been killed by some other mechanism, a bad fall on the slick ground or an explosive aneurysm.

As she had the night before, Juliet went to every window in the house, looking out for any sign of the animal. The sun was just cresting the ridges to the east, and its slanted light would have picked out tracks. She saw some that might have been birds and maybe rabbits, but no canines, large or small.

That task completed, she went into the kitchen and put a pot of water on the stove to boil for tea. She chose a box of Earl Grey and shook some into an infuser, which she lowered into an enameled teapot. She knew she should eat something, but her headache was affecting her stomach, making her nauseous. *Maybe a slice of toast. Or two. With just a little butter.*

When the water screeched its boil, Juliet shut off the stove, poured some into the teapot, and set the boiling pot down on a cool burner. While her tea steeped, she went to the front door. She pressed her ear against it, listening.

There was no sound at all, not even birdsong. With the boiling pot off its burner, it was as if sound had ceased to exist, or she had gone deaf during the night. She knew that wasn't the case, since she'd heard the whistling pot. Just in case, she tapped her fingertips against the wooden door. They made noise. *Nothing wrong with my hearing, then. It's just awfully quiet.*

Her restless mind filled in the cliché. *Too quiet.*

Placing her hand on the doorknob made her heart pound. She held it there for a long moment, willing the noisy organ to quiet itself. She took three deep breaths, letting the air out slowly. Her heart calmed. She jump-started it again by flicking open the thumb latch. More breaths, more waiting. This was taking too long; her tea would be bitter by the time she got back to it.

It had to be done, though. *If* the beast was gone, *if* there was a way out of here, she had to take it.

Holding her breath altogether, Juliet opened the door. Just a fraction of an inch, at first. Enough to peer out through the crack. She could see the walkway in front of her house, some snow, a tiny splash of red over where Stu was. She pulled it open more. Nothing attacked her. Nothing moved.

Juliet stepped outside, pulling the door to but not releasing the outer knob. There was no breeze at all, no flutter of wings or chirping or any of the other morning noises she was accustomed to hearing. Absolute stillness. The air was cold, as on a crisp winter morning. She associated days like it with shopping on Chicago's Miracle Mile, the stores decorated for the holidays, Marshall Fields standing like a warm, welcoming beacon that would happily take her money and make her appreciate it.

She hadn't decorated for Christmas since Ross died, and hadn't planned to this year, either. The holidays felt empty without him.

She released the knob, took a few steps away from the door. Now she could see Stu better, and the sight brought with it a wave of nausea.

What she still didn't see was the wolf.

Maybe it had gone. She had ascribed nearly supernatural powers to it, but what if it was, after all, just a big canine? It had been hungry, had attacked a few cows, and then had seen Stu as a threat because he came between it and its dinner. It couldn't have magical powers, couldn't read her mind or know her intentions. Last night she had believed it could do all those things and more, but that had been panic talking, not reason. By now it was probably forty miles away and still going.

Juliet began to formulate a plan. She had to have some food, and her tea. Had to settle her stomach a little. Then she would put on some good snow boots, fresh clothes, long underwear, her down parka. With gloves and a cap, she would be ready for the long walk to the neighbors' place. They kept to themselves and she hardly knew them, but they'd let her use a phone. That was all she needed now. Just a phone call to the sheriff and this whole thing would be behind her.

She turned back toward the house and her head swam, black dots crowding her vision from the fringes, and her stomach lurched. Thinking she might vomit, she stopped in place. Better to do it in the snow than on her living room floor. She put her hands on her knees and rested for a moment, hunched over, waiting. The feeling passed, and the blackness moved out of her eyes again.

Straightening, she let her gaze travel up, past the door to the edge of the roof.

The wolf hunkered there, gazing down at her. A surprisingly pink tongue slipped from its mouth, washed across it. Then the canine's muscles tensed.

Juliet bolted. She burst back inside, slammed the door behind her, and locked it again. Outside, she barely heard the crunch of the animal's landing in the hard snow.

With the door secure, she rushed to the bathroom, certain that the vomit would come this time. All the way there, she thought, *Stupid, stupid, stupid! You cannot go outside! To go outside is to . . .*

To go outside is to die.

TWENTY-ONE

The deputy's SUV was pulled off to the side of the road and its driver's side door hung open. No lights burned inside or out. Someone said that the vehicle had run out of gas and then its battery died, but it only sat there for a couple of hours, so Sam thought the real explanation had to be more complicated than that.

They had heard about its discovery on their police band radio, shortly after returning to the motel following the eventful trip to Heather's and back. By the time they made it to the scene, the deputy's body had already been bagged and hauled away. Sam overheard another deputy talking about bugs, but that didn't make any sense; he hadn't seen so much as a housefly since coming to town.

Yellow tape reading SHERIFF LINE DO NOT CROSS in big black letters had been strung around the SUV and off into the brush around it. Uniformed deputies bustled around behind the tape, taking photographs and measurements. Others stood in grim little knots, talking among themselves in low voices under the gray light of an overcast morning. Nobody seemed to pay any attention to Sam and Dean until Sheriff Beckett detached himself from one of those clusters and stalked toward them. He didn't look like a happy man.

"Who are you people?" he asked as he drew near them. "And don't give me any crap about the *National Geographic*, because I only see you at crime scenes, and neither one of you is ever taking notes or pictures. I've just had a man killed who was a deputy and a friend of mine, and I'm not in any mood for foolishness, so either I get a straight answer out of you or we might just have ourselves a constitutional test case on unlawful arrest."

"We're not here to make any trouble," Sam said.

"That's not what I asked you."

Dean dug a leather case from his pocket that Sam hadn't seen him put there. "We're trying to stay low profile," he said, lowering his voice as if inviting Beckett into a conspiracy. He opened the case. Sam saw a flash of a badge and a plastic window showing an ID card. "Homeland Security," Dean said quietly.

Beckett took the badge case and studied its contents. "Nice job," he said. "Looks like the real deal. It'd convince me if I was feeling persuadable, which I'm not." He eyed Sam with suspicion. "You got one, too? Or maybe you're from the Department of Agriculture."

"He's not buying it," Sam said to Dean.

"Doesn't seem to be."

"I say we tell him the truth."

"Okay," Dean said. "We're with DEA," he began. "Deep undercover."

The sheriff reached for his handcuffs.

"We're here because of the murder cycle," Sam said quickly. The sheriff stopped, hooked his thumb through his belt. "We investigate things like this. Paranormal events, particularly the violent kind. Folklore, myth, what some people would call monsters. I can't give you verifiable statistics, but we have a very good track record at what we do. By now you've got to admit that there's something going on here that's outside the scope of your expertise."

"So you two are some kind of ghostbusters?"

"Except they're not real," Sam said. "We are."

Sheriff Beckett ticked his eyes back and forth between them. "I don't know which story is more ridiculous."

"So when you said tell him the truth," Dean said quietly, "you meant the true truth."

"That's right," Sam said. "He needs our help, and we could use his."

"We really are here about the murders," Dean said. "Every forty years, like clockwork. Unusual weapons. Even animal attacks. You have a better way to explain it?"

"Better than what?" Beckett asked. "I haven't heard you explain it yet. You've only *described* it."

"Well, truth is, we're still working on that part."

"I see," Beckett said. "So all your expertise is good for what, exactly?"

"At least we're not running around pretending it's something you can solve by the book."

"Son," Beckett said, looking weary, "I haven't been pretending I could solve any of this for about thirty hours now. Maybe a little longer. I'd like to be able to keep ahead of it, prevent some people from dying if I can. But solve it? Hell, I just want to keep the town together until it passes. Forty years from now it'll be some other cop's problem."

"But we can make it stop forever," Sam said.

"How are you going to do that?"

Sam cleared his throat. "That's the other thing we don't know yet. Depends on what it is. We'll get there, though. We really are good at this sort of thing."

Beckett shook his head slowly. "I can hardly believe what I'm going to say. You think you can do something about all this? We're supposed to have a shopping center opening at noon today. It's—" He consulted his wristwatch. "It's seven-ten now. You were there when Mayor Milner said that nothing would delay the opening."

"But that many people all gathered together in one place might be an irresistible target for whatever's behind all this," Sam said.

"Exactly. If they can get here." He inclined his head toward the SUV. "Apparently, we can't get out. That's what Trace was trying to do, trying to get to Flagstaff to fetch us some reinforcements. We can't call or even e-mail outside of town. But if people can come in, then once they're here they'll be trapped too, and like you say, piled up in the mall, they'll be easy pickings. So if you think you can do something to stop it, you have till eleven. When noon comes around, I'll be at that mall. If I see you and you haven't put a stop to all this, I'm holding you both as material witnesses. You have any outstanding warrants?"

Sam and Dean caught each other's glances, then looked away.

"I thought maybe," Beckett continued. "Look, that's five hours away. You're the experts you claim to be, that should be plenty of time."

"We'll do what we can, Sheriff," Sam said. "You have our word on that."

"I hate to admit it, boys, but I'm counting on you."

Beckett was turning around to go back to his car when police radios crackled. After a moment's conversation, one of the deputies called out to him. "Sheriff! Jodi Riggins has spotted that old man, she thinks, heading east down Second!"

"On my way!" Beckett replied.

Sam caught him by the arm. "Let us go first," he said. "You said you'd trust us, so give us five minutes. It's just a sighting, right, no one's been killed? We think that old man might be the key to it, and if you go in with lights and siren, he's going to vanish again."

Beckett looked constipated, like he'd eaten his own

words and they disagreed with his gut. "Three minutes," he said. "You get on out of here, and I'm three minutes behind you. You better move your asses."

They moved. Sam reached the Impala first, so he got in behind the wheel. Dean slid in beside him without comment, and before his door was closed Sam was peeling out.

On the way, Dean slid his nickel-plated .45 from the glove and checked the magazine.

"What are you doing?" Sam asked.

"Making sure I'm loaded." He reached into the backseat, brought up a pump-action Remington from the floorboards. "For anything."

"We probably just want to talk to this guy," Sam said. "Not kill him."

"We don't know that. All we know, he might be the soldier. Or the Indian. Or both."

"Yeah, and we'll know that if we see him."

"When."

"When we see him. But if he's none of those things, he might be a witness. He might know something. He might even be a hunter."

"He doesn't sound like a hunter," Dean said.

"Only because so few of them live to be old. But showing up around the scenes of these incidents? That sounds like a hunter to me, and a better one than we are, so far."

"Okay, you could be right, Sam. We won't shoot on sight."

The car cornered well considering the roads had frozen over during the night and were just beginning to thaw, and within Sheriff Beckett's three-minute window they were cruising down Second Street. A mailbox on the right had RIGGINS painted on the side.

"Okay, along here somewhere," Dean said.

Sam slowed. He watched the houses and yards on the left while Dean took the right.

They had covered two blocks when Dean shouted, "There!"

Sam screeched to a stop. "Where?"

Dean pointed to a gap between a single-story bungalow and a larger, shingled A-frame that looked like it had been built during the seventies. "I saw him right in there, going behind that wannabe ski lodge. Old guy, carrying a rifle he must have had since birth. I think there was a knife or hatchet or something tucked in his belt, too, but I couldn't get a very good look."

"You go up behind him," Sam said. "I'll go around the other side. We'll try to pinch him in the middle. And don't let him get us caught in each other's cross fire if we need to shoot."

"I thought you didn't want to shoot him."

"I don't. I'm just saying . . . if we have to."

"No cross fire," Dean repeated. He got out of the car and started jogging toward the A-frame. Sam sprinted past it, then hooked around toward the back.

Behind the A-frame the woods grew thick again. At first Sam didn't see anyone except Dean in the yard. *Lost him again*, he thought, disappointment welling up in him. But then Dean gave a shout and pointed, and Sam saw the old man trying to sneak off through the trees.

Both Winchesters started running, relying on long legs to propel them over short, prickly underbrush, dodging low-hanging branches as they went. The old man broke into a run too, but his legs weren't as steady as theirs, and the length of his rifle slowed him because he kept catching it in fir branches.

Within a minute they had caught up to him, one on either side. He leveled the rifle at Dean's belly. In the distance, Sam could hear approaching sirens.

"You take one more step, either of you jaspers, and I'll open you up like a can of tuna," the old man said.

From the glint in his narrow-slitted eyes, Sam believed he meant it.

Wanda Sheffield was disappointed to see that the snow had stopped during the night. She'd curled up under her down comforter the night before, hoping that when she opened her eyes again a blanket of white would cover the land, flocking all the trees and creating the winter wonderland effect that would help put her in the Christmas spirit.

Christmas was Wanda's favorite time of year. She loved the music, the decorations, the general good cheer. She even liked shopping in crowded malls, as long as the stores were dressed for the holidays. She wore bright clothes, heavy on the reds and greens, and she seemed, on those occasions, to have a perpetual grin on her face, like some kind of happy idiot.

This year the mood hadn't quite caught her up yet. It would, she had no doubt of that. And it was early in the month yet.

Still, a good heavy snowfall would have set her nicely down the Christmas road.

She would survive the disappointment, she figured, one way or another. To that end, she brewed a small pot of fair trade organic French roast and put a couple of croissants she had picked up the day before in the oven to warm. She got some boysenberry jam from the refrigerator, along with a container of heavy cream. If one intended to pamper oneself, she had long believed, half measures weren't worth the trouble. From a cabinet, she took a real china cup, the kind that came with a saucer and seemed so out of vogue these days, and she put a spoonful of sugar into the bottom of it.

Wanda didn't like a lot of clutter around, so although she would decorate for the holidays, she hadn't done so yet. She kept her home, a 1970s A-frame, neat and clean, and as she worked in the kitchen, she put used utensils and dishes into the sink and ran a little water over them. After sitting at a pine dining table and consuming her breakfast, she carried those dishes back to the sink, rinsed them, and put the whole lot in the dishwasher.

While she was straightening up after bending over the dishwasher, she thought a shadow passed across her back window.

She closed the dishwasher's stainless steel door and walked over to the window. It looked out onto a quarter acre of flat yard, then a thick expanse of trees. A few birds—the kind she called LGBs, for "little gray birds," because she didn't know their real names—jumped and flitted about on yesterday's snow, pecking through it for bugs or seeds or whatever it was they ate off the ground. Grass poked through the snow in tufts here and there, and one scraggly bush, its reedlike branches bent toward the ground by late fall's snow and ice, offered shelter to a couple of the tiny birds.

None of those looked big enough to have cast such a shadow on the window. Wanda pressed her face against the cool glass, leaving an oval of steam there as she scanned this way and that for some larger creature, a hawk or maybe even a rare visitor like one of the black bears seen once in a great while in town—although surely they'd be in hibernation by now?

Seeing nothing, she gave the tiniest of shrugs. Just a cloud across the sun, maybe—or the sun breaking through the cloud cover, more likely, for a second, and her mind misinterpreting it.

She gave the room a quick once-over. Nothing out of place, no missed croissant crumbs on the table, no splashes of water on the tiled kitchen counter. Satisfied that all was as it should be, she headed upstairs for a bubble bath. She was off work today—she was a checkout clerk at Swanson's, which wasn't exotic but paid the bills—and except for the mall opening in the afternoon, she had nothing on the agenda except relaxation.

At the top of the stairs, a sitting area overlooked the kitchen and living room. She had a couple of cushy, comfy chairs and a reading lamp there, along with a low bookshelf containing her to-be-read books. After the bubble bath, maybe she would tear into that new Laura Lippman thriller. Beyond the sitting area was her bedroom—on a corner with dormer windows on both sides, the lightest room in the house during the day—and her bathroom.

She went into the bathroom first and started the water, shaking in some scented moisturizing bubble bath flakes. She took a thick white towel from the antique cabinet at the end of the tub, where they were rolled and tucked into cubbies, and set it out, folded neatly, on top of the cabinet. While the water splashed in the nearly empty tub, she thought she heard a noise downstairs. Just a thump or a bump, hardly worth notice, except that she didn't have any pets or visitors and she hadn't left a radio or TV on down there. Maybe a bird had flown into a window. She went to the bathroom door and listened.

The sound wasn't repeated.

But now there was something else strange. At the doorway, the air felt cooler than it had a few moments ago. She remained there long enough to be sure.

Yes, there was moving air wafting up the stairs, and the scent of the pine forest outside had intensified, battling with the floral smell of her bath flakes.

Someone had entered through the back door.

She had a phone in her bedroom. Barefoot, walking as quietly as she could, she hurried in there.

But she hadn't made it yet when she heard a tread on the steps . . .

TWENTY-TWO

"Lower your weapon, Grampa," Dean said. "We just want to talk to you." He wasn't sure if that was true, but it seemed like the right thing to say. He was tired of civilians pointing guns at him.

"And those sirens I'm hearin', boy, they're just the wind in the trees? Do you think I'm some kind of an idiot? I still got all of my senses, including hearin' and common sense."

"I'm sure you do," Sam put in. "Believe us, we don't want to be here when the sheriff gets here, either. We'd rather be long gone, but with you along for the ride."

"Why? What've you got to say to me, stripling?"

"You're not behind these attacks, are you?" Dean said. The more he watched the old guy, the more convinced he was that the man was nothing but human. He wasn't flickering or vanishing from sight, and although he was dressed oddly—a little like Elmer Fudd on a wabbit-hunting expedition, in fact—he wasn't the soldier they had seen at the mall. "You're trying to stop them. So are we. I think we'll all do better if we can compare notes."

"And why should I believe that? Answer me that one if you can."

"Do we look like Indians, or bears, or soldiers, or whatever to you?" Desperate, Dean zipped his leather jacket up and then unzipped it again. "Have you ever seen one of those creatures wearing a modern leather jacket with a zipper?"

The old man narrowed his eyes even more than they already were—just tiny black balls behind fleshy folds—and peered at Dean's jacket. He came a few steps closer, pushing through the underbrush, his rifle held out before him. What Dean thought he had seen at first glance now proved correct—the guy's coat was belted shut, and jammed under the belt was a small hatchet. A smell like old cheese wafted off him in waves. His breathing was ragged and wet, as if he had fluid built up in his lungs. *Guy's got to be at least ninety*, Dean thought. *Unless he's thirty-five and lives* really *hard*. Still, for such an old coot, he got around well. He had, after all, managed to elude him, Sam, and every cop in town until now.

"Sir, all we want is to talk to you, compare notes," Sam said. "But if we're not out of here by the time those sirens arrive, we won't have the chance."

The old guy looked confused, or maybe uncertain—Dean didn't know how to read his ancient, creased face. His mouth was open a little, with a wedge of pink tongue flitting out and running across his lips. Those BB eyes twitched back and forth. His chin quivered a little, but that might have been because all of him was locked in a state of continual tremor.

Dean hadn't minded landing on the kid before. It had been kind of a shame to dent the hood of that old wagon, but at least he hadn't dented the Impala—that would have required a more punitive beating.

Laying into an old geezer like this, though . . . it just seemed wrong. He'd do it if he had to, particularly if the guy looked like he was going to pull the trigger on his blunderbuss, or like his hand might spasm on it. Things would be much easier if they could, for a change, *talk* the man into lowering his weapon.

Meanwhile, the sirens closed in. Beckett had prolonged the head start beyond the promised three minutes, but not by much.

"Sir . . ." Sam said. Always polite. They must have taught him that at Stanford, because manners hadn't been high on John Winchester's lesson plan. "We've got to hurry."

Finally, the man lowered the barrel of his weapon. He flashed a quick, unconvincing smile—showing teeth as small and yellow as baby corn—and then his face seemed to collapse, cheeks sinking, forehead drooping, as if he had held out hope until just this instant that he and he alone would somehow save the day. "All right," he said, his voice as creaky as a rusted gate hinge. "Let's go."

"We have a car," Dean said. *Although I don't know if there's enough air freshener in the world to get the stink out of it after I give you a ride.* "Let's go."

Hustling toward the Impala, the word "spry" came to mind. The old guy stepped lively, and by the time the sheriff's department vehicles appeared in Dean's rearview, he was already turning the corner.

"I'm Sam, and this is my brother Dean," Sam said, twisting in the front passenger seat to talk to the old man. "We're here to try to put a stop to this murder cycle once and for all."

"Murder cycle," the old guy said, chuckling wetly. "That sounds like a kind of motorcycle."

"The usual response is to tell a person your name," Dean pointed out.

"Oh. I'm . . ." He paused, as if he had to think about it. Dean knew the feeling. " . . . I'm Harmon Baird."

"Pleased to meet you, Mr. Baird," Sam said. "You've been spotted around a lot of the murder scenes. That's why the cops are looking for you. Us, too, at first, but we just wanted to make sure you weren't another guy, this old soldier we saw once."

"Oh, right," Baird said. "We should go back there."

"Go back?"

"The reason I was there in the first place. They

come out of the woods, you know. If you're quiet and you watch the woods you can see 'em coming, like wraiths or the dire wolf."

"Is there going to be an attack?" Dean asked. "Is that what you're saying?"

"It came as a raven," Baird said. Dean hated people who answered questions with riddles. "Then it became a snake. Now it's a man, or the shell of one, without a soul. His heart is twisted and black as coal."

"Dude!" Dean snapped. "Is he gonna kill someone?"

"Oh, yes," Baird said. "Unless he's stopped, most certainly. He'll kill 'em dead as they can be."

Dean hit the brakes and spun the wheel, pulling the Impala around in a screeching power 180. Fortunately the streets were still mostly empty at this hour.

"How can they be stopped?" Sam asked.

"Shoot 'em," Baird said. "Simple as that."

"You can just shoot them?"

"Can shoot anything. Some it don't stop, some it does. Them it does."

"Shoot 'em," Dean said under his breath. "Like we couldn't've thought of that."

"So they're not spirits," Sam said. "What are they? The reanimated dead?"

"Reanimated dead shapeshifters," Dean added. "Just to make it that much better."

" 'Course, not with just any bullets."

"What kind of bullets do you use, Baird?" Dean asked.

"I carve crosses into mine. Let the power of the Lord work through 'em."

"Crosses?" Sam asked.

Dean slapped the wheel. "He's making them into homemade dumdums, dummy! Cut an X into the lead and the slug explodes on impact. It's the oldest trick in the book."

"But if they're spirits, or reanimated dead, or whatever, why would exploding bullets work any better than regular ones?" Sam asked. "Maybe it's the crosses themselves, the symbolism of those, that's stopping them."

"All I know is it works," Baird said.

"I'd still feel more comfortable with rock salt," Sam said. "But whatever they are, Dean, if we can shoot them, we can beat them."

"If we can believe Grandpa Munster here," Dean said. "Where are we going, Baird?"

"That house with the pointy roof," Baird said. "He was heading in there last I saw him, so that's where he's looking for his victim."

"Right where the sheriff's people will be," Dean said.

"Unless they've already moved on," Sam said. "They're looking for Mr. Baird, not whoever it is he saw. Even if they see the killer they won't know what he is."

"Unless he's doing that whole flicker in and out of sight thing," Dean replied. "That's pretty much a dead giveaway."

"He was flickering like a Christmas tree," Baird said. "One of them blinky kinds."

Dean slowed as he reached Second Street again. There was one sheriff's department SUV parked about halfway down the block, in front of the house with the name Riggins on the mailbox, but the others had come and gone. Dean couldn't see any officers; presumably they were inside interviewing the woman who had placed the call.

Dean stopped in front of the A-frame. "That's the place, all right!" Baird shouted. "Feller's in there right now."

"How can you be sure he's still there?" Sam asked.

"I've developed a kind of nose for 'em," Baird said. "This is the third time I've gone up a'gin 'em, after all. I know what they're thinkin', almost, except thinkin' ain't exactly what I'd call what they do."

"Come on," Dean said. "We can talk about it later." He reached into the back and drew out the Remington. Sam chambered a shell in the sawed-off. They locked eyes briefly and then clambered from the car. Harmon Baird followed, still wielding his antique.

The front door of the house was closed, but through floor-to-ceiling windows Dean could see that a door in back was ajar. He couldn't see any movement inside or any signs of struggle, or much of anything in the house. It seemed that whoever lived here had adopted a minimalist lifestyle, which was probably appropriate for someone whose house had a lot of windows.

"Cover the back!" he shouted. "I'm going in!"

Sam sprinted around the house. Baird hadn't quite reached the yard yet. Dean tried the doorknob, which was locked. He reared back and kicked the door just beneath the knob. With a loud splintering of wood, it flew open.

"Anyone home?" Dean called into the silence.

For a second he thought no one was home and the old guy had been mistaken all along. But then, from somewhere on the second floor, up a flight of open-faced stairs, came a piercing scream.

"I guess someone is," he said to himself. He raced for the stairs. As he reached them, he saw Sam appear at the open back door. Dean jerked a thumb toward the upstairs, then pointed at Sam and made a palm-out "stay" signal. Sam nodded his understanding. Dean raised the shotgun and continued up.

The upstairs was a loft, only occupying a third as much floor space as the downstairs. The stairway's wooden banister became a railing at the top, and behind it, after a small sitting area, were two doorways. One of the doors stood open, and through it Dean could hear frightened whimpering. Running bathwater sounded through the other.

He swung into the doorway, bracing his right shoulder against the jamb, shotgun leveled.

Inside the room a slender brunette in her fifties or so stood up against the far wall with tears running down her face. Between her and Dean was a soldier—not the one they had seen at the mall, but a younger guy, from about the same era if the uniform was any indicator—holding a wickedly huge knife in his right fist. A genuine bowie knife, Dean thought. The soldier advanced toward the woman, but the bed blocked his way. He stepped to his left like he would go around it, then raised his leg like he would step up on it. He lowered the leg again, apparently undecided.

"Ma'am," Dean said softly. "You might want to duck now." He backed up his words with a hand signal.

At the sound of his voice, the soldier turned around. He was just a kid, maybe seventeen or so—or that's how old he had been when he died. His throat had been slit, and the wound still gaped, dry and papery. Something had been gnawing on him, too—holes in his cheeks and forehead showed bone beneath. As he looked at Dean, he flickered, and for an instant it was like his bones were illuminated from inside by a bright lightbulb made from transparent black glass. Then he looked whole, as he must have in life, and then he flashed back to the slit-throat dead man Dean had first seen.

As indecisive as he had been before, he didn't seem to have any trouble recognizing that Dean—while not his initial target—represented the greater threat. He lunged toward Dean with the big blade.

Dean pulled the Remington's trigger. The rock salt blast obliterated what remained of the young soldier's head and much of his chest. The woman, hunkered down in her corner, screamed as bits of him pelted her like rain.

The soldier's lower part teetered and fell, landing in a seated position on the bed for a few seconds before slumping to the floor. There he blinked in and out, in a pattern that was growing familiar to Dean, and vanished.

All the other parts of him disappeared at the same time. The walls were marked with rock salt, but not with the bits of flesh that Dean had just scattered all over.

"It's okay now," Dean said. "He's gone."

The woman, sobbing almost hysterically, wiped her hands at body parts that had been on her a moment before and were no longer.

"No, I mean completely gone," Dean said.

"But . . ."

"I know. Don't try to understand it," Dean suggested. "It's a lot easier that way."

The woman tried to smile through her tears. She rose and wiped a sleeve across her eyes. "Thank you. Whoever you are."

"No problem," Dean said. "And, uh, you might want to have someone come out and install a new door in front. I kinda broke yours."

TWENTY-THREE

As Dean had directed, Sam waited downstairs. Coming back down, Dean saw that he'd been able to hold Harmon Baird there.

"What happened, Dean?" Sam asked.

"There was another one of those soldiers," Dean said. "Just a kid. His throat had been cut, and he was trying to do the same to the woman who lives here. But the old guy's right—if you shoot them, they go away. Blink a few times and poof, gone, like they got stuck in a transporter beam."

"If you shoot them with the right load," Sam said. "Anyway, we should probably get Mr. Baird out of here before someone comes to investigate the gunfire."

"What I was thinking." Dean called back to the woman upstairs, who still hadn't left her bedroom. "Ma'am, we're taking off. There's a sheriff's officer down the street at the Riggins place. You might want to see if they can stick around until you get that door fixed."

She didn't answer, but comprehensible conversation was not yet within her capabilities. Dean thought she'd be okay once she got over the fright of the dead guy—and he had been ugly dead—trying to ice her.

Dean shrugged. He and Sam and Baird exited through the destroyed front door and hurried to their car. The sheriff's vehicle was still parked in front of the Riggins house. By the time Second Street vanished from the rearview for the second time that morning, no one had come out.

The summer that Dean had been fourteen and Sam ten, their father had taken them on a long hike into the Rocky Mountains. They'd been staying at a cabin in Colorado for a week, and it seemed almost like paradise to Dean. Blue skies, a swift creek running past the place where trout could be caught, a meadow on the other side of the creek, reached by crossing a rustic wooden bridge, that bloomed with thousands of wildflowers.

The thing that had prevented it from actually being paradise was that Dean was fourteen, and would rather have been meeting girls and playing sports and sleeping in than continuing what seemed like lifelong boot camp. Dad hadn't offered that option, though, and Dean went where Dad went and did what Dad said.

On this particular day Dean, Dad, and Sam shouldered heavy backpacks containing rations and equipment for a three-day stay in the wilderness. Dad had packed them both, and said Dean's weighed eighty pounds and Sam's sixty. With their respective burdens, they struck off into the higher elevations. They walked all morning, stopped for a quick lunch of peanut butter sandwiches and raisins from Dad's pack, then kept going. The meadows thinned and disappeared altogether. Deciduous trees were left behind. Eventually there were only scattered firs on hard, rocky slopes. The air was thin and cool.

Most of the way, Dad kept up a running patter, telling his sons lessons he had learned in the Marines or since their mother had died, on his hunting trips. He told them about the *loup garou* and the Manitou, Assyrian *ekimmu*, Greek *keres*, about mummies, golems, zombies, and much more. He described the tests and traps and traditions they would one day rely on. He had already taken the boys on several hunting trips, of course, but he told them that he was preparing them for the day when they would go without him.

Finally, as the day grew late, the side of the mountain they were on shrouded in shadow, he told them to take off their packs and sit. They obeyed, as they usually did.

Dad didn't remove his backpack. He remained standing. "The main thing I want you boys to learn from this," he said, "is never to trust anyone. Even me. Always verify what you're told. Taking a few minutes to check might save you hours later on. It might even save your life."

"What do you mean, Dad?" Dean asked. An awful thought had already risen up in the back of his mind, and he realized that he hadn't paid much attention to the route they took to get here, counting on Dad to know the way back.

"I mean, neither of you checked your backpacks before we left. You just trusted that I put in the things you'll need out here."

"That we'll need?" Sam asked.

"You boys sit there for one hour," Dad said. "By then it'll be almost dark, and you'll need to make camp. Tomorrow you can head back to the cabin—if you remember the way. I don't expect I'll see you until the day after, or maybe the day after that."

"But . . ." Dean started to protest, then held his tongue. Dad tested them. That was what he did. He taught them and he tested them, and so far they had failed this particular test. He wasn't going to make it worse by complaining.

"Dad, you can't—" Sam began.

Dean cut him off. "Zip it, Sammy. We'll be fine."

Sammy zipped it, and Dad headed back down the mountain. Dean figured he'd be able to follow their tracks back—unless Dad took pains to erase them, which was the kind of thing he would do.

When he was gone, both boys opened their backpacks. The top layer looked legitimate—rolled-up tarps that might have passed for tents under a cursory examination. Beneath those, though, Dean's held a box of baseball cards, some cans of pork and beans but no can opener, a couple of bricks, a plastic bag full of wadded-up paper, and miscellaneous other objects of absolutely no use in the wilderness. Sam's was similarly packed. Neither one of them had a match, a sleeping bag or tent, a compass, or any accessible food. They had water in separate canteens, strapped across their chests and clipped to their belts, so Dean wasn't worried on that score.

But it was getting dark, and they would soon be starving and sleepy.

"What are we going to do?" Sam asked. He was only ten, so Dean tried to cut him some slack, but if the kid started to blubber, he was going to toss him off the nearest cliff.

"I'm going back down the hill," Dean said. "Try to get as far down as I can before it's dark. Inside the tree line it'll be warmer, and maybe we can find some berries, or a rabbit or something, for dinner."

"But we're supposed to stay here for an hour," Sam protested.

"That's what Dad said. He also told us our backpacks held supplies for three days. You want to believe everything he says, or you want to eat tonight?"

"Eat, I guess."

"Then let's get going."

They ended up getting back to the cabin just after dark on the next day—hungry, tired, and mad. But, Dean had to admit, having learned a valuable lesson.

He tried to apply that lesson now, listening to Harmon Baird's story.

The old man had been right about two particulars.

He had known which house was under attack, and that shooting the attackers put an end to them. Dean had verified both by going into the house and confronting the young soldier.

Sitting on Sam's bed in their room at the Trail's End, though, he told a story that would be difficult to verify. If Dean hadn't seen what he had—both throughout his life, and specifically since arriving in Cedar Wells—he wouldn't have believed a word of it.

"I'm ninety-one years old," Baird began, once they had turned up the heat in the room to a level he found comfortable and brought him a Dr Pepper from the soda machine. He had taken his hat off, and his head was nearly bald, just a few wisps of hair spreading across pink, tissuelike skin. "So I've already lived through two of these, what you call murder cycles. I just think of them as the forty-year."

"Forty-year what?" Sam asked.

"Nothing. Just forty-year. Ain't like I talk about it to other folks, and I know what I mean when I think it in my own head, right?"

"I guess that's true."

"Damn straight it is. So like I say, I've lived through two before. This one marks my third time. First one, I was just a sprout, of course. But I saw it happen. Saw my own father cut down with a tomahawk. My aunt shot in the back. My neighbor—this was the worst—my neighbor tied behind a horse and dragged, facedown, until all the skin was flayed off his front side."

"Yeesh," Dean said. "That's harsh."

"Harsh it was, young man," Baird agreed. "But it left an impression, I can tell you that."

"Bet it did."

"Forty years later, as I reckon you know, it all started up again. This time I knew what was happening, because I saw the same sorts of attacks I remembered from the first go-round. Attacks by Indians and soldiers dressed in clothing and uniforms that had stopped being worn before the first set of murders. People who were there one second and gone the next, like you were opening and closing your eyes. And animals who changed their forms from one second to the next, who became people, people who became animals. It was all so familiar, and so terrible, seeing it happen a second time."

"What did you do?" Sam asked.

"Well, I fought back as hard as I could, that's what I did. The first time, none of them came for me, else I wouldn't be here now, most likely. But the second time? They came for me, all right. Nine times I was attacked. I used my rifle and my pistol and an ax and even a flaming log, in one case, to fight 'em off. I had seen what they could do and wasn't about to let 'em do it to me. Some of them I killed, if that's what you can call it, and others I just chased off. They like to have turned to easier prey, after tanglin' with me."

The old man rubbed his left eye, hard, as if trying to pry it out of its socket. Then he scratched at the end of his nose, leaving red marks. "I had married by then, and they did get my lovely Betty. I only left her alone at home for a short while, long enough to run into town for supplies and ammunition. I left a gun with her, too, but somehow they got her anyway, split her open from collarbone to breast. I buried her in the back and went out lookin' for whichever one had done that, but of course they can't really be followed."

"Why not?" Dean asked. "Don't they leave tracks?"

"Sometimes yes, sometimes no. Sometimes the tracks just trail away into nothing at all. Sometimes they change into other tracks. They don't really come from anywhere, you see. They . . . what's the word?" He snapped his fingers with a dry clicking sound. "They *materialize*, that's it, they materialize out of nowhere, then they do their dirty work, and then they vanish again."

"You've seen this?"

"After Betty was killed, I didn't go back into the house. I buried her and then I went out into the woods, because I'd seen 'em coming from there. I lived in that forest for days, as much animal as human I guess, trying to learn where they came from, if they had a leader, that kind of thing, you see? And what I found out was that they weren't there and then they were, and there wasn't any kind of sign you could see, anything that would tell you when or where they might materialize. One appeared right in front of me one night—almost on top of me—and I wondered what would have happened if he had appeared exactly where I happened to be standing instead of an inch away. Didn't ask him, of course, I tore his head off with my ax. That worked as good as shooting, seemed like. They ain't all that sturdy anymore, is the thing. They're strong, but they've been dead and they seem happy enough to go back to it."

"So we were on the right track," Sam said. "They *are* the reanimated dead."

"All we gotta do now is figure out who's reanimating them, and maybe why, then," Dean said. "And put a stop to it."

"Which isn't exactly right back where we started," Sam said. "It's just back in the same neighborhood. Mr. Baird, do you know of anyone who would have a grudge against Cedar Wells? Anyone who might be behind these attacks?"

Baird gripped his right elbow with his left hand and clicked the index finger of his right hand against his small yellow teeth. "I moved away from town after that second forty-year. Nineteen and sixty-six, that was. There was an element coming to town I didn't much care for—besides the dead folks, that is. And I couldn't see staying in town without Betty anyway. I didn't go far away, about fifteen miles as the crow flies, longer on the roads. But I kept track of the dates, of course, just in case it happened again. I was ready, I'll tell you that. Knew what I had to do, too. I had to come back to town and try to stop it."

"And you've been doing that," Sam said. "Which is why you've been spotted around some of the crime scenes. But what we need to know is, who do you think is behind it in the first place? There had to be someone who started the cycle of murders every forty years, and if we can find out who, we might be able to put a stop to it forever."

"I guess I didn't tell you up front," Baird said. "The first time, in 'twenty-six? My family worked on a big cattle ranch, and lived there, too. The attacks that killed my pa, my aunt, and our neighbor all happened on ranch property. My ma, afterward, she was convinced that the ranch had something to do with it all. That something had happened there that brought this evil down on the place. She wouldn't have anything to do with it after that, moved to town—even though I told her the killings happened in town, too, that the ranch wasn't alone in that regard, no way, no how."

"Do you believe her now? Do you think the ranch is behind it all?"

Baird grinned. The effect reminded Dean of a cartoon vulture eyeing a particularly tasty morsel. "Heck, boys, I don't know. I don't care much for Cedar Wells or the ranch or any of it. The only reason I've stayed alive and come back for the forty-year was that I hate those ghosts or whatever they are more than I hate everything else. I've thought on it and thought on it, though, and I suppose the ranch might be where it all started."

"Can you take us there?" Dean asked him.

"Oh, that old ranch was sold years ago. Split up into smaller parts, developed into housing areas and whatnot, I don't know. Whatever might have been there once, it's most likely plowed up, cut down, or paved over by now."

TWENTY-FOUR

Howard Patrick unlocked the door to his realty office on Main Street, stepped inside, and flipped on the switches that not only illuminated the overhead fluorescent fixtures but also the Christmas tree, animated Grinch, and electric menorah he kept in the front window from December first to January fifth every year. If he could have found an electrical Kwanzaa display, he would have put that in too, particularly since he and his wife and two kids had taken to celebrating Kwanzaa four years before, in addition to Christmas, wanting to instill in the kids a firm sense of their African heritage—but mainly because he wanted his business, Kaibab Realty, to be all-inclusive. Everyone needed a place to live, and he wanted to be the guy who helped everybody buy or sell theirs.

On the way to his desk he stopped and turned on the radio, to a satellite station that played nothing but holiday tunes. Johnny Mathis came on singing "The Christmas Song," and Howard smiled. He liked comfortable things; the comforts of a well built home, a fat bank account, family, and the comfort of a familiar song. He tapped the thermostat's Up arrow and the furnace kicked on.

His desk was made of oak, blond and polished, and it was a good thing it had sides because he hadn't seen the top of it in years. Paper completely obscured it: listings printed from online, flyers, notes, a couple of contract packages waiting for people to drop by the office to sign, folded newspaper classifieds, and more; once, he found a commission check that had worked its way to the bottom of a pile and stayed there for two months. The only place there wasn't paper was under his phone.

After hanging his coat on a hook, he sat down and put his briefcase on the floor by his feet. From it, he drew a laptop, which he set on the desk on top of several random paper objects. He opened it up and turned it on. Another day at the office.

The first thing he did was to check his e-mail account. More and more business was done online every day. He hadn't yet reached the point where he could show and sell a house without ever leaving his desk, but that day was coming, he believed. Already online listings replaced the miles and miles of driving to every possible home that had once characterized the job. Clients often came to him with specific properties in mind that they had found on the Web and wanted to see in person once before making the offer they'd already decided on—sometimes with the help of online mortgage calculators.

Today he had nineteen e-mails in his in-box. Three were spam, which he deleted. Four were personal. The rest were related, in one way or another, to his business. Reading those and trying to respond— growing increasingly frustrated that everything he sent out bounced right back, and when he tried to call tech support he found that call wouldn't go through either—took an hour and eleven minutes. He closed the window, looked at the clock, leaned back in his desk chair, and stretched his legs out.

Eight fifty-six. At nine he usually liked to walk around the block, stop in at the Wagon Wheel for a cup of joe and once in a while a doughnut or a slice of apple pie. He'd greet friends and neighbors, leaving them with the impression that good old Howard Patrick was a great guy with whom they should do business whenever they found themselves in the market.

Time for one quick phone call before he went. He had tried yesterday to get through to Juliet Monroe, because he had a party coming in from California on Monday who was interested in a ranch property like hers. She hadn't answered her phone, which was unusual for her. He'd left a message on her voice mail but gotten no call back, which was even more unusual. He'd tried Stu, her ranch hand, at his place in town, again with no response. Finally, he dropped her an e-mail, but there had been no reply in his in-box.

She could have gone out of town, although ordinarily she would tell him if she had any such plans. But even when she did, she usually checked her voice mail. And she was anxious to sell the place, so she'd jump at a chance to show it.

He had a key, of course, and could show it without her there, but he always liked to have express permission before going into someone else's home.

He checked her number and dialed it. Four rings, then voice mail picked up. He listened to the outgoing message, then the beep, and said, "Juliet, this is Howard again. It's Saturday morning, and this fellow will be here on Monday morning to look at ranch properties. I've shown him your listing and he's very interested, so please get back to me and let me know if it's okay to bring him around on Monday. Thanks, and have a terrific weekend."

People in town sometimes called him "Mr. Terrific," because he tended to use that word when anyone asked him how he was or how business was or how the family was or how did he like the weather. "Terrific," he'd say, "just terrific!" He didn't mind the nickname. It helped instill a positive impression of him, and success in life was about positive impressions. *That good old Howard Patrick, good old Mr. Terrific, he's got a good business going there. He could probably sell my house for me.*

Maybe Juliet had simply forgotten to tell him that she was going away for the weekend. No harm, no foul.

But then again, something sour was going on in

Cedar Wells. Everybody was talking about it, and the whispers had become full-blown exclamations since early yesterday. People were being killed, but nobody knew by whom, or why. And Juliet, living alone on that ranch, would be as vulnerable as anyone. Then there was the trouble with the e-mail and phones.

Instead of going to the Wheel, he would take his half hour and run over to Juliet's. Just to put his mind at ease.

Verify. Never mind trust, just verify. That had been Dad's advice, Dean argued, and Sam remembered the lessons, too. In a hushed conference, with Harmon Baird waiting outside the motel room door—even there he carried his rifle, but coming through town they had seen other people bearing visible weapons, so no one was likely to pay much attention to that—they had discussed what he'd told them, finally agreeing that they needed to see if he was just blowing smoke or if he knew what he was talking about.

He seemed pretty certain of his statements. And he had been at multiple scenes, which indicated a better understanding of the attackers than most people had. But they had to make sure.

So they were standing in the woods. Tall pines blocked the morning sun, which was only now beginning to burn through the clouds. A breeze from the north carried a chill and the threat of more bad weather. Dean carried the pump-action Remington, Sam the sawed-off. Both wore sidearms as well, and had stuffed their pockets with rock salt shells and extra bullets.

With the sawed-off tucked under his left arm, Sam held an infrared thermal scanner. He trained the double green laserlike beams this way and that, and they spiked off on separate paths into the trees. As he moved it around, he watched the device's small screen for any indication of paranormal activity.

"Anything?" Dean asked.

"Nothing." They might as well have been hunting deer, except if they had, they probably would have found something by now. As it was, Sam couldn't shake the feeling that they were wasting time. Baird said they came out of the woods, but there were a lot of woods around here, so even if he was right, they might simply have been in the wrong spot. Then again, Baird was also ninety-one years old, and the fact that he sounded mostly coherent didn't mean that he wasn't suffering dementia of some kind. "Maybe there's somewhere else we should try, Mr. Baird?" he asked. People could be dying while they froze their asses off in the forest.

"Plenty of places, yeah, boy," Baird said, that weird spaced-out smile he sometimes wore flashing across his face. "But one's as good as the next. Can't know where they're comin', or when, so you just have to guess. Guess and hope, that's what it is. Guess and hope."

"I'm getting a little tired of hoping," Dean said. "I want to shoot something."

"You'll get your chance, young one. Believe that, yessir. You'll get your chance, 'fore too much longer."

How can you be so sure, Sam wanted to ask, *if you don't know where or when they'll show up?* He had already learned that it was hard to get straight answers out of Baird most of the time, so he didn't bother asking. Baird knew what he knew, it seemed, and didn't worry about the rest of it. Same could be said of anyone, Sam supposed. Maybe Baird's conviction was something like religious faith. Sam believed in a higher power, and Dean didn't. Sam didn't have any special knowledge that Dean lacked, hadn't seen or heard or met God. He just felt like there had to be something more than science could describe, because so many of the things they had seen and fought also seemed to exist outside of scientific understanding. So, without Dad's much-vaunted verification, he believed.

As Baird seemed to believe that killing spirits would materialize in these woods.

Sam was about to switch off the ITS device when one of the green beams flickered, becoming as jagged as a bolt of lightning for a second. The machine gave a soft beeping sound. He couldn't see anything that would have disrupted the beam, but disrupted it was. "Dean."

"Gotcha," Dean said softly. He raised his shotgun. Sam clicked off the device, shoved it into a deep coat pocket, and readied the sawed-off.

Harmon Baird grinned like a loon.

Where the beam had flickered, a deer stood, looking at them with its big, empty brown eyes.

It hadn't been there a second ago. Then it was. Then it bounded away, like a deer would.

They followed. Sam lost it behind a tree for a second, and when he had it in sight again—

—well, what *might* have been it—

—it was a rangy coyote, shaggy coated, with ferocious looking fangs it showed when it snarled at them.

"Shapeshifter," Dean said.

Baird raised his rifle to his shoulder, eyeing down its length at the coyote. "Hold on," Dean told him. "Give it a minute."

Baird looked confused, but moved his finger away from the trigger.

The coyote blinked from sight, flashed black, reappeared. Repeated the sequence. *Like a TV set just before you get up off the couch and smack it one*, Sam thought.

It stared at them, still snarling, like it might lunge. All three put their fingers inside their trigger guards, ready to fire.

Instead of attacking, it turned and sprinted away.

The three men gave chase. Dean let out a whoop as he hurtled a bush, following the coyote's course. Baird cackled like a madman.

The animal went around a pine and disappeared behind an outcropping of big granite boulders, green and orange lichen coating their shadowed lower surfaces like corrosion on an old battery. Sam cut left, pushing ahead of Dean, and went behind the rocks. Up ahead he saw a flash of the coyote's dun pelt and switching tail, cutting through the brush.

But he didn't see where it went, because a man reared up from the rocks and swung a downed tree limb right into his face. Sam saw flashing lights, and went down among the rocks.

TWENTY-FIVE

When he opened his eyes again, the light seemed way too bright. It hurt. He shut them tightly, and that hurt too. Eyes still closed, he touched his face.

His hand came away wet, tacky with blood. He risked opening them again and saw the red on his fingers.

"Good. You are alive," Dean said.

"I'm still trying to decide if that's good or not," Sam answered. "So far it's a toss-up."

"He whacked you good," Dean said.

"Glad his form was so impressive," Sam said. "Who was it?"

"Just some guy," Dean said. "Might have been a cowboy or a logger or something, hard to tell. He had one of those flannel shirts, suspenders, heavy beard."

"Yeah, well, he hits like Paul Bunyan." Sam realized he was lying on his back, and tried to sit up against one of the granite rocks. The motion sent a wave of nausea through him. "Oh, that was a bad idea."

Dean helped him to a sitting position, but none too gently. "You'll be okay. Nice goose egg on your forehead, though. It should be a good shade of purple by tomorrow."

Sam touched his forehead again. His hair was glued to the wound. "Glad one of us is getting some pleasure out of this, Dean. What happened to the lumberjack?"

"I shot him," Dean said.

"And?"

"And it happened just like the other one this morning. Splattered him all over the forest, and then he vanished. Back where he came from. I grabbed the ITS out of your pocket and scanned, but it didn't show any activity anymore."

"What about that coyote?"

"Harmon's following it."

"You let him go by himself?"

"He was doing okay before we found him. Maybe better than us. I didn't want to leave you alone in the woods playing Rip Van Winkle, and I sure didn't want to drag your ass around with me. You might want to look where you're running next time."

"He wasn't there, and then he . . . he just appeared. How long was I out?"

"A minute, maybe two. That's all."

Sam tried to push off the rock, to get his feet under him. "Help me up. We should go after him."

Dean hooked his hands under Sam's arms and yanked him to his feet. "You're right."

Sam swayed, unsteady. His knees wobbled and he thought he'd fall, but he managed to remain upright.

"Wow," Dean said with a grin. "That green face looks really good with the purple. You just might start a new trend."

"Which way?" Sam asked, ignoring the comment. The swat to the head had taken a lot out of him, but he didn't want to let Baird and the coyote get too far away. If he kept standing around he might fall over again, but he thought that if he were in motion he would be able to keep going, at least he might be able to fall in a helpful direction.

Dean pointed through the trees, back toward town.

"Makes sense." Sam tried walking, and was pleasantly surprised to find that it wasn't impossible. "You coming?"

Juliet was making toast when the power went off. One minute the inside of the toaster glowed, red-hot, and the familiar toast smell filled the kitchen. Then there was a click and the sudden quiet that accompanies a power failure, and all the things she didn't ordinarily think of as making noise—the low rumble of her refrigerator, the faint hum of light-bulbs—abruptly went silent.

The wolf, she thought. She knew it wasn't a power line or a breaker. Down at the neighbor's place—assuming it hadn't targeted them as well—the power would still be on. It was just her, and the canine had done it.

She popped the toast out manually, put it on a plate, and spread margarine over it. She already had hot water in the teapot, so the animal hadn't completely succeeded in ruining her breakfast. And since she hadn't eaten any dinner last night, she was famished.

Before she dug in, though, just in case, she found a flashlight in the kitchen drawer where she kept batteries and spare bulbs and went into the laundry room. There, she opened the breaker box and scanned the switches, but they all looked fine. She tested each one in turn, wiggling it to see if it was loose. None of them had been tripped.

So, like the phone service, the wolf had somehow cut the line from the pole into the house. She closed the box and headed back to the kitchen to get her breakfast.

But then another thought came to her. How would a wolf cut a power line? By biting it, most likely. But if it bit through a high voltage line, it would surely electrocute itself!

She bypassed the kitchen and went upstairs again. From the spare bedroom, the one that Ross had claimed as his home office, she believed she'd be able to see the pole. If there was a crispy canine at its base, she would dance on its corpse.

She hadn't gone into Ross's office much since his death. His desk, computer, various certificates and diplomas, and even the stupid power tool calendar with photos of nubile young things in skimpy outfits, holding tools they could barely lift, still filled the room. She had donated most of his clothes except his long underwear—she kept thinking, impossibly, that if he came home he might be cold and would need his long johns—and his little bit of jewelry, some of his books, and all the magazines he'd always insisted on saving. She had taken over the dresser they once shared, and spread her things out to use up most of the closet, but left this room virtually intact.

She crossed it now, glancing at the calendar, two years out of date (a gag gift from a stockbroker buddy—much as Ross admired young nubiles and power tools, he hadn't been very skilled with either), and went straight to the window.

She was correct; the pole was there, just to the right a little. By standing on her tiptoes she could see its base. And there was a heavy cable, drooping from the pole, its end—obviously torn off—lying on the ground.

Shouldn't it be sparking? she wondered. *Isn't that what live wires do? They spark and jump around and people have to be careful about getting near them.*

This one looked absolutely lifeless, though. A dead wire.

Juliet didn't know how the beast had accomplished that—not only breaking it, but somehow making sure that no charge came through the cable that could have threatened it.

Then again, she had already decided that her persecutor was no ordinary wolf. The things it had done were far from instinctual in the animal world.

She was turning away from the window when motion in the distance caught her attention. A light, she thought, then she realized it was the sun glinting off glass. She watched as it came into sharper focus. A windshield threw sunlight toward her.

She opened the window just a crack and listened. Through the morning stillness she could hear the rumble of an engine, getting closer every moment.

She shut the window quickly, locking it. This was what she'd been waiting and hoping for with every beat of her heart, every wakeful moment! Someone with an operating vehicle, coming down the long dirt driveway toward the house. She didn't want to give the wolf a chance to hook a paw inside the open window and force it wide enough to enter. Now that salvation was near, she didn't want to give it a chance to do anything to get in the way.

Standing in the window, she watched as the vehicle approached. After another couple of minutes she recognized it. Howard Patrick drove a red Jeep Grand Cherokee, a couple of years old but with power everything and a smooth ride. He spent a lot of time on the road, he'd once explained to her, and liked to ride in comfort. Soon she could even see Howard through the windshield, squinting into the sun as he drove toward the house.

When he drew inside the barbed-wire fence that defined what she and Ross had always thought of as their "yard," Juliet turned to leave the window and go downstairs.

But again, something drew her back. Something that was not as it should have been. At first she didn't know what, but after a moment's close observation, she saw it.

It crept through the tall grass just beyond the fence. Its coat almost blended with the dry grass. The markings on it could have been shadows, but she got a glimpse of its golden eyes and its pink tongue, and she knew. The wolf watched Howard. She had to get him to drive right up in front of the door, across the grassy swath of yard where the snow still melted and Stu's body lay.

At least she knew the wolf wasn't near her window. She threw it open and leaned out. "Howard!" she screamed. "Howard, up here!" She waved her arms. Inside the Jeep, she could see Howard remove the key from the ignition and start to open his door. "No!" she shrieked. "Howard, drive closer!"

Now he saw her. He gave an awkward wave and smiled. Clearly, he couldn't hear what she was saying, didn't have the slightest idea what her arm signals meant. She tried again, making a come-hither motion with her hands. He pointed at her, and she nodded her head vigorously, shouting, "Yes, yes! Come closer!"

He still couldn't hear. He cupped his hand to his ear, then reached to lower the car window. But with the key out of the ignition, it wouldn't go anywhere.

He started to put it back. "No!" she shouted. Then she realized that he couldn't drive forward without turning the key, so she started nodding again. "Yes! Drive up closer!"

The animal had moved again, bellying under the lowest strand of barbed wire. It was ten feet from the Jeep now, maybe less. From his angle, Howard wouldn't have been able to see it unless he knew it was there. But she could see it clearly now, the muscles of its shoulders and haunches moving under the sleek fur, the fangs in its partly open mouth.

"Drive up to the door!" she screamed, and pointed to it.

Howard followed her pointing hand. She could tell when he spotted Stu's body because his rich dark skin turned ashen and his mouth fell open.

Then he opened the car door and stepped out into the driveway.

"*Nooo!*" Juliet cried.

The beast struck. Faster than her eye could follow, it was *here*, and then it was *there*, with no apparent in-between. Howard saw it only at the last instant, before its bulk drove into him. He had time to let out a brief scream, and then he was down.

Mercifully, the Jeep blocked Juliet's view of most of the carnage. But in front, she could see limbs flopping now and again, like a puppy worrying at a rag doll, and that might have been worse.

The wolf—she thought it was a female, but refused to acknowledge any gender, to think of it as anything more than a monster—kept Howard there for several long minutes. Juliet stayed by the window, unable to look away. Tears ran down her cheeks, snot bubbled from her nose.

Finally, the animal emerged from behind the Jeep, its muzzle again slathered in red. It looked up at her in her window, blinked twice. She had the distinct sensation that it was just biding its time, toying with her.

It knows exactly where I am, she thought.

It knows . . .

TWENTY-SIX

The sound of gunfire helped Sam and Dean find Harmon Baird. The coyote had apparently led him on a chase through the forest parallel to the town's eastern edge, instead of right into Cedar Wells. The animal's tracks in the hard snow had been obliterated by the path that Harmon Baird had cut, so they knew which direction to take.

When they heard the loud cracks of rifle shots echoing toward them, Sam and Dean glanced at each other and picked up the pace. In spite of his injury and the fact that he had sustained it by running headlong through these same woods, Sam raced alongside his brother, the sawed-off once again ready in his hands.

A few minutes later they spotted Baird himself, prone on the forest floor behind a big fallen tree trunk. He had his rifle propped on the trunk and was sighting down its length when a shot fired from off in the distance spat tree bits all around him. He ducked, belatedly, and swore.

Sam and Dean threw themselves down behind the tree on either side of him. Another slug chewed into the trunk. Acrid gray smoke hung in the air around them. A shaft of sunlight sliced between the pines onto the fallen log, and tendrils of steam rose where it touched down.

"Who's shooting at you?" Dean asked. He put his own shotgun barrel over the tree, looking for someone to aim at. Sam's wouldn't be much good unless whoever was shooting at them came a lot closer, but he drew the Glock semiautomatic he carried.

"That coyote was meeting up with some others," Baird said. "I saw an Indian and a couple of soldiers. The coyote changed into an eagle and flew around them a few times, then took off toward town. I tried to shoot it on the wing, but I missed and then those others pinned me down here."

Sam raised his head to see the attackers, but they must have been watching because he heard a shot and ducked just in time to miss having wood and bark chips fly into his eyes.

"We've got to flank them," he said. "Before they flank us."

"Works for me," Dean agreed. "I go right, you go left. Harmon, you stay here and keep them firing at you."

"Sure," Baird said. "I've lived plenty long enough anyway, right? Outlived my usefulness, haven't I?"

"That's not what I meant," Dean replied, a sharp

edge in his voice. "I just don't think you'll be as quick or quiet as we are."

"I've hunted these woods for more'n eighty years," Baird argued. "Know every tree and twig. I think I can be as quiet as the next guy."

"Look, we're wasting time," Sam said. And the snow on the ground was seeping through his clothes, cold and uncomfortable. "Dean's right, we have to be the ones to go. You keep your head down and shoot in their direction every once in a while. If you can take one of them out, it'll help our chances."

He and Dean rose to crouches and took off in their respective directions. As he went, Sam could hear Baird mumbling, "Taking orders from a jasper young enough to be my great-grandson. Why, I remember . . ."

Sam darted from the cover of the downed trunk to a bushy pine. From there he'd have to cross a relatively open space to the next tree substantial enough to offer protection. There were a few scraggly bushes in between, so he ran low, hoping they would shield him from view.

They didn't. A bullet whipped through the branches of one, six inches behind him. He threw himself down and belly-crawled the rest of the way to the next big fir.

Stopping there, he peered through the trees, hoping to see where the men—or spirits, or whatever they were—hid. He knew they would be phasing in and out, but figured they probably couldn't shoot unless they were in material form.

Another volley sounded, and Sam saw muzzle flashes ahead and to his right, amid another rock outcropping. These shots seemed to be aimed at Baird's position, and Baird had fired back—Sam saw his bullet chip the gray rock.

He was pretty close, then. He hoped Dean was closing in on the far side of them. Getting the three assailants in a cross fire would be their best bet.

Keeping his gaze glued to the rocks, he raced at a steady, uncomfortable crouch to another bushy pine, then darted toward a limestone boulder of his own. Hunkered behind it, he holstered the Glock again. He was almost in shotgun range, and his rock salt shells would do more of the kind of damage he needed done.

Sam took a deep breath, preparing himself to charge the unworldly beings. Just before he did, though, in a moment of odd quiet, he heard someone sobbing quietly, close by. He couldn't tell if it was someone injured or simply terrified, trying not to be overheard.

Attack, or check the crying person?

The last time he'd heard someone crying in the woods, it had been Juliet, the widow. He decided he should check fast. He didn't want whoever it was trying to make a run for it and stumbling right into a firefight. He stepped carefully through the brush and around a tree, and he saw, curled into a ball with his face in the snow and his butt in the air, a small, terrified boy, his skinny shoulders spasming with each sob.

"Hey," Sam said softly. "You need to sit tight here for another couple of minutes and everything will be okay. All right?"

The kid gave no indication of having heard him. If anything, his crying got louder.

"Are you okay?" Sam asked. "Are you hurt?"

This time, the kid moved. He raised his head from his arms. His face had been sliced open down the right side, hairline to chin. Snow rimed his eyebrows. Under them, big blue eyes met Sam's gaze.

"We'll get you to a doctor right away," Sam said. "Just—just stay put for a few more minutes."

The kid didn't say anything, but he continued to unfold from his fetal position. He was maybe nine years old, Sam guessed. He looked like a poor kid, rural. Probably spent a lot of time in these woods.

Sam wished he'd say something, because the murderous spirits never spoke, and—

The kid jumped to his feet, a nasty, gleaming knife clutched in his little fist, and rushed at him.

Is he real? Sam wondered. *Having a breakdown of some kind, as a result of the injury?* He hadn't seen the kid flicker out. He didn't want to be stabbed, but he also didn't want to shoot an innocent boy.

The boy closed the gap and sliced toward him. Sam dodged the cut, caught the kid's arm. The boy did phase out then, leaving Sam with nothing but air in his grip. A moment later the boy reappeared, a couple of steps away, driving the knife blade toward Sam's kidney.

Sam spun around and lashed out with the shotgun's butt. It connected with the kid's jaw, snapping his head back. He still hadn't made a sound other than breathing and crying—no vocalizations, anyway.

But he came back for more. He didn't lose his grip on the knife, and he lunged at Sam again. This time Sam lowered the sawed-off's barrels and squeezed a trigger. The gun roared and rock salt shredded the little boy.

A second later every trace of the kid was gone. Gunfire sounded behind Sam, by the big rocks. Dean, he guessed, had engaged the enemy—and he wasn't there to back him up.

Dean crouched behind a thick-trunked ponderosa pine. He wished now that he'd brought a decent hunting rifle, like a 30.06—or maybe a bazooka—instead of the shotgun. He hadn't anticipated a full-on firefight, though, and anyway, it was rock salt that killed the spooks, not lead. If you didn't count Baird's dumdums, which he refused to do.

Not that he minded. A good gunfight could be nearly as cathartic as a no-holds-barred brawl. At the moment, however, he was worried about Sam, who hadn't shown up to carry his part of the fight.

He wouldn't be able to check on Sam until the bad guys were down. He swung the barrel of the Remington around the tree and fired a blast at the rocks, then ducked back again. He wished the spirits would say something—their preternatural silence was one of the creepiest things about them, and if they screamed or cried out, at least he'd know he'd hit something.

With his back against the tree, he felt the impact of a bullet *thunking* into its trunk. Just one, though, not the two or three that had come before. He took that as a good sign. Counting to three, he pushed himself upright and swung around the other side of the tree, his head and the shotgun at a different height than before. This time he could see one of his opponents, a blond soldier with no hat on, lifting his Winchester '73 to fire. Dean squeezed off another shot and waited around to see the spray of rock salt turn the soldier's face into hamburger a moment before he vanished altogether.

All clear, then? He ducked partway behind the tree and reloaded, watching the rocks as he did. Something moved there, a flash of blue serge. The older soldier, he thought, a captain, still hid among the rocks. If the soldier didn't show himself soon, he would have to find a new position from which to shoot.

And he had to hope that while he was moving, old man Baird didn't mistake him for one of the bad guys.

Dean was waiting, watching the rocks, reloaded shotgun at the ready, when he heard the rapid flutter of wings and a rush of air. He looked up just in time to see an eagle stooping toward him, talons extended, beak open in a soundless screech. He threw his left arm into the air to fend off the bird's approach, but the eagle dug one clawed foot into the sleeve of his coat and pecked at his face. The bill, razor-sharp, bit into his cheek.

"Damn it!" Dean cried, swatting at the thing with the shotgun. "Get off me, you freakin' bag of feathers!"

The beak shot toward him again, aiming for an eye this time. Dean spun around, dropped the shotgun and caught the beast by its legs, then hauled off and dashed its head against the pine tree trunk. The third time he hit it, the eagle's left eye popped out of its socket and its skull fractured. Just when Dean was struck by the horrible certainty that this was a real bird, not some magical construct, it vanished from his grip, leaving his hand empty.

He heard a gunshot—not directed at him, and not the crack of a Winchester, but the duller boom of the sawed-off—and snatched up his shotgun again. He had been in some strange fights, but this one was shaping up as among the oddest. At least it sounded like Sam was back in it.

Risking a glance around the tree, he could still see the smallest bit of the soldier through a tiny gap in the rocks. No sign of Sam. If he fired from here, only a few grains of rock salt would likely pass through that gap. But the soldier could stick his gun barrel out at any time and have a reasonable shot at him.

He had to get closer.

He scanned the sky, hoping no more birds would swoop down on him. Seeing none—the gunfight had even scared off the real ravens, which seemed as common in these parts as pigeons in Chicago or

New York—he ran at an ungainly crouch toward the rocks. *Don't shoot me, Harmon!* he thought as he covered the space from his tree.

When he was almost to the rocks, his foot plunged through the snow onto an old branch, which snapped with a resounding crack. At the same instant, though, the soldier fired a round into the distance. *At Sam, maybe?* The report from his rifle covered the sound of the branch breaking.

Dean allowed himself a quick peek through the gap. The soldier was in there, aiming into the trees—they never had to reload, that he could tell—and Dean shoved the barrel of the Remington into the gap and pulled the trigger.

When he looked again, through a cloud of gray smoke, the soldier was gone, the rock hideout empty.

"Sam!"

"I'm okay, Dean!" Sam shouted back. "What about you?"

"I'm fine! It's all clear! Get your ass over here!"

The branches across the way parted and Sam came into view. His expression was grim, his cheeks pale despite the cold and the exertion. Whatever he'd been doing instead of engaging the enemies among the rocks, he hadn't liked doing it.

Dean touched the wound on his cheek, where blood leaked out from under a torn flap of skin. *Makes two of us . . .*

TWENTY-SEVEN

"We are *not* postponing the opening," Mayor Milner insisted. He had long since moved from simply raising his voice and was at the point of outright, window-rattling yelling. Red blotches rose in his cheeks and he kept tugging at the knot of his necktie as if it was cutting off circulation to his head.

"Donald, you know I've done everything in my power to make sure we don't have to," Jim Beckett argued. He sat in a comfortable leather chair in the mayor's office, which was decorated with Navajo and Hopi crafts and antiques—some of which, Beckett was pretty sure, had been acquired outside legal channels—and at the moment he wished he was pretty much anywhere else on the planet. "I just don't know what else to do."

"You can't get the National Guard here to help out? Have you tried the governor?"

"You know we can't call outside of town," Beckett

said. He'd been over all this with Milner already, but the man had reached a point where he no longer saw reality for what it was. He wanted things to be his way because he willed them so, and nobody could tell him it didn't work that way. "And we can't drive out, either. Trace died trying."

"So you're telling me, what, that there's some kind of magical barrier all around Cedar Wells? Funny, I could have sworn I saw a UPS truck drive by an hour ago. That must have come from somewhere."

"That's right," Beckett said. "We've intercepted the driver and told him he can't leave town until further notice. He's not happy about it, but he tried to call his dispatcher and couldn't get through, so he's on board with us for the time being."

Milner picked up a small clay pot, an artifact from the ancestral Puebloans, from the edge of his desk and turned it around in his hands. "So we'll have to put up signs on the way into town warning people that if they come in, they won't be able to leave again? Do you have any idea what that would do to our tourist business? Not to mention the shopping center's sales?"

"I think it's unfair to let people come in not knowing about it," Beckett said. "Warning them away might be bad for the town's reputation, might even make us a laughingstock. But is that worse than letting people get trapped here and killed, when we could have kept them out?"

"You know there's no way to get the word out, right, Jim? The mall has been advertising today's opening for weeks. Even if we could reach the local radio stations, they'd only be able to notify a fraction of the people who have seen ads and flyers and heard about it on radio and television. But since Cedar Wells doesn't have its own radio station, apparently we can't even inform that many. The best we could do would be to station officers on the roads and have them wave people off before they got too close."

He put the pot down angrily, scowling at it, at Beckett, at the world in general. "Have you ever heard anything so stupid? Can you even believe we're having this conversation?"

"I wish we weren't, Donald."

"Did you try satellite phones? Shortwave radio?"

"I've tried everything short of smoke signals, Donald." He had considered those, but didn't think he could count on anyone to read them. He'd even considered just lighting a huge fire and letting forest service firefighters come in to check it out. Finally, he'd decided against that, because chances were they would just get stuck, too.

"Why couldn't this have happened when Janie Jennings was mayor? I'd love to have seen her trying to deal with this sort of thing. She got off easy."

"Every forty years, Donald. It only lasts a few days, then it's over. By Monday, probably, everything will be back to normal."

Milner tugged at his shirt collar. "By Monday? How many people will be dead by then? How many lives ruined? Will the mall ever be able to attract shoppers after something like this soured its opening?"

"There's no way to know any of those answers," Beckett said. "And honestly, they're not my first concern."

"Well, I'd like to know what the hell *is* your first concern then, Jim."

"Saving as many lives as I can. And so far the only way we know how to do that is to spot the killers before they reach their victims and kill them first." He didn't point out that they had to be killed with rock salt, of which there was a sudden shortage as more people got the word. Those Winchester boys had called to tell him, and he'd told his deputies, and before long every container of it in town seemed to be spoken for.

"So either way, people are getting killed."

Beckett shook his head, astonished by the mayor's ability to completely fail to understand the situation. "They're not real people, Donald. They're . . . I don't know, ghosts or something. But they can kill and they can be killed."

Milner buried his ruddy face in his hands. His fingers were thick enough to be Ball Park franks. Beckett remembered the catch phrase and could barely suppress a hysterical giggle. *They plump when you cook them!*

"Terrific," Milner said from behind the fleshy cage. "You want to put up signs on the roads into town saying, 'Closed on account of ghosts.'"

"I don't think we need to be that specific," Beckett said. "In fact, maybe we could come up with a more plausible scenario. An outbreak of some kind, or a chemical spill. Something that would make people want to stay away, but that we could then announce was over, once we know the danger is past."

"If there are any of us left to make that announcement."

"That's a given, Donald. And, unfortunately, it's a real concern. We don't know for sure how long it'll last or if there's any limit to the number of people they'll go after."

"God, I wish one of them would kill me," Milner said, lowering his hands. "Then this would be someone else's disaster."

Don't wish too loud, Beckett thought. *It just might come true.*

Reunited with Sam and Harmon Baird, Dean took another look at the rock hidey-hole the spooks had used. No sign remained that anyone had been there— the snow was disturbed, but only by rock salt, not by footprints or bodies.

"I'm thinkin' spirits, for sure," he said. "Just not ones that are like any we've encountered before." He touched his raw cheek again. "And I don't like 'em messing with my manly good looks."

"Seems the likeliest bet," Sam said. "Which still leaves us with the big questions of why and how do we stop them. Harmon, are you sure you can't remember anything else about that ranch?"

"Oh, I remember lots about it," Baird said. "Just nothing that seems like it's connected to the forty-year."

"Like what?" Dean pressed. "Anything might help, even if it doesn't seem like it at first."

"Let's get back to the car while we talk," Sam suggested. "We need to keep an eye out for more of them, just in case."

The others agreed, so they started crunching through the snow, back toward the road. On the way, Baird talked. "It was called the Copper Bell Ranch," he said. "Brand was the C Circle B. I think it had some other name before that, but that's what it was when I was growin' up there. Outside the ranch house there was a big copper bell made outta copper from the Orphan Mine, right there below the South Rim."

"In the national park?" Sam asked.

"That's right."

"I didn't know there were any mines inside the park."

"Not anymore. Used to be. They took copper outta the Orphan, then uranium."

"Grand Canyon National Radioactive Park," Dean said with a dry chuckle. "I like it."

"Used to be," Baird said again. "Miners'd come out after a shift and drink at the Bright Angel Lounge, right alongside the tourists. Some of 'em probably woulda set a Geiger counter to tickin'. Anyway, I don't remember what the ranch was called before the folks who owned it when I grew up there took it over, or if it had always been the Copper Bell. But that mine didn't get going until eighteen and ninety or thereabouts, and the ranch had been around at least forty years at that point."

"So the area was settled as early as 1850?" Sam asked.

"Some folks was here then. Not many. Which was why the first owner was able to claim such a big spread. More people showed up later on, harder it got to hold onto all his land. Then the Murphys, who owned it when my folks worked there, came in and bought a piece of it. The Murphys had twelve thousand acres, but that was just some of the original spread."

"And the first murder cycle, the one in 1926, that happened while you were living on the ranch? And the Murphys owned it?"

"That's right, Sam."

"But you don't remember anything that happened before that, anything that might've set someone off, made them mad at the town or the other settlers?" Dean asked.

"I've been tryin' to," Baird said. "Come up blank ever' time."

They reached the car and Dean opened his door, let Baird in back. Sam climbed into the front passenger seat. "Why did your mother think the ranch was involved, then?" he asked.

"I'm not too sure about that neither," Baird said. "Seems like someone told me a reason, either in 'twenty-six or 'sixty-six, but I'll be doggoned if I can remember who or what it was."

Dean started the Impala and fed it some gas, enjoying the satisfying growl. When everything else was going to hell, it was good to have something he could count on.

"Sometimes people write histories of those big old ranches," Sam said. "Even if they're not published professionally, they're privately printed. The library might have something like that."

"Don't think so," Baird said.

"Why not?"

"He never finished it."

"Who?" Dean asked, his tone abrupt. "Someone started one? What happened to it? Who was it?"

"His name was Neville Stein," Baird said. "I remembered it yesterday."

"Is he still alive? Would he talk to us?"

"He won't talk," Baird said with certainty.

"Why not?"

"I shot him yesterday. That's when I remembered his name. 'Course, he was already dead—died before the first forty-year, back in nineteen and twenty-three or twenty-four, I think. He was a teacher, and some of the local boys didn't think much of teachers in those days. His last mistake was asking a cowboy's sister out on a date. A picnic lunch, I think is what he had in mind. Cowboy shot him in the face. I did the same, yesterday. He won't be talkin' to anyone."

TWENTY-EIGHT

"Where did he teach?" Sam asked. "Here in town?"

Baird gazed out the car window as they cruised the quiet streets of Cedar Wells. A couple of times they saw people carrying guns, and had to watch them for a minute or two—long enough to make sure they weren't flickering and didn't have any visible fatal wounds—before deciding they were real people and not a threat.

"No," Baird said finally, after waiting so long that Sam couldn't remember for a second what he had asked. "No, he had a little schoolhouse on the ranch itself. There were a dozen of us kids, most times, that needed schoolin', so they took care of it right there. Too far to come into town for school."

"How far out was it?"

"Oh, no more than six or seven miles, I guess," Baird said. "But you can cover that a lot faster now than we could when I was young."

"But it's still within the range of the killings," Sam said. "And the distance from town people can travel."

"I think the sheriff said the cutoff was fifteen," Dean said. "That's about where the deputy got it."

"Yeah, it's within the town limits of Cedar Wells," Baird said. "Always had a Cedar Wells mailing address, anyhow."

Sam's mind raced, trying to find another way to unlock the secrets that must have died with Neville Stein. "Did he have any notes, that you know of?" he asked. "If he was planning to write a book, he must have had some notes, right?"

"Now you mention it, I believe he did," Baird said. He scratched his temple and blinked his tiny black eyes. "He used to have some journals or something like that, in the schoolhouse, that he always warned us kids away from. Most probably that's what it was, the things he was keepin' for his history of the ranch. Sometimes I'd see him talkin' to some old cowboy or another for hours, writing down things the cowboy'd tell him." He chuckled. "Lies, like as not."

"Maybe they were," Sam said. "But even so, he'd have to keep the records of those interviews somewhere. Do you know who would've ended up with them after he died?"

"I can't imagine anyone would have wanted 'em. Most folks thought he was crazier'n a jaybird, even talking to those old cowboys. Much less writing down what they said, or thinkin' anyone would ever care to read what he wrote."

"Then where would they be?" Dean asked. "Had to end up someplace, right?"

"They're probably still there."

"Still where?" Sam asked.

"In the schoolhouse."

"The schoolhouse is still there?"

"Sure it is," Baird said.

Dean braked the car to a sudden stop and slammed his open palm down on the wheel. "We asked you before if the ranch was still there!"

"It ain't," Baird said. He didn't look like he even understood that Dean was angry with him, much less what had prompted that anger. "Ranch has been divided and subdivided, made into a housing project and smaller ranch properties and little ranchettes and what have you. But part of the land is still there, and some of the buildings. Schoolhouse was put in a rocky canyon nobody much cared about because there wasn't no good grazing back there. You don't build a school on land that has commercial value, do you? Same reason, nobody else has bothered to build on it, so what's left of the building is still standin' there. Least, it was last time I went through there. That's ten, twelve years gone by, now, but I can't imagine anyone much goes back there."

"Can you take us to it?"

"You're drivin', Dean," Baird said. "And I reckon your eyesight is a lot better'n mine. Why don't you take us to it?"

Sam could almost hear the sparks of Dean's fuse

burning. "Because . . . I . . . don't . . . know . . . where . . . it . . . is."

"Well, I can *tell* you that."

"That's a good idea, Harmon," Sam said, hoping to intercede before Dean threw Baird into the road and ran over him. "You tell Dean where to drive, and he'll drive there."

"That's right." Dean's voice carried the false cheer that he used to disguise sheer fury. "You tell me where to drive. I'll drive. Okay?"

"Sure enough," Baird said. "Turn left up here at the corner."

As it turned out, they couldn't drive all the way. Paved road led to within a few miles of the old schoolhouse, and then dirt road—which hadn't been traveled much lately, by the looks of it—got them another mile or so closer. After that they had to travel on foot, cutting across snow-covered fields, climbing barbed-wire fences, all while carrying their weapons.

Baird directed them toward a rocky ridge. When they reached the ridge, they had to scramble up it at a relatively low point. It looked like Kaibab limestone to Sam, like the upper layer of the Grand Canyon itself. From its peak they looked down at a short drop to a wide valley with another, similar ridge maybe a mile or two away. Both semiparallel ridges ran into the distance, where they grew closer and seemed to funnel the valley floor into a canyon.

"That there, that leads right to the Grand Canyon

after a few miles," Baird said. "We used to have to make sure the fences out that way was sound because we didn't want any beeves to get away and fall down the big drop. Some of 'em found pathways down, and that was even worse because then we'd have to go down ourselves and try to herd 'em back up."

"But you were just a kid, right?" Dean asked.

"Sure. Anybody ever tells you kids don't work on ranches, you can tell 'em what they're full of."

"And the schoolhouse is around here?" Sam said. He'd been scanning but hadn't seen anything that looked like a school.

"This is called School Canyon on the maps. You can't see it from here, though." Baird started down the slope again, picking his way among the rocks like a mountain goat.

His words took a minute to sink in, but when they did, Sam asked, "You said it's called that on the maps. Does that mean the locals called it something else?"

"You betchum. We called it Witch's Canyon."

Dean stopped short, crossed his arms over his chest. "And it didn't occur to you to maybe mention that name before now? Considering what we're dealing with?"

Baird shielded his eyes with his right hand, looking back upslope at Dean. "No. No, it sure didn't. I apologize if that was an oversight, young man, but you didn't ask me about no witches, and anyhow, it's just a name, isn't it? Lot of places around here have names that don't mean nothing."

"But it might mean something," Sam pointed out. "It's as solid a lead as anything else we've come up with so far. Where's that school?"

"Follow me," Baird said. He started down the slope again. Sam followed. After another moment's petulance, so did Dean.

The canyon floor was mostly tall yellow grass poking up through the snow. Frequent boulders jutted up from the floor, a few scrubby junipers among them. They trudged down the canyon, and finally Sam could see what Baird had insisted all along was there. Almost up against the wall of the ridge they had crossed was what remained of a log structure, its roof caved in, its log walls partially collapsed. Logs stuck out at odd angles. Forget about structural integrity—the place looked like it would fall apart completely if a visiting sparrow flapped its wings too hard.

"That's a school?" Sam asked.

"It was in better shape when I went there."

"Hard to believe," Dean said.

If Baird caught the cutting sarcasm, he ignored it. He approached the ramshackle building, at once anxious and somehow reverent. Sam had the impression that the place had meant a lot to him, once upon a time. It probably hurt to see it in this condition. If it had been within the national park boundaries, it might have been preserved as a historical monument, but instead it had been ignored, left to the not so tender mercies of wind and weather.

There might have once been a door in the doorway, Sam thought, but if so, it was long gone. The building stood open to the elements. The beam over the doorway had collapsed, so instead of being seven feet tall, the opening slanted down at a forty-degree angle, and even Harmon Baird had to stoop to go inside. He didn't hesitate, though. Sam fished a penlight from his coat pocket, clicked it on, and followed him in, with Dean close behind carrying his own flashlight.

Inside, it looked more like a home for rodents and bats than a place of learning for humans. The floor was covered with dirt and animal feces and vegetation that had been blown through the open doorway, some of which had taken root amidst the ancient benches and desks. Webs clotted the upper reaches, some hanging low enough that Sam had to dodge them or brush them away with his arms. The air was thick with the stink of ammonia and the earthy, fecund aroma of manure.

"Looks like summer vacation lasted a little too long," Dean said.

"I don't think anyone's used the place since I was young," Baird said. "The Murphys started dividing up the ranch in the early thirties, after the park started drawing people to the area and the demand for real estate started to grow."

"It's almost too bad no one took the furnishings out," Sam said. "They could have been preserved in a museum or something."

"Been plenty of schools abandoned over the years, I expect," Baird said. "Some things can't be hung on to, just got to be left to rot."

"I suppose that's true. Do you have any idea where your teacher would have stored his records?"

Baird stood still, looking at the place in the dim light filtering through the door and the openings in the walls and roof. "Mr. Stein, he had him a big old chest made of cedar wood," he said after a while. "Used to keep schoolbooks and those old journals of his in it, and just about any other treasure he needed to keep safe. Had a big padlock on it, and he kept the key on him all the time."

"Where was the chest?" Dean asked.

"Front of the room, behind his whatchacallit. Lectern. I remember starin' at it, day after day, sometimes wonderin' what marvels he had inside, sometimes wishin' I could hide in there myself."

Sam couldn't quite determine the room's original layout. "Where was the front?"

Baird pointed immediately to the worst area in the room, where the roof had completely fallen in. It looked like part of the canyon that the schoolroom had been built around. "That's the front. Right there."

TWENTY-NINE

"I guess we start digging," Dean said. "Wish I brought a hazmat suit." He turned off his flashlight and shoved it back into his pocket. There was enough ambient light for manual labor, if not for reading some long-dead schoolteacher's notebooks. He hoped they didn't unearth any dens of rats in that mess, though. He hated rats.

Hated them a lot.

Sam put his light away, too, and soon they were shoveling through the accumulated debris of the decades, digging their hands into cold mud, decomposed branches, animal dung, and probably the corpses of small creatures of various kinds. They'd need to sterilize their hands after this or risk all sorts of unpleasant consequences.

The task was disgusting, but before long they had unearthed a large wooden chest that had to be the one Baird described. Its hinges and hasp were rusted through but still visible. Dean kicked at the old lock, still fastened in place, and it crumbled to dust. "You really think anything in here is gonna be legible?"

Sam shrugged. "Won't know until we look." He opened the trunk's lid. Dean found his light again and shined it inside.

On top, there was indeed a layer of paper that had gone to pulp. As soon as his fingers touched it, it disintegrated. But underneath, as if that layer had protected the important stuff, were school records, with each student's name neatly handwritten on the outside. Under that were the journals Baird had described, leather-bound and still mostly intact, although insects had nibbled at the edges. Dean lifted one out gingerly and turned its brittle, yellowed pages. The same neat handwriting filled the pages.

"This has got to be the journals," he said.

"Looks like it to me," Baird said.

"There must be twenty of them," Sam said. "He must have collected a lot of oral histories."

"A lot of lies," Baird reminded them.

"But with some truth mixed in, we hope."

"No promises."

"We going to read them right here?" Dean asked. Reading wasn't his favorite activity by any means, and he had found that people in the past often used way more words than they had to. And funny handwriting.

"If we try to transport them, we run the risk that they'll fall apart," Sam said. "Besides, given the urgency—"

"Then I guess we read them right here. Better get started." Dean sat down in the muck, figuring it was already too late to salvage any of the clothes he was wearing. The books all looked alike from the outside, so he didn't see how to choose where to begin.

It didn't take long for him to decide that he'd started with the wrong book. He was immediately immersed in some old ranch hand's account of a particularly dry summer, with grass dying, fires burning up what hadn't died, and cattle starving. Unpleasant reading, but nothing that struck him as even remotely supernatural. And the old-fashioned handwriting, while precisely formed, was in ink that had purpled on the yellow paper, hard to read even with a flashlight clutched in his left hand.

He skimmed the pages, looking for any mention of a witch or any event that might have led to antagonism against the town. There were plenty of small slights—trips into town for supplies that ended in a fight, or someone feeling they'd been overcharged for merchandise, that kind of thing. Dean had learned not to underestimate how petty people could be, but he didn't get the sense that anyone would have launched an ongoing murder cycle because of such minor disagreements.

He reached the end of that first book and picked up another. Sam was turning pages just as quickly as he had. Baird sat with a book open on his lap but his gaze wandering around the room, as if in his mind's eye he was seeing all the children he had gone to school with in this little room. Dean wondered if the old guy understood the stakes here. Then again, he had armed himself and faced potential danger in order to help out the residents of a town to which he didn't feel any genuine attachment anymore. In the long run, Dean guessed, no one had done more than Harmon Baird to try to stop the killings from happening again.

Still, he felt the minutes ticking by as if each one carved a notch in his arm.

When Dean was on his third book, he heard Sam issue a low whistle. "What?" Dean asked.

"I might have something here," Sam said. "Hang on." He read further, tracing his finger along underneath the lines in the book. Dean ignored his own book and watched his younger brother's face cloud over as he read.

After another few minutes Sam stopped and looked up from the pages. "I think this is it. Harmon, do you remember ever hearing about a woman named Elizabeth Claire Marbrough?"

"The Marbrough family owned the ranch before the Murphys," Baird said, snapping his fingers. "Couldn't remember that name, for the life of me."

"But what about the woman? Does that name ring a bell?"

"Not specifically," Baird said. "Jens Marbrough, I think he was the first owner. My people, they worked for him for at least a generation before I was born, then my folks stayed on when he sold out to the Murphys."

"Who is this Marbrough lady?" Dean asked, wanting Sam to get to the point.

"According to this account, given by one of the

young women who worked as a maid and laundress on the ranch, Elizabeth Claire Marbrough was a witch," Sam said. "She came here from back East someplace, and there were stories about her before she even got here. Once she was here, though, the stories got worse. This woman, Mary Beth Gibson, said she once saw Elizabeth turn a horse that had thrown her grandson into a lizard."

"Sounds like the kind of scare stories they used to tell in Salem," Dean said.

"But we know there was a certain amount of truth to some of those. Not that the practice of witchcraft is necessarily inherently evil, but some of the people drawn to it as a way to gain and exercise power are happy to misuse it."

"Some witches are plain evil, though," Dean added. "And whatever's going on in Cedar Wells is the work of someone or something evil. You see anything in there about her cursing the town or anything?"

"So far, just this one reference."

Dean turned his attention back to the book on his lap. "So we need to look for more stories about Elizabeth whatshername."

"Elizabeth Claire Marbrough," Sam said again. "And yeah, that seems like a good idea."

Paging through more of the volumes—always with an appreciation for the time slipping by—they put together an idea of Elizabeth Claire Marbrough's history, at least as described by the rotating cast of employees and family members interviewed over a twelve-year span by schoolteacher Neville Stein. These memories had been related years after the fact, in most cases by people who had not witnessed them firsthand but had been told about them. In the telling and retelling, stories had a tendency to grow, and Dean suspected these were no different.

Some of the tales sounded like pure fantasy. Elizabeth zooming across the rangelands on a flaming broom. Elizabeth striking down Apache shaman Geronimo through a long-distance spell, although according to Sam, historians said he died of pneumonia at Fort Sill, Oklahoma, and not—as this story claimed—from having his head explode suddenly at the dinner table. Elizabeth taking multiple werecats, in their human forms, as lovers. Okay, Dean allowed that this one could have some basis in truth—he had heard some pretty kinky stories involving witches.

But even setting those aside, a clearer picture emerged. Elizabeth was the mother of Jens Marbrough, the original owner of the ranch. She had lived somewhere in New York or New England until a scandal of some sort caused her to need to get away from that region. With some reluctance, Jens arranged for her to move to the ranch.

In those days, running a ranch in Arizona Territory sounded like a struggle. Indian raiders were a constant threat. There was little in the way of real law enforcement, so Jens had to take matters in his own hands when it came to theft, cattle rustling, and the like. Soldiers on the hunt for Indians could be as destructive as the Indians themselves, cutting fences and trampling fields.

The local population was small at the time, since the Grand Canyon had not yet become a national park, but Jens made efforts to be a good neighbor and a community leader. This became harder to do when his ill-tempered, spiteful, malicious mother moved in. Her occasional forays into town brought complaints and cost Jens friendships he had spent years cultivating. Finally—and on this story, multiple accounts agreed—she had caused the withering death of a Basque ranch hand named Bacigalupi because he had failed to bow sufficiently low when he ran into her between the house and the stable one morning. That day, he had been hale and hearty, but by the end of the week he looked as if a wasting disease had had its way with him for months. He died a week to the day after the original encounter.

For Jens, this was the last straw. He couldn't get rid of his own mother, but he wanted her far away from him. Telling her that it was for her own privacy and peace of mind, he built her a cabin of her own, in an isolated canyon far from the main ranch headquarters.

She protested from the first day she learned of the plan, and her attitude—not to mention her relations with other local settlers—soured even more. After some additional run-ins, she was finally banned from the little community that would become Cedar Wells. Not long after that, the new cabin was finished and Jens hauled all her belongings there before going back for her.

A horrific argument followed. Apparently, Elizabeth was unwilling to use her witchy powers against members of her immediate family, but witnesses claimed that only that fact curtailed her response. One said he had never seen her so furious, and this was a woman to whom rage seemed a first response to any provocation. And there was no second response.

She agreed, Jens leaving her little choice, and moved to the little cabin. There, by all reports, she stewed and plotted her revenge, on the ranch and on the town that grew up nearby.

"I found this one account of what that revenge would be," Sam said. He sat awkwardly on what had once been a student's desk, although the years had made it resemble a vaguely desk-shaped mound of mud and sticks. "And it sounds familiar."

"Spill it, Sam," Dean said. "We're burning daylight."

"According to this, she had one confidante on the ranch, the wife of one of the hands, who took pity on her and visited her in the cabin when no one else would. This woman says that Elizabeth told her that she had cast a spell that would bring to life everyone who had ever died violently on the ranch's property, human and animal alike."

"That does sound familiar," Dean said. "Does she say what this pissed-off bitch wanted the undead to do?"

"This is where it gets good," Sam said. "Every forty years, they would attack the town, killing indiscriminately, in the ways that they had been killed. Some would come back in their own forms, but some would be skinwalkers, able to take animal forms at will."

"The forty-year," Baird said. Something like awe tinged his voice.

"The forty-year," Sam agreed.

"I don't suppose there's a schedule in there," Dean said. "When we can count on this thing to be over."

Sam shook his head. "It says Elizabeth Claire Marbrough died in 1886. The cycle was supposed to begin after her death. So 'eighty-six, 'twenty-six, 'sixty-six, and 'oh-six. But if her confidante knew how long it was supposed to last, she didn't say."

"It'd sure be good to know," Dean said. "Because if it's not ending soon, we could be staring at a massacre at that mall opening."

THIRTY

"I think these books have told us what we need to know," Sam said. "If it was really a spell and not a curse, then we should be able to counter it."

"Yeah," Dean agreed. "Let's get out of this dump." He glanced at Baird, who looked sad to hear his beloved schoolhouse described in such terms. From Dean's point of view, "dump" was too good for it. "Sorry."

Sam put the books back in the chest and closed the lid. "Maybe when this is all over," he told Baird, "we can come back here and get them out, take them to your place. They should be preserved even if nothing else is."

"Okay, sure," Baird said. "That'll be fine."

Dean picked up his shotgun and headed for the door. The light, with clouds blocking the sun, hadn't changed since they came in.

Baird beat him to it, though. Maybe he had been disappointed in the place after all, the way people some-times were when they went back to locations they'd known as children and found that they didn't measure up to the memories. He seemed in a hurry to leave.

But as soon as he was outside, he backpedaled, in a greater hurry to get back in.

"What is it?" Dean asked.

"We got a visitor," Baird said. "Not the friendly kind, neither."

"A visitor?" Dean checked his shotgun, made sure a shell was chambered, and crossed to the slanting doorway.

Baird wasn't kidding.

The bear had to be seven feet tall, standing up on its hind legs. A grizzly, a species probably long since wiped out in this area, with light brown fur and teeth that dripped menace and claws like daggers.

"Dean?" Sam said. "What is it?"

"It ain't Smokey."

"Smokey . . . Dean, is there a bear outside?"

Dean was about to respond, but the grizzly gave a silent roar that he believed would have shaken what remained of the schoolhouse, its head thrown back, its paws flailing at empty air as if trying to swat away imaginary bees.

"I'll take that as a yes," Sam said, shouldering up beside Dean in the doorway and seeing the bear's furious stance. "Wow."

"Yeah," Dean said. "That about sums it up."

"It looks fierce," Sam said. "But we can shoot it, right?"

"If it's a spirit bear, I guess," Dean replied. "But if it's real, we might just tick it off."

"Chance I'm willing to take." Sam fired his sawed-off at the thing. The boom echoed in the small schoolhouse, and Dean could taste the bitter smoke.

The bear flickered when the rock salt hit it, flashed its glowing black form. But it didn't vanish. Instead, it returned to its original material shape, dropped down to all fours and glared at the Winchesters like it had just decided on lunch.

"My luck," Sam said. "It's a spirit bear *and* I pissed it off."

Dean leveled his own shotgun and let off a blast at the thing before it could charge. This time the rock salt hit it square in the face. At a distance of less than twenty feet, it should have taken the bear's head off.

Instead, the bear flickered again, and when it stabilized it was no longer a bear, but a Native American warrior in buckskin leggings and war paint. He carried a spear with a finely chiseled stone head. Near the center of his chest gaped an open wound that might have been made by the same weapon. He glowered at Dean and Sam as if he had felt the blast and didn't appreciate it.

"One more for good measure," Sam said, firing his other barrel. The rock salt hit the Indian. He dropped his spear, flickered, disappeared, and came back as the grizzly again. The fallen spear had vanished.

"This is not good," Dean said.

He didn't get a chance to say more, because the

bear charged. Not wanting to get caught in the doorway, Dean darted to the left, Sam to the right. The bear stopped short, swinging its huge head both ways, then settled on Dean and started toward him.

Great, Dean thought. *I can probably outrun it, but for how long? And what about the old coot?*

He decided to stay and fight.

As the bear closed on him, he pumped the shotgun again. The old shell ejected, a new one in the chamber, he held his ground, waiting, waiting . . .

He could smell the bear now, a smell like old dirt and death, the smell of the grave, worse by far than the animal stench inside the schoolhouse.

The bear thrust its giant head at him, teeth gnashing, spittle flying.

Dean shoved the barrel of the shotgun against the bear's neck and pulled the trigger. The gun boomed.

The bear flickered, fell back, flickered again. For a moment the Indian sat in the snow instead of the bear, but with another blink the bear returned.

If the shotgun blasts were having any lasting effect, Dean couldn't see it.

The bear shook like a wet dog and raised up onto its four paws again. Gave a head-shaking snarl. Lunged.

Dean sidestepped the charge, but his foot came down on a patch of frozen snow and skidded out from under him. He went down on his right knee just as the bear's slavering mouth came at him. Its breath hot on his face, Dean ducked under the attack. The bear hit him with hundreds of pounds of fur-covered muscle, bowling him over. Sharp claws jabbed into the ground around Dean as he writhed to avoid them.

That wouldn't work for long, though. The bear was playing a game of Twister, and Dean was the mat. Left paw, yellow, might be the one that landed the animal's crushing weight on his skull. He was stuck wriggling and dodging, unable to get past the bear's sturdy legs.

Then, over the sound of the bear's huffing breath—saliva dripped onto his face, hot as coffee—Dean heard the thumping of Sam's feet as he ran toward them. Sam jumped and landed on the bear's back. The bear reared up, and Dean scrambled out from under it. Sam piggybacked on the beast, jabbing it over and over with a knife as the bear tried to shake him off.

Since the shotgun blasts hadn't worked, Dean scooped the weapon off the ground, reversed it, and swung it by the barrel, clubbing the creature in the head while Sam stabbed it.

The bear let out a soundless wail of pain, flashed, becoming the Indian again momentarily, then reverted to bear form. When it changed, Sam fell off its back. As a bear again, it whirled on him, clawing at him with those giant paws. One swipe with those would decapitate Sam. Dean wondered what Baird was up to while they battled it.

But the creature's quick transformation gave Dean an idea. "Hang on another minute, Sammy!" he shouted.

"I don't see much choice!" Sam returned. He tried to stab with his knife, but his arm and the knife seemed like feeble weapons compared to those ursine claws.

The bear had its back to Dean now, as it sparred with Sam. Dean took advantage of the chance to pump another rock salt shell into the chamber, raise the gun to the back of the bear's head, and fire.

As before, the buckshot didn't even seem to penetrate the animal's thick fur, but the beast blinked out of existence. The Indian appeared, empty-handed. Sam stabbed at him and the Indian dodged, as nimble as his other form was powerful.

While the Indian was visible, so was his spear, still where it had fallen on the ground. Dean dove for it and snatched it up. By the time he had his footing again the Indian was already changing back into the grizzly and reaching for Sam. This time, as it changed, its claws caught in Sam's coat and it began to draw Sam toward its gnashing teeth.

Dean threw himself at the creature, driving the spear forward with every ounce of muscle he could put behind it.

Its stone point pierced the grizzly's fur and flesh with a sound like wet fabric tearing. Dean met resistance, pushed harder. The spear went deep, glancing off bone, finding organs.

After what seemed like days, the grizzly fell forward into the disturbed snow, flickering faster and faster. Bear, Indian, bear, Indian. When it was bear, the spear vanished from sight—although Dean knew it was still there, since he had felt it, although not seen it. When it was human, the spear jutted from the warrior's back. Dean didn't turn him over to check, but he guessed the spear's point would have hit approximately the same spot in the Indian's chest as whatever made the wound on his other side had.

Within seconds it was gone.

Dean dropped down into the snow, panting heavily. Sam rested, hunched forward, hands on his knees for support.

"You okay?" Dean asked between breaths.

"Y-Yeah," Sam said. "Thanks."

"No . . . no problem."

"Anyway," Sam said, "what the hell?"

"What do you mean?"

"I thought the spirits were supposed to be easy to kill with rock salt loads. Not this one."

"Not so much," Dean agreed. A sentence as long as Sam's still seemed beyond his capabilities.

He blew out a couple more big breaths, sucked in great lungfuls of air. "Maybe . . ." he said. One more breath. "Maybe because we're close."

"Close how?"

"Close to where the witch cast her spell. Maybe there's a distance factor involved. The farther from the ranch, or from her cabin, the weaker the spirits get. Closer in, they're more powerful because her magic is stronger here." He allowed himself a quick grin for having gotten all the way through that without fainting. Emboldened, he tried standing again.

His knees felt a bit wobbly but he kept his feet under him.

"That could be," Sam agreed. "Makes as much sense as anything else."

"Your definition of 'sense' appears a mite questionable," Baird said from the schoolhouse door, "if you think any of this makes sense. I don't doubt what my own senses tell me, but I've long stopped thinkin' it's sensible."

Dean shrugged, noting that Baird had not participated in the battle against the big beast. "I guess we stopped worrying about that distinction a long time ago," he said. "Anyway, we've got to get to Dad's journal, in the car, and see if there's a way we can undo her spell."

"We'd better do it fast," Sam said. "The mall's opening in less than an hour."

"Fast as we can," Dean agreed. "I'm sure my legs'll work again sometime today."

He just hoped he wasn't being overly optimistic.

THIRTY-ONE

"Elizabeth Claire Marbrough. That was the witch's name, right?" Dean asked.

"That's what the schoolteacher's notebooks said," Sam replied. He remembered the precise, elaborate way Stein had formed his capital letters. "Why?"

Dean smacked the pages of Dad's journal. "Dad's heard of her."

"He has? Would have saved us a lot of trouble if we'd known that."

"It wouldn't have done any good," Dean said. "There's an entry about her in here, but it's about when she was back in Darien Center, New York. Before her son brought her out here."

"What's it say?"

Dean read further in the journal.

"I guess this is what got her shipped out to Arizona," he said after a while. "A series of girls went missing around Darien Center. One of them turned up in the nearby forest and said she had escaped from good old Elizabeth. But while a captive of the evil witch, she had seen other girls in various stages of dismemberment."

"A one-woman *Chainsaw Massacre*?"

"Only without the power tools," Dean said. "Townspeople went to her house to investigate. Only two of them made it back to town alive, and one of the two had turned into a gibbering idiot. When they went back, it was in force. But apparently she clued in and booked before they got there."

Sam took this all in. "Easy to see why Jens wasn't so thrilled to see Momma come to town."

"No kidding. Dad wrote that she was eventually suspected of more than seventy disappearances, of people ranging in age from three to eighty. After she was gone, the disappearances stopped."

"Maybe she really did try to reform when she got out here," Sam speculated. "If there weren't any reports of the same kind of thing happening. I mean, sure, she was a pain, she was rude and obnoxious, and maybe she even killed a handful of people, but we haven't heard about anything like that."

"And maybe there just weren't that many people around for her to pick on," Dean said. "Or maybe because they were more spread out, the disappearances weren't reported."

"Either way, when she went bad again, it was in a big way."

"Got that right, Sammy. A real big way. One we have to put an end to."

"Does Dad have any suggestions on that?"

"There's a counterspell in here that might work," Dean said. "But it sounds like it'd be most efficient combined with the good old burning and salting of her bones."

"Always a classic. Do we have any idea where she's buried?"

Harmon Baird had been standing by the road, swaying a little as if in a stiff wind. "Maybe Elmer Fudd knows," Dean said.

"Mr. Baird," Sam said. "Do you know where Elizabeth Marbrough's house would have been? Or is there anyplace else she'd have been buried?"

"Her house?" he said, sounding startled, like Sam had just woken him up. "It's farther back in Witch's Canyon. Almost to the Grand. I think the old man wanted her as far away as he could get her without dropping her into the river."

Dean grabbed a duffel bag of weapons and tools from the Impala's trunk, unzipped it, and added a folding shovel. "Let's go."

"You should go," Sam said. He'd been thinking a lot on the walk back from the schoolhouse, and although he knew this moment would come, he'd delayed it as long as he could. "I want to go to the mall. You may not get to her in time. Or even if you do, the counterspell might not work. I want to be there to help, just in case."

"Your call," Dean said. The change in his tone was subtle, not something just anyone would catch. Sam wasn't just anyone, though. He was the only person, besides Dad, who had ever been truly close to Dean. They had spent so much time together in the last year that, to Dean, it was probably almost like having a real social life. But he wasn't used to being honest with people, and he wasn't used to being read by anybody.

Sam could read him, and he knew that while his brother pretended to be aloof, Dean was, in fact, disappointed.

"Me, I want to be where the real action is," Dean continued. "I want to nail that witch once and for all."

So did Sam. But he wasn't in the hunting business for the nailing, although that was a fine perk. He was in it to protect people, to save lives. "I guess I'll have to miss out on the fun," he said. "I think there's going to be real trouble, maybe panic, when everything starts to go down, and the people there won't know how to deal with it."

Dean gave a little shrug, still without meeting Sam's gaze. "You're probably right."

Sam knew he was. He also believed that the idea never would have occurred to Dean. His brother was a hunter through and through. Nothing wrong with that—the world needed hunters. But he knew that would never be him. He'd been headed down that road, but got lucky, tasted real life—the lives most people led—and couldn't leave that behind. Not entirely. Not like Dad had. Dean had been a kid, hadn't ever had a chance to become anything other than what Dad had made of him.

That, finally, was the gulf between them—the canyon that could never be bridged. Dean knew only one way of life, and it kept him separated from the world that he fought to protect. Sam, through his years at Stanford and the love of Jessica, had been brought into that world for a time, and the part of his soul that it claimed would always be with him.

Without saying more, he loaded up his pockets with rock salt shells and conventional ammo for the .45 he carried.

"I'll go with you, Dean," Baird said. "I'd like to see an end put to this, once and for all."

"Cool," Dean said. He also restocked his ammunition, and the Winchester brothers' shoulders brushed as they both reached into the Impala's deep trunk. "You be careful with my car," he said. "And pick us up when you're done. I don't want to have to walk back to town after this."

"Don't worry. I won't leave you stranded."

Without more conversation, Dean finished reloading and started back toward where they'd come from, toward Witch's Canyon. Baird looked at Sam a couple of times, as if for some sort of validation, then followed Dean.

Sam knew full well that any time he and Dean separated might be the last time. When they were together, they had each other's backs. Apart, any battle might be their last.

He watched until Dean and Baird were out of sight, then started the Impala and headed for the mall.

Juliet's attention kept being pulled back to the window. Howard Patrick's Jeep sat out there in the drive, the door open. The keys—*unless that damn overgrown hound has eaten them or something*—were probably still on the ground next to it, or else clutched in Howard's fist.

The wolf might have disabled the vehicle, as it had the others, but Juliet couldn't see any signs of tampering, no parts littering the ground beneath the engine compartment, no pools of gasoline or other liquids in the snow.

Which meant, less than fifty yards away, was an escape vehicle. *More like thirty*, she thought. *Twenty-five.* She had tried to warn him away, but he just kept coming closer.

She regretted that she hadn't been able to communicate more clearly. But how? If she had written a sign on a piece of paper and held it up to the window glass, he wouldn't have been able to read it at that distance. She couldn't call him on his mobile phone.

She'd hoped that someone would drive up, but now she prayed they didn't. She didn't want anyone else to die because of that damn wolf. *Present company definitely included.*

She scanned the property for as far as she could see, hoping for a glimpse of the beast. If she saw it and it was far enough away, stalking a cow or a bird or something, maybe then she could run for the Jeep.

How far was far enough? That was the tricky part.

The wolf could cover ground much faster than she could. But could it cover, say, a hundred yards in the time it took her to go twenty-five? Could it do two hundred? She had to acknowledge the fact that she didn't know where the key was. If it had fallen under the vehicle, finding it and retrieving it would take extra time. She shuddered, visualizing herself on her knees, pawing under the Jeep, and the beast coming down on her back . . .

She shook the image away. Worrying about that wouldn't do any good. If she could see the animal and it was at a good distance, she would try it. But a very good distance—if the key was gone, she needed enough time to get back into the house. Locking herself in the Jeep wouldn't help—surely the wolf could break through the window glass in no time when it saw her inside. And getting Howard's mobile phone wouldn't help, either—his signal here would be no better than hers.

She didn't think he carried a gun in the Jeep. If he did, that would be the Jeep's main advantage, without keys. Its only advantage.

Otherwise, she was better off where she was.

She climbed the stairs again and made the circuit, window to window, looking for the canine. No sign of it to the west. None to the south. To the east, she thought for a second that she saw it in the snow, then realized it was just a beavertail cactus poking up through the snow and stirred by a sudden breeze. Back to the room from which she had watched Howard's death. She looked out past the red Jeep, combing the distance, then focusing lower, covering the ground. Nothing.

At last her gaze crossed over the Jeep.

Howard stood in front of it, looking at the house.

He was alive! She started to throw open the window, to call to him.

Caution stayed her hand. She couldn't see the wolf, so it might be on the roof, just waiting for her to open a window or stick her head out.

And as she watched Howard, she realized something else.

His chest had been torn open, his viscera tugged out. Bits of intestine dangled like rope from above his belt. Could he possibly be alive, in that condition?

Besides, she could still see his corpse, on the ground beside the Jeep. Behind where the other one stood.

There couldn't be two Howards. Two dead Howards.

She thought she would begin to weep again, expected to feel tears filling her eyes.

They didn't come.

She was beyond crying, she guessed. Beyond even more than mild shock at seeing Howard upright and lying down dead at the same time. Numb.

The idea crossed her mind that she ought to just open the window and climb out. If the wolf got her, fine. If it didn't, she could make a beautiful swan dive—she had loved high board diving, ever since high school—off the roof. That might not kill her, but it would incapacitate her long enough to let the wolf finish the job.

What was the point of going on without emotional response to the world outside? Wasn't she already dead? Dead where it counted?

Her hand was actually on the window, ready to push it up, when she saw Stu, also on his feet, his own wounds red and gaping. And Stu behind him, a mess in the melted snow.

Howard was closer now, trudging toward the house with apparent purpose. His head leaned toward his right shoulder, his mouth hung open, and his steps were unsteady, faltering.

But he came.

Stu came, too.

The wolf, it seemed, had reinforcements.

THIRTY-TWO

Covering the short distance to the mall, Sam saw evidence of carnage on a scale he wouldn't have imagined even a day ago. He passed a minivan that had gone off the road, fresh black tire marks giving evidence of sudden braking, with corpses strewn around it like beer cans after a beach party. Another quarter mile up the road he spotted what looked like a backpacker, or a backpacker's clothing and gear, although the person inside them appeared to have been beaten badly enough to break every bone in his body, so that the clothes might have contained a bag of water rather than an actual person. A cabin a hundred feet from the highway was on fire, but nobody moved to do anything about it.

Apparently, the sheriff's officers weren't even bothering to respond to murder reports anymore. Or else there were so many, they couldn't get to all of them. He didn't like either option.

That's why they were here, though. Why he and Dean traveled the country, investigating the bad stuff and defeating it where they could. So far they hadn't managed to save many lives in Cedar Wells.

Maybe they still could. There was no telling when the murders would end. But if Dean and Harmon Baird could destroy the witch's bones and break the spell, and he could prevent mass slaughter at the mall, then the trip here would have been worthwhile.

If they couldn't do those things, it would be a spectacular failure. One he didn't think he could get over. He wasn't sure Dean could even survive it.

He pressed down harder on the gas, and Dean's car responded immediately. The trees blurred together and then the mall loomed ahead, its vast parking lots already filling up.

Sam pulled into a slot, grabbed a zippered duffel bag containing his weapons and spare ammo, and ran for the structure.

Even though it was not quite noon, the crowd had already been let inside. A few stragglers wandered through the parking lot, but he had expected to see hundreds milling around outside, given all the vehicles parked there. He didn't think they would have moved up the opening ceremonies, so maybe they were being held inside because of the threatening skies.

As soon as he pushed through the heavy glass doors, he discovered where they were. The center court was thronged with people. Others window-shopped, since the stores weren't open yet but every display window was decorated with merchandise.

Holiday decorations seemed to cover almost every visible surface—huge ribbons and bows, snowmen and candy canes, Santas and menorahs. Live Christmas trees stood everywhere, in planters and along walkways, as if the decorators had just gone outside and moved the forest in.

The crowd's mood seemed cheerful. Clearly, no general announcement had been made that they were all in grave danger. Sam tucked the zippered bag under his arm, hoping he didn't look too much like one of those disaffected youths who occasionally opened fire in shopping centers or schools. He saw some of Sheriff Beckett's deputies mixing with the crowd. As he pushed his way into the center court, he saw Beckett himself, standing near an empty dais, locked in conversation with the mayor; Carla Krug, the shopping center manager; and Lynnette from Security. Lynnette wore a holstered gun on her hip. He noticed other mall security guards who were also armed.

He worked his way forward until he caught Beckett's eye. The sheriff gave him a barely perceptible nod and a glance that could only mean *Wait there.* Sam waited.

A couple of minutes later, Beckett stepped away from the others and walked toward him. Mayor Milner spotted him, too, and his face blanched. Sam wasn't a good enough lip reader to see what the man said about him to Carla and Lynnette, but it didn't look like a compliment.

"You hold up your end?" Beckett asked as he approached.

"Trying," Sam said. With everything else that had happened, he'd nearly forgotten the bargain they cut with the sheriff. "Dean is on his way to end this thing, but something like that is always trickier than you hope. In the meantime, I thought I might be needed here."

"We have things under control, I think."

Sam kept his voice low, not wanting to stir up panic if anyone overheard. There were at least thirty people in close range, and several hundred in the court. "How much control will you have if things go bad?"

Beckett scanned the crowd. "It could get ugly," he admitted.

"There's no guarantee that Dean will succeed before we get some . . . unexpected shoppers," Sam said. He was pretty sure the sheriff would catch his drift. "If that happens . . ."

"My people are loaded up with rock salt," Beckett said. "And I've got more posted in the woods on the edge of the parking lot. Hopefully they'll be able to intercept before any of 'em make it here. You're right, random gunfire could shake this crowd up, and I'd hate to see a panicked mob on the mall's opening day."

"You might have been better off keeping them outside."

"Ms. Krug wanted them to be able to look at the store windows until the opening ceremonies. Then they'll be able to get right to spending. I went along with it, because I figured in a pinch we could lock the doors."

"How are all these people supposed to get home?" Sam asked. "Are the roads open again?"

"Not so's I know. We're just hoping they will be by the time people start to leave."

"There's a lot of wishful thinking going on around here," Sam observed.

"You don't know Mayor Milner like I do," Beckett said. "He's the king of wishful thinking. It's gotten him this far—mayor of a little mountain town—so he thinks it's the most powerful force on Earth. I don't think he's ever had a real setback. I recognize that he could have one today, if we end up with a few thousand people stuck in Cedar Wells because paranormal murderers don't want them to leave." His face broke into a wry smile that vanished just as fast. "And I know how nuts that sounds. But it's what you believe, right?"

"I don't just believe it," Sam said. "I know it. I even know why. That's why we think maybe we can end it."

"If wishful thinking has any power at all, I'm wishing you fellows can."

"If not . . ." Sam shook his bag so the sheriff could hear the contents clanking together. "If not, then we're going to have a real mess on our hands."

Kid's right, Jim Beckett thought. If there was an attack on the mall—even by a single one of those ghost killers or whatever they were—the ensuing panic would do a lot more damage than the ghosts. He had covered this with his deputies, and they were all ready to do whatever they could to keep order, but the fact was that a crowd of even a thousand or two could be plenty destructive.

The plan was to isolate the ghost and divide the shoppers into manageable chunks by closing off sections of the mall. It was arranged in great hallways off the center court, so it could easily be chopped into three parts. Smaller groups could be reasoned with more easily than big ones.

That was the hope, at any rate. How it would work in reality, Beckett wasn't sure. During his years as sheriff, he'd never had to deal with such a large group of people. He doubted if any law officer had ever dealt with this precise situation.

One thing he knew for sure: When this was all over, if he walked away from it, he wouldn't be writing it up for any law enforcement publications or talking about it at conventions. Not only would it be unbelievable to anyone who hadn't lived through it, but he wasn't particularly proud of his performance. He had let the politicians—Mayor Milner, to be precise—walk all over him. He, not the mayor, was responsible for securing the public's safety, and he had let the mayor handcuff him.

Just a couple of minutes ago, before the kid had interrupted, it was happening again. He'd found himself agreeing to keep a low profile and to do everything possible to allow the mall opening to go ahead as planned. Milner and Carla Krug were still locked in intense conversation—the mayor no doubt arguing for a greater role in the festivities than had been agreed on, now that he saw a fair-sized crowd had gathered.

Maybe Beckett could reclaim some of his self-esteem after all. He stalked back to the pair of them, bureaucrats from public and private sectors, with determination settling in his gut like a hearty breakfast. They broke off, mid-sentence, at his approach.

"I want to make one thing clear," he said, not waiting for an invitation to speak. "If there's one sign—I mean, a single solitary shred of likelihood that one of those things is on the way—this whole place is mine."

"Meaning what, Jim?" Carla asked.

"Meaning it's a crime scene and I control it. Not you or Mayor Milner or your security people. Me. Is that clear?"

"Now, Jim," Milner said, in that conciliatory tone he took that made it sound as if he was trying to calm a three-year-old throwing a tantrum. Beckett had to resist the impulse to smack him one. Maybe before the day was out, he'd get a chance. "Let's get down off that high horse, okay? We're all together on this thing."

"I don't think we are, Donald. In spite of everything that's happened, bodies piled up like cordwood around town, I don't think you have quite grasped what we're dealing with here. This isn't something you can make go away by spreading some favors around. And if there's a chance of a panic that might cost lives, I'm taking over. No argument, end of story."

"Believe me, Jim," Carla said. "The last thing I want is a panic. I just want to know that if the worst doesn't happen, that your people won't be out there stirring things up."

"I don't think you need to worry about my people," Beckett said. "How many of the store employees here live in Cedar Wells? Probably most of them. The ones who don't, who we had to keep here in town last night, will be complaining about that, and the ones who do will be talking about the murders. All it'll take is for a few customers to hear the wrong thing. You remember the game of telephone? Someone whispers something in the first person's ear, and by the time it makes the whole circle it's transformed into something else entirely? With all the people in this building, you're going to have one hell of a telephone game going on, and it might not even take an attack to set off a panic. So this is how it's going to be, and if you don't like it, I don't particularly care. In the event of any sort of incident, your security people will look to me and my people for guidance. I'd like to meet with Lynnette again and make sure she understands this. I want to know that she has transmitted the instructions to her crew. What I don't want is for even one of those security guards to do the wrong thing when I'm trying to restore order. Is that all clear?"

Mayor Milner looked like he wanted to complain, to throw his weight around. But he clamped his lips together so tightly they almost disappeared and nodded his head gravely.

Carla watched his reaction, then gave in, too. "I'll get Lynnette for you," she said. "Why don't you meet her in the security office so you can talk about the specifics without being overheard?"

"That's a good idea," Beckett said. "I'll see her there directly."

Sam made a quick tour of the mall's interior, eyes open for anyone who looked out of place or antique, or who was flickering the way the spirits did. Although they were inside, everywhere he went people were bundled up in coats and hats and scarves, the coats open, scarves worn loosely about the neck, hats sometimes stuck into pockets. The crowds milled around the shop windows as if they couldn't wait to get inside and start spending money. Sam saw a few things he wouldn't mind picking up either. He wasn't a materialistic guy—Dad had raised them both with a disdain for people who let their possessions rule or define them—but that didn't mean he couldn't use a new jacket or sweatshirt or pair of boots from time to time. If he'd made it through law school, he probably could have brought down a healthy salary. Now he got by on Dean's credit card scams and justified it by knowing that society as a whole was better off because hunters were out there killing the bad things.

The food court already smelled like pizza and sweet and sour chicken and cheeseburgers and fries. It had been hours since he'd eaten anything, and the aromas made his stomach grumble. Some people already stood in line, and the counter workers bantered with them, although no one was selling until the official ribbon cutting.

He glanced at a clock on the wall behind the counter of the taco stand: 11:54. Not much longer now.

And he still had plenty of ground to cover in here before he checked the outside. He picked up the pace.

His hunger could wait.

THIRTY-THREE

"Dude, you do know where the witch's cabin was, right?" Dean asked. They had passed the old school-house a while ago. The snow had drifted deeper here, and Dean's boots and jeans were soaked through.

" 'Course I do," Harmon Baird replied. "We kept away from it, even though she'd been dead and gone long before I was born. Sometimes the older kids would try to convince us to go inside. I did once, about three steps inside the door, before I turned around and ran out again. Lucky I didn't wet my drawers just out of general principle."

"And this is the best way to get there?"

"Hell, all I know, there's a road right to it now. Might be a high-rise apartment complex built on top of it, too. Ain't a place I've been back to since I was a tyke. Or wanted to go back to."

Dean didn't respond. He couldn't have been po-lite. This guy was old, sure, but most of the time he seemed relatively coherent. Since he had known they were looking for some unnatural evil, he might have mentioned this witch house sooner. The certainty that people had died while Baird was playing Lone Ranger in the woods, or traipsing around with him and Sam once they found him, made Dean physically sick. Being an amateur hunter was fine if you took the task seriously. Letting people be killed because of your absentmindedness did not fit that description.

There was an undeniable beauty to the landscape out here. Something Sam would probably have appreciated more, since admiring scenery wasn't high on his own list of hobbies. The whitish-yellow canyon walls rose around them as the valley floor sank. The fields were snow-covered but with pale yellow-brown grasses poking out, and every now and then a gnarled, twisted tree whose branches were weighted down with the white stuff tried to stand up. The scene would have been peaceful, except that as they trudged along, more and more wildlife started showing up. Ravens and doves, gray-backed with black spots and pale-breasted, stood on the branches or on the ground, watching them. Gray squirrels, with tails less bushy than some he'd seen in cities, joined the birds. Brown coyotes, like scraggly dogs, stood beside animals they would happily eat under other circumstances. A couple of deer showed up a little after that, including one stag with an impressive rack. Three bighorn sheep came next, stepping gracefully out of the rocky canyon wall. Rats and mice and snakes—snakes, in the snow—emerged from underneath the layer of white. Before long there must have been fifty pairs of eyes gazing at them. More.

Seeing the animals out there, watching them but apparently not spooked by them, was strange enough.

Stranger still was the fact that the animals seemed to track their progress, following along like the gallery at a golf tournament.

"You ever see anything like that?" Dean asked finally, nodding toward the woodland creatures.

"Seen all of 'em, one time or another," Baird replied. "Just not all together like this. Like they're here for some kind of party or barn dance."

"That's what I was afraid of. You think they're real or you think they came from the witch?"

"I thought witches had black cats."

"There's a lot more to witches than that," Dean said, still impatient with the geezer. "If they attack, we could use up a lot of ammo fighting 'em off. Leave us vulnerable later on when we get to the witch's house. How much farther?"

"Not too much," Baird said. "I think."

"You *think*. That's encouraging. I feel a lot better now."

"You coulda just bought a map from Mr. Rand McNally," Baird shot back.

"Maybe I should have."

The fine hairs on the back of Dean's neck were standing up. All those little eyes staring at him—it was like the usual sensation of being watched, but multiplied and made weirder by the fact that the eyes weren't human.

There seemed to be a sort of intelligence operating there just the same. At least, they weren't behaving like wild creatures, which would have run at the sight of the two humans, and which would not have hung around together like old friends. Real animals would have made some kind of sounds, too, but these were utterly silent.

Dean knew his shotgun was loaded, and he resisted the impulse to check it. The air seemed fraught with menace, as if the attack would come any time. He didn't want to take his attention away from the renegade petting zoo for a second.

"We could shoot first," Baird said after a few minutes. "See if we can spook 'em."

"They've got me plenty spooked," Dean replied. He kept hoping the explanation was something else—that they were responding to an impending earthquake or other, more natural, disaster. He had stuffed plenty of rock salt shells into his pockets, but they were for dealing with the witch and maybe a handful of guards. And he couldn't exactly dash to the car for more, since it was at the mall.

The birds came at them first.

One moment they were standing with the others on the ground, and the next—with no signal Dean could identify—they were in flight, wings beating at the air, silently screeching their bird cries and headed right for the two of them.

Dean snatched a couple of shells from his pocket and tore them open, pouring rock salt on the snow, forming a circle around himself and the old man. He had a plastic bag of salt, but that was for the witch's bones. "Stay inside this circle," he said. "No matter what." He tore open one more shell and kept pouring. The salt melted the snow's crust but he was able to make a solid circle around them, about three feet in diameter.

He finished it just in time. The ravens flew fastest, their big black wings flapping steadily and hard, and the birds dove at them with claws extended, beaks ready to gash and cut. But when they hit the line above the circle in the snow, they fell away, flapping madly to remain airborne. The doves—*no geniuses, those*, Dean noted—did the exact same thing a few seconds later.

By this time the other animals were on the advance, too. The deer and bighorn sheep thundered across the ground. In their wake came squirrels, skunks, raccoons, ringtails. Behind them, rats and mice and snakes.

First of the mammals to reach the circle was the buck with the big antlers. He lowered them on the charge and sprang toward them, but when he hit the invisible wall of the circle, he staggered back as if electrocuted. He flashed black light, flickered, fell into the snow looking like a ranch hand who might have been from Harmon Baird's era, then transformed back into a deer and pranced away from the circle, staggering a little, like he'd downed a few too many tallboys.

"He's smart enough to be scared," Dean said.

"He oughta be," Baird said. "That's my pa."

Two of the bighorn sheep did the same thing, in tandem—rushing the circle, then falling back with silent squeals of alarm.

"Your father died on the ranch?" Dean asked.

"I told you that."

"That's right, you did." Dean felt bad about his tone just then. For a change, the old coot hadn't been withholding information; Dean had simply forgotten what Baird had told him.

"I gotta get to him," Baird said. "He looks hurt."

Dean caught the old man's coat just before he broke the circle and dragged him back in. The man, surprisingly strong, fought him. Dean held on, though, drawing him back an inch at a time. Finally, Baird stopped struggling against him.

"That's not your dad," Dean said. "Not anymore. Believe me, I know what it's like to want to be there for him. But your dad's dead. A long long time now. What did you say got him? A tomahawk?"

"Split his back clean open."

"See? That's just a spirit that takes his shape sometimes, but it's not really him. He's under the witch's influence. We get to her, then you'll be able to give your dad some rest. If you break the circle, though, those animals will tear us both apart and we'll never make it."

Harmon Baird stood, breathing hard, his jaw defiant. But as Dean spoke, his eyes softened and he let his mouth drop open, blew out a breath. "How we going to get to her?"

The animals had completely surrounded the salt

circle, some of them testing its integrity from time to time. The birds flew rings around it, just outside its perimeter. Dean could smell them all now, erasing the clean, fresh aroma of the snow-filled valley.

"Yeah, I haven't figured that out yet."

"Looks like you better get to it pretty soon."

"I know that!" Dean snapped. "I know people are dying. My brother's at that mall, and he's in danger, too. I'm not an idiot, you know."

Baird just smiled at him. He nodded toward the ground. "I just mean the snow's melting a little under the salt," he said. "You made a nice neat ring, but if it don't all melt exactly evenly, then some of that salt could shift or slide. That happens, your circle ain't so neat. What happens then?"

"Oh," Dean said. "Sorry. If that happens, then I guess Bambi and friends eat us up."

THIRTY-FOUR

"Sam?"

He turned at the voice. Heather Panolli came toward him, wearing a fake fur coat and snug jeans, her hair pulled back into a loose ponytail. She looked fresh-faced and very young. "I didn't think I'd ever see you again," she said. "Where's Dean?" When she came closer, a wave of vaguely floral perfume washed over him.

"He's . . . somewhere else, trying to bring a final end to the whole . . . situation we talked about," Sam said. "What are you doing here?"

"Are you kidding? It's a mall!"

"I know, but . . . it's not exactly safe around here yet. And I don't know how much intelligence the . . . the murderers have, but if they have much at all they'll realize what a prime target this mall is today. You shouldn't be here."

"From what I hear, no place is much safer than any other," she said. "Besides, my boyfriend Todd got a job here." She pointed to a chain bookstore. "In there."

"Todd with long dark hair?"

"That's right. Do you know him?"

Apparently he hadn't told Heather about their encounter, even though he'd promised that he would. "We've met," Sam said. "It might be better if he doesn't see you talking to me."

"Why?"

"He can explain. Let's just leave it at that." If that didn't force the issue, then he didn't know what would.

She didn't follow up on it. "So you think I should be on the lookout for any bow-and-arrow wielding Indians?"

Sam nodded. "Among other things."

"What's in your bag?" she asked. "Is it guns?"

"Heather, listen—"

"You can tell me, Sam. I won't blab."

Like you kept your dad's big secret so well, he thought. He was glad she hadn't—although it turned out to be a blind alley, you never knew in this kind of case which information might be invaluable. But that didn't mean he wanted to trust her with any of his own.

"Heather, I need to keep going. I'm trying to cover a lot of ground here, and there's not much time."

"Okay, I won't keep you, Sam." She looked a little disappointed. "Maybe I'll see you later on."

"Maybe so," he said, breaking free as fast as he could.

The disappointment wouldn't kill her.

The witch's spirit army just might.

He was trying to cut through one of the balconies surrounding the center court, but the crowd had grown so thick it was hard to make any progress without ramming people out of the way with his bag.

A squeal of microphone feedback explained why. *Guess it's showtime.* He hadn't even finished the upstairs circuit, much less made it out to the parking lot.

Instead of fighting his way through the throng, he dropped back, until the front window of a lingerie shop was at his back. He wanted the wide view so he could see if anyone flickered or flashed.

From his angle, he could see only a small section of the lower level. He hoped the sheriff's officers were alert instead of watching the dais.

"Ladies and gentlemen," Carla Krug's voice rose up from speakers that had been turned up a bit too loud. "Thank you all for coming to the grand opening celebration of the Canyon Regional Mall."

A swell of applause came from the crowd, and Carla quieted to lavish in it. After almost a full minute it subsided enough for her to continue. "I see you, like me, have been waiting anxiously for this day to come. The day we don't have to drive to Prescott or Flagstaff or Phoenix to see the latest fashions, pick up the new best-seller, catch a movie, or have a nice dinner in comfortable surroundings. The day that people from across the region can come together in a climate-controlled shopping environment featuring the latest in retail technology, the best stores, and the greatest salespeople—your neighbors and mine—found anywhere!"

Another burst of applause met this statement, although it was not as sustained as the first.

"My name is Carla Krug, and for those of you who don't know me, I'm the manager of this shopping center. My office is on the second floor, and if you ever have a comment or a compliment, or God forbid, a complaint, you'll be able to find me there. I want to hear from you. And if I'm not there, it'll be because I'm out shopping in some of these fabulous stores!"

Eyeing the crowd, Sam spotted Eileen, their waitress from the Wagon Wheel Café, Heather's dad, Peter Panolli, Mrs. Frankel the librarian, and several other people he'd run across in town. It almost seemed like everyone who was still alive in Cedar Wells had come today. Maybe they thought there was strength in numbers.

There could be, but there could also be unexpected danger.

"I know you want to get busy shopping," Carla continued. "So do I. And I'll warn you, there's a pair of red Manolos in the window at Freddie's Fashion Footwear that has my name on it, so keep your mitts off those!" After a hush, the crowd laughed,

good-natured and enjoying her banter. Sam hoped
they stayed that way. "So I'm going to stop talking
and get my credit cards warmed up. We do have a
special guest today, so I'll ask you to offer a great big
Canyon Regional Mall welcome to Mayor Donald
Milner of Cedar Wells. After his brief remarks, the
stores will open and you can shop till you drop!"

Another round of applause, another squeal of feedback, and then Sam heard Mayor Milner's voice. He
wondered how the politician would gloss over the
murders and the fact that until they were solved, none
of the people at the mall would be able to leave town.

"Thank you, Carla," Milner began. "And thank
all of you for braving the elements and joining us here
today. The great thing—one of the great things, but
there are a lot of them, as you'll learn—about Canyon Regional Mall is that you can shop in climate
controlled comfort no matter what the weather's like
outside. We all know that's going to come in handy
in the months and years to come."

He waited for polite laughter and a smattering of
applause to die down. "A lot of people worked really
hard for a long time to make this thing happen," he
went on. "I'd like to thank them today. There were
plenty of times people thought the project would
never get off the ground, but I had faith, and so did
Carla and some others, and I'm happy to say that
today we can sit back and say, 'I told you so!'"

This brought more laughter and a few hearty
whoops. "Cedar Wells is the greatest small town in

Arizona. Maybe in America. And as of today, Cedar Wells has one more claim to greatness—the newest, greatest shopping mall in the country. Just up the road is an American landmark, the Grand Canyon, which we all know and love. Today, ladies and gentlemen, I give you America's newest landmark—Canyon Regional Mall! Thank you for coming, and enjoy!"

The applause swelled again, more sustained this time. So that was how he planned to deal with the issue, Sam recognized. By pretending it didn't exist. Dad had been no fan of politicians. At Stanford, Sam had developed a more nuanced view, recognizing that some of them had the public interest at heart, while some had only their own interests.

Mayor Milner seemed to reinforce Dad's beliefs quite nicely.

After a little more than a minute, the applause died. People started to move away from the balcony's edge as the shops threw open their doors and invited people inside.

Sam blew out a sigh of relief. He had been most afraid of an attack while almost everyone was congregated in one confined area, but it looked like that wouldn't happen.

Maybe Dean and Harmon Baird had already made it to the witch's house. Maybe she was salted and burned, the counterspell performed. Neither of them had had mobile phone service at the schoolhouse, so Dean probably wouldn't be able to call him to let him know.

Suddenly, the tenor of the crowd changed, the babble of cheerful conversation stopping abruptly.

"What's that?" someone asked, terror registering in his voice.

Then again, Sam thought, *maybe Dean's not there yet after all.*

THIRTY-FIVE

"What we don't want to do," Dean said softly, "is run out of ammo."

"Makes sense," Baird said.

"But we may have caught a break. They're packed in pretty tight around us now. With this scattergun—"

"I gotcha." Baird waved his own rifle. "I can back you with this but it ain't gonna take out bunches of 'em at once."

"Wouldn't hurt, though," Dean said, wishing the old man had a shotgun instead of his antique rifle and homemade dumdums. "Just be stingy with lead."

"Son, I can squeeze a nickel so hard Thomas Jefferson weeps real tears. You don't have to tell me to be stingy."

"Let's do it, then." Dean already had a shell chambered and the gun completely loaded. The animals milled around outside the circle, prodding at it now and then, testing to make sure it remained whole. As he had said, they were packed in tight, for the most part. The difficulty would be that they were on several different levels: rodents and reptiles close to the ground, deer and sheep higher, birds above that.

He had to make his move fast, though. The trampling of the snow around the circle would shift the salt ring even faster than the melting. If he used up eight shells, that would still leave him with sixteen.

Of course, the possibility existed that when they got to the witch's cabin, this force would seem like a small platoon out of a much bigger army. In which case sixteen shells might not be enough.

Then again, a hundred might not be enough. If he died here, he'd never find out.

"Here we go!" he shouted. He aimed high with the first blast, hoping to take out a good number of the birds. The shotgun roared and the air filled with flying feathers and bird parts. As they fell to the ground, the pieces flashed and glowed black. Very few of them actually landed; most blinked out of existence on the way down.

The other creatures reacted with a start—most freezing in place, some scurrying for cover behind larger animals. That was okay with Dean. The more they were bunched together, the more he could take out with a single spray of rock salt. He wished they were farther back, so the salt would have more time to spread, but beggars, they said, couldn't be choosers. He lowered the shotgun's barrel and shot toward ground level, on the theory that rock salt even hitting the ankles of the bigger animals might be enough to destroy them.

Rats, mice, ground squirrels, skunks, were obliterated instantly—the skunks leaving behind, oddly, traces of their familiar burnt rubber stink as they vanished.

The larger ones, the coyotes and raccoons and deer and one bighorn sheep caught in the blast, were not destroyed, but crippled, falling to the snowy plain and releasing unheard screams toward the sky. As they writhed and bucked in evident agony, some of them blinked and flashed while others changed form, strobing back and forth between human and animal shape.

One of these was the deer that had the form of Baird's father.

"Pa!" Baird shouted again. This time he lunged before Dean could catch him toward the spirit that resembled, momentarily, his long-dead father.

Doing so broke the circle.

"Crap!" Dean said. He whirled and fired a blast, mid-level, behind them, to forestall a charge from the rear.

The spirit animals were momentarily confused. The path to attack was cleared, but so many had died in the three blasts so far that it took them several seconds to decide what to do.

Which—*of course*, Dean thought—was to charge.

He chambered another shell, fired. Baird had reached his father, who had already changed back into the big buck. The animal tried to gain its foot-

ing, and swung its antlers in a ferocious arc toward
Baird. Dean dove, plowing into the old man and
knocking him clear just in time. The buck brought
the antlers back around, and Dean ducked beneath
the swipe, feeling the wind whistle past his scalp. He
fired from point-blank range into the deer's muzzle.

Five, he counted. *Three more to go.*

But he and Baird were both on the ground now,
exposed, and the remaining spirit creatures had re-
grouped. Birds gained elevation to drop down toward them in precipitous dives. Snakes and rats burst
from drifted snowbanks at them.

God, I hate rats. Dean fired a blast at ground
level, taking out what seemed like dozens more of the
crawling, creeping, and writhing vermin.

He heard a sharp *crack!* and saw Baird, on one
knee, firing his old rifle. His slug hit one of the remaining sheep, destroying it. He shot again and
eliminated the other deer.

Dean aimed at the largest remaining clutch of
animals and fired. Fur flew from raccoons, skunks,
squirrels, and the last of the bighorn sheep, and they
disappeared.

One of the remaining coyotes rushed at Dean with
his mouth open, fangs bared in a soundless snarl.
Dean couldn't bring the shotgun around fast enough,
but there was another report from Baird's rifle. Even
as Dean braced for the inevitable impact, the beast
blinked away, and all that hit Dean was a brief rush
of air.

Then it was over. The remaining animals sprinted

or skittered or slithered away. Dean and Harmon Baird both sat back in the snow, catching each other's eyes and breaking into smiles, then outright laughter.

"I guess we showed them somethin', eh?" Baird said between fits of hilarity. "You see the way they turned tail and skedaddled?"

"I did," Dean said, striving to catch his breath. "I did indeed."

The moment passed. Dean knew they weren't in the clear—far from it. This had been an advance guard, that was all, meant to kill them or at least delay them before they could reach their goal.

The good part was that an advance guard wouldn't have been required if there hadn't been something worth protecting. More than ever, he was convinced, the answer lay at Elizabeth Claire Marbrough's cabin.

If she had been buried somewhere else—one of those cemeteries he and Sam had visited on their first day in Cedar Wells, for instance—then he and Baird would have been wasting time here.

The fierce defense by the animal spirits was the best thing that had happened in hours, because it gave Dean hope that they were on the right track after all.

"Come on," he said, standing up. He extended a hand to Baird, who grasped it with his own rough, workingman's hand, and drew the old man to his feet. "Let's burn us a witch."

Baird chuckled again, the amusement still strong

in him. "Best invitation I've had all week," he said.
"Hell, all month, it come to that."

Juliet Monroe shivered uncontrollably. She had never
imagined anything so terrifying. She'd watched horror movies all her life, and read scary books, and she
was present when a fatal automobile accident had
strewn body parts all over a street corner and left
behind a bloody streak that stayed for weeks.

None of those things, however, had affected her
like the sight of two men she knew standing up and
stepping away from their own dead bodies.

She tried to take slow, deep breaths, to calm the
hammering of her heart and the quaking of her
hands. Every time she did, the image of Howard
Patrick walking toward her house came back to her,
and her breathing became swift and shallow and every muscle in her body seemed to go into hyperactive
mode. Sweat ran down her sides and collected at her
hairline.

Although she was perspiring—maybe because of
it—she felt cold, and decided to turn up the heat,
if that was possible with no electricity. That meant
going downstairs again, and downstairs was closer
to where the not-Howard and not-Stu were, and she
thought that if she saw them through the windows
she would start screaming and never be able to stop.
But the longer she thought about it—and this was
over the space of seconds, not minutes—the colder
the house felt. Maybe something had happened to

the heat. Either way, she had to go to the thermostat at the base of the stairs.

Because she had drawn all the curtains, the house was dark. She flipped the light switch at the top of the stairs. Nothing happened. She tried it a couple more times, down and up and down and up. Nothing. The power hadn't magically restored itself.

She hurried down the stairs, trying to both look and not look at the living room window, where the curtains didn't quite come together in the middle at the same time. That was hard to accomplish, so she found herself looking and glancing away, glancing and turning her head, until she reached the wall with the thermostat. It was an old-fashioned kind where you pushed a tiny lever in the direction you wanted. She pushed it toward warmer and waited to hear the heat cycle on.

Nothing happened.

Well, she was in here for the long haul with whatever was in the house. There was a fireplace in the living room, with a few logs stacked on the hearth, but most were outside in the woodpile, where she couldn't get to them. She had space heaters, which would do no good at all without electricity. She did have candles and matches, flashlights and blankets, even a battery-operated radio. No household in snow country should be without those things, even though the snow here rarely got deep enough to strand anyone for long. In the barn there was even a gasoline-powered generator. But she wasn't about to go out to the barn with that wolf out there.

And now, it seemed, its once-human allies.

She was downstairs now, but didn't intend to stay there for long. She would live upstairs, where she could keep a better eye on the wolf, Stu, and Howard, and they would have less of a view of her. She gathered the things she thought she would want—the kitchen matches, a heavy-duty flashlight, and the portable radio. The radio didn't have any batteries in it, but she had a bunch tossed into a coffee can on another pantry shelf. She fished some out and installed them on the kitchen counter.

Juliet was on her way back to the stairs when she heard a rattling at the front door.

She froze. From here, she could see the door. Anyone outside could take five steps to their right, look through the gap in the curtains and see her.

The doorknob turned, to the extent that it could with the knob latch locked. She had fastened the dead bolt, too. When she'd taken those measures, she felt like she was at least doing something, however small, that would help protect her.

Now, though, knowing that the wolf had figured out how to turn off her phone and electricity, knowing that it wasn't a natural canine at all but some sort of monster with magical powers to raise the dead, it seemed unlikely that two simple mechanical devices could do much to keep it at bay.

The door rattled in its jamb, harder than before. She could see it moving this time. Some small part of her had hoped that Stu and Howard—the ones that weren't dead, not the ones still lying where the wolf had left them—were just figments of some kind, without material form. But a canine couldn't try to turn a doorknob and then use it to shake a door.

That could only mean the wolf's allies had human shapes and human attributes. Solidity, maybe intelligence. So far she had heard no voices, but that might be next.

Before that could happen, she ran back upstairs. Any sense of security she achieved by doing so would be fleeting. The doors up there had knob locks, but that was all, and they were flimsy interior doors.

At this moment, however, even a little security—false security, if that's what it was—seemed better than none at all.

She dashed back into her bedroom and closed the door, locking it behind her.

When that was done, she leaned her back against the door, her hands still full of the things she had brought upstairs. The flashlight remained on, even though plenty of light washed in through the open curtains. She liked the feeling of the hard wood against her back, though she knew it wasn't thick or strong—the wolf's claws could probably shred it, and a good swift kick would break it down. It was a barrier, though, and it offered the slightest little bit of emotional comfort. Juliet was surprised to discover that her tremors had passed. Once things had started happening, once she was acting instead of just reacting, she'd gained more control over herself.

She had just allowed herself a faint smile when she heard the living room window shatter.

THIRTY-SIX

Unable to see what people were reacting to, Sam raced to the stairs and started down, unzipping his duffel bag as he went. When he was about a third of the way down, he could finally get a glimpse of it, through the crowd—most of which was running in his direction, expressions mixed between terror and outright panic. One of the sheriff's deputies was screaming instructions at the top of his lungs, but Sam couldn't make out his words over the frightened shrieks of the shoppers.

They ran from an Indian man wearing an open shirt, cavalry pants, and a red headband. The right side of his face was mostly missing—Sam guessed he'd been shot in the back of the head, and the exit wound had taken out his upper jaw and cheekbone. In his hands he held a rifle, which he pointed into the crowd.

None of the other sheriff's officers were in sight.

With people flooding up the stairs and Sam trying to push through them, he couldn't get a shot at the Indian. From this vantage point, he could only see one clear shot—from ground level, almost right beside where he was now. But by the time he could salmon his way down the stairs against the flow, the Indian would be able to get several shots off.

Which left him with just one choice. It would hurt, but Dad had drilled them over and over again on how to fall and come up shooting. He reached into the bag and brought out the sawed-off, then tossed the bag over the side. It hit with a heavy clank. He followed it over.

He fell straight down, landing on his feet, but pitched forward, rolling, head and weapon tucked safely, then came up into a steady crouch and aimed by instinct. When he squeezed the trigger, the rock salt shell blasted toward the Indian (his own finger tightening on the rifle's trigger, its barrel aimed into the throng on the staircase). The window of a dress shop beside the Indian exploded, spraying glass inside and dropping big shards onto the mall's walkway. But the rock salt did the trick, and the Indian blinked away before he could make his shot.

Snatching up the bag, Sam ducked beneath the slanting bottom of the staircase, which was partially blocked by decorated Christmas trees in large wooden planters. He shoved the shotgun back into it and zipped the bag again. Surely people would have seen him, but he hoped the sight of the dead Indian would make more of an impression.

The sound of feedback from the P.A. system filled his ears, then Jim Beckett's voice boomed from the speakers.

"Attention, everyone!" the sheriff called. "There's been an incident near the east entrance to the mall, but it's been dealt with. There is no risk to any of you except panic. Please, stop where you are, take a deep breath, and then look around you to see if any of your neighbors have fallen down or been hurt."

From underneath the staircase, Sam couldn't watch the crowd's reaction. From the sound of it, though, Beckett's announcement might have made things worse, at least in the short term. It sounded like some people obeyed and stopped in their tracks, causing those who were still in motion to run into them.

"Halt!" Beckett ordered, yelling into the microphone. "Everyone just stand still, please!"

This time the response sounded more orderly. Other sheriff's officers picked up the cry and spread it through the crowd, and suddenly the place was almost still.

"There's a little girl up here who's been hurt, Sheriff!" someone shouted from upstairs.

"My mother got knocked down!" someone downstairs called. "Her cheek is bleeding!"

"We have paramedics right outside," Beckett announced. "They're coming in now. Show them anyone who's hurt. The important thing is to keep your cool, don't panic and run around, because that's how people get injured. I'll repeat, the situation has been dealt with, and there doesn't seem to be any more immediate danger."

"Doesn't seem to be? That's not very encouraging," someone called.

Sam scooted out from beneath the stairs and worked his way into a clutch of people standing around watching the dais. Beckett was consulting with Mayor Milner and Carla Krug again. Probably, Sam guessed, debating the wisdom of evacuating the mall versus keeping everyone confined where at least the enemy could be watched for.

Enemy was the right word, because this had become a war, with casualties at critically high levels. Like all wars, the longer it went on, the more people would be hurt or killed.

I really hope Dean is at that witch's cabin, he thought, *because I could use some good news here.*

A man in a ball cap and denim jacket grabbed his shoulder. "You the one shot that guy?" he asked. "I seen you shoot him."

Sam tried to give a grunt instead of an answer, smiling all the while.

"What the hell was that? Some kind of Indian, it looked like."

Paiute, I'd guess, Sam thought. But he really didn't want to get snared in a conversation about it, so he shrugged and started to walk away.

"Hey, this here's the guy shot that Indian!" the man shouted, pointing at Sam. "You got your gun in that bag, cowboy?"

Within seconds a mob had gathered around Sam,

people calling out questions at him like he was a celebrity on a street corner. He was trapped, hemmed in on every side.

Sheriff Beckett saved him.

"Sam, you want to step over here?" he said into the microphone.

Sam looked over the heads of the crowd—not hard to do at his height—and saw Beckett gesturing him to the dais. "Excuse me," he said to the people immediately around him. "Sheriff needs me."

The crowd parted for him, and he walked through a tunnel, some people quietly complimenting him on his act while others continued to ask questions all the way. Finally, he climbed the steps to the dais.

"People," Sheriff Beckett said, "I know you all have a lot of questions about this, and I'm sorry such a great day in Cedar Wells got spoiled by this. Just keep shopping and having a good time, and we'll answer your questions as quick as we can."

When Sam neared him, he clicked the microphone off and set it back in its stand. The mayor and Carla joined them. "That was quick work, son," Beckett said. "Thank you."

Sam shrugged again. "Didn't look like anyone else had a shot at it."

"My people didn't. If you hadn't done what you did, I don't know what. It would have been a lot worse."

"I'm not sure private citizens should be walking around my mall with firearms," Carla said.

"I'll second that," Milner said. "It's a recipe for disaster."

"Unless you've got guards and metal detectors at every entrance," Beckett pointed out, "you're going to have people coming in with firearms from time to time. In this instance, Sam might have saved several lives."

"I suppose," Carla said. "But—"

"Look, you've got much bigger problems than whether or not I'm armed," Sam interrupted. "This crowd is still on the verge of all-out panic. And there are more of those—those killers out there. One has already come inside, past whatever security perimeter you set up around this place. More might follow. If they do, this place is going to go crazy."

"He's right," Beckett said. "I have to recommend that we evacuate in an orderly fashion while we still can."

"Hold on," Carla said. "Lots of people are already leaving—have you seen the parking lot in the last few minutes? There are still cars coming in, but not nearly as many as are going out. For the sake of my merchants we have to stay open as long as possible."

"Besides," Milner added, "where are the people going to go if we do evacuate? They can't leave town, can they? We'll just end up with traffic jams on the roads, and they'll be just as vulnerable, but harder to protect."

"That's a good point," Beckett said, tugging on his ear. People had gathered around the dais, trying to listen in, so the four spoke in ever lower tones. "Maybe it's time to separate them into smaller groups and—"

"You want to imprison them in different areas of the mall?" Carla asked. "That's as good as shutting us down, except maybe for the food court."

"We already had this discussion once, Carla," Beckett said. "Far as I'm concerned, this is my mall now, and I make the rules."

She nodded. Her hair had come out of its neat arrangement and her face looked drawn, her eyes tired. She probably hadn't had much sleep, and now the stress of disaster on opening day was showing. "I know," she said. "I won't argue. You can do whatever you need to. I just want it known that it's under protest."

"It's known," Beckett said. "You got any complaints, Donald?"

"I just want everybody out of here alive," Milner said. "And for this whole damn nightmare to be over."

"My brother's working on that," Sam told him.

"Why aren't you, Jim?" Milner asked.

"I don't have anyone to spare, Donald. My people are either here or out on the roads already, with a few responding to emergency calls."

"It's okay," Sam said. "Dean has all the help he needs. He's the best there is at this kind of thing."

"I'd ask just what this kind of thing is," Milner said, "except I don't think I really want to know."

"I don't think you do, either."

Carla put her hand to her ear, and Sam realized she had an earpiece and was no doubt keeping in touch with her security team. Her mouth dropped open and her face went white. "Oh," she said into a mike clipped on the collar of her blouse. "All right."

She looked up again. "There's a situation outside, in West parking," she said. "It sounds like a bad one."

"How bad?" Beckett asked.

"Eight or nine of them," she said. "They said it was hard to count."

Beckett immediately thumbed his own microphone. "Anyone in the west lot? How come I haven't had any reports?"

"That's the thing, Jim," Carla said, her voice strained. "They shot your officer first."

THIRTY-SEVEN

An occasional raven flew past them, but no more than on any other day Dean had experienced out here. Still, he couldn't help suspecting they were spying on the progress he and Baird made. If they were, let them. Nothing the witch could do now would prevent him from accomplishing his task.

The old classic "or die trying" couldn't be allowed to enter into it.

After they'd chased away or destroyed the animal spirits that had surrounded them, Baird had picked up his pace. It soon had him huffing and panting, and a sheen of perspiration coated his face. Dean desperately hoped the old codger didn't have a heart attack before they were done.

As they got closer to where Baird insisted that Witch's Canyon intersected the Grand Canyon, the walls grew wider apart, until the land looked like a valley with some gently rolling hills. About a mile away, Dean guessed, he saw a dirt road, and a ranch house, a barn, a corral, and some other outbuildings.

"Someone lives there," he said. "Are you sure we're going the right way?"

Baird considered this for a long minute. Dean found that encouraging; if the man had simply snapped an answer, he would have assumed it was a lie.

"See that old pine by the side of the ranch house?" he asked finally.

"What about it?"

"That was a sapling in those days."

"Dude, that was eighty years ago. How can you be sure it's the same tree?"

"I can't be certain. But judging by where it is in relation to the canyon wall behind it, I'd just about swear to it."

The canyon wall was a good half mile behind it, which seemed to Dean like it would make it hard to judge the relative position of anything. "I don't know . . ." he began.

"I know what you're thinkin', Dean. You're thinkin' I'm an old fool whose memory is playin' tricks on him and I've brought you out here on some damn goose chase while your brother's in danger. All I can say is you're wrong. Remember those animals? They wouldn't have attacked us if we weren't getting close—"

"I thought the same thing myself."

"—and my memory may not be as good as it once was, but for some things—like that witch's cabin—

it's just fine. That place scared the hell outta me, and I'll never forget it while there's a breath in my body."

"Then where is it?"

"It's gone!" Baird stared at Dean with those small black eyes. "That's what I'm tellin' you! It was right there. Someone knocked it down and built a ranch right on top of it."

"Well, that's always a bad idea." It seemed like everyone knew not to build on Indian burial grounds these days, but people needed to be more careful about building on top of the bones of evil witches, too.

If the house was literally on top of her grave, he'd have to tear up floorboards or jackhammer a concrete slab to get at it. All the while, Sammy and everyone else in Cedar Wells remained in danger.

"All right," he said finally. "Let's get over there and see what's what."

They started forward again. As they got closer to the place, Dean could see a few vehicles scattered around. A truck was parked beside the house, a red SUV in the driveway and a white one in a carport. *Somebody's probably there, then*, he thought. *That might make the home-destruction part of this more complicated.*

The ranch house was two stories, with a fenced yard around it that was neatly groomed. In a distant pasture some cattle grazed. The whole scene looked peaceful, even idyllic. Except for the vehicles, it could have been from a hundred years ago.

Dean didn't trust it for a second.

He took his electromagnetic frequency reader from his pocket and switched it on. They were maybe a quarter mile from the ranch house when it started to react like crazy, squealing and beeping, the lights across the top flashing red.

"The hell's that thing?" Baird asked. "One of them pod things?"

"EMF reader," Dean said. "There's been an anomaly in the electromagnetic frequency around here. Recently."

"Which means what?"

"Paranormal activity isn't the only cause, but it's a major one. And I don't see anything else around here that might cause this kind of reading."

"So there's been spooks around here."

"Probably some spirit activity, yeah."

They kept walking as they talked, reaching the gate through the fence that surrounded the house.

Dean noticed the broken front window about the same time that he heard a woman scream inside.

After the crash and the rain of glass onto her living room carpet, Juliet didn't hear anything. She wasn't sure what to make of that. If Stu or Howard had been rattling the door, then they had to have physical bodies—even though she could still see their ravaged corpses out her window, where they had fallen. She couldn't imagine either of them walking across the glass that must surely be littering the living room floor without making noise. So if anyone had come inside, it had to be the wolf.

She hadn't had time to formulate much of a plan, and she didn't have many weapons handy. She had a couple, though, and intended to use everything at her disposal before retreating into the master bathroom, locking that door, and waiting for the end.

Maybe this was her day to join Ross in the grave, or beyond it. She'd decided that she would go out fighting.

To that end, she took a bottle of nail polish remover from her bathroom cabinet. *Extremely flammable,* the bottle said. *Contents and vapors may ignite.* Sounded good to her. She upended it into a plastic bag full of cotton balls, then sealed the Ziploc closure of the bag. The balls turned blue and the whole thing had a satisfying weight in her hand.

She had a can of hair spray, too, but was a little concerned about the whole thing exploding on her. She would save that as a last resort.

Next she yanked down the shower curtain rod, dropping one end and letting the plastic curtain fall off into the tub. She gathered the curtain and the rod—separate weapons, for separate uses—and put them both on the bed. Doing so, she noticed the curtain rod over the bedroom window, part of the rustic design Ross had wanted for their ranch house. It was twisted wrought iron with an arrowhead point at each end. Shorter than the shower curtain rod by several inches, it would be much stronger. Screws through welded-on L-brackets held it into the wall, and the curtains dangled from matching black iron hooks. Juliet tipped over a solid oak nightstand and stood on it, wrenching at the rod until the screws pulled from the walls and she held the thing in her hands.

She looked out the window again. The bodies remained where they had been, but she could see no sign of the duplicate Stu and Howard. If they were on the covered front walkway, however, she knew she wouldn't be able to see them from up here. She scanned for the wolf without success. Just on the far side of the fence, though, she saw two men headed toward the house. She thought they both carried guns. Assuming they were real, and not impossible constructs like Stu and Howard, they could be her best bet of surviving this nightmare. If, that was, they could reach her in time, without being killed themselves.

No way to communicate at this distance in any kind of comprehensible fashion. Maybe they'd respond to an old-fashioned distress call, though. And what did she have to lose? She pushed open the window and loosed the loudest, most ear-piercing B-horror movie scream she could summon.

As she pulled the window shut, her bedroom door shook like someone had punched it.

"Okay, you bastard," she said. Her jaw was tight, her fists clenched, her legs poised and ready to spring. "Might as well get this over with."

The door rattled as someone tried the knob. *Wolf or person?* She couldn't tell.

But then it shook again and a paw punched through the center panel, tearing downward for about eight inches, as easily as if it had been paper.

Wolf, then. Good. She didn't want to waste time with intermediaries.

The beast clawed at the door again, this time punching out a bigger opening in the panel. Now she could see its silvery head, golden eyes regarding her steadily through the hole in the door. She stood behind her bed, hoping it couldn't determine her intentions.

Or, given its other abilities, read minds.

Something moved behind the canine, and a human hand—Stu's, from the look of it—reached inside and turned the knob, unlocking it.

Juliet braced herself for anything, and lit a match.

The door swung open.

The wolf stood in the doorway, mouth open just enough to show its huge teeth. Its head was vaguely wedge shaped, triangular ears flared away from the big head, alert, turning slightly as it examined the room, its eyes drawn to the flaring match Juliet held.

Stu and Howard flanked the canine, a few steps behind it. Both were dead, their bodies ripped open by the animal's teeth and claws. They looked at Juliet without expression.

She touched the match to the plastic bag of soaked cotton balls, and the flame melted through the plastic. The fluid-soaked balls ignited as she hurled the bag.

She could hear it flaring and burning hot as it sailed across the short distance between her and the wolf. It hit the animal's right front shoulder and burst, spreading flames across its back and up onto its head.

Next, Juliet snatched up the shower curtain and took a few steps toward the startled beast. Opening the curtain, she sailed it over the animal's head and back. She didn't think it would choke out the flames, but hoped it would hold the bulk of fiery cotton against the wolf's shoulder where it had landed. Confusing the wolf would be a good fringe benefit.

It seemed to do both. The beast batted at the curtain with its paws, shook its massive head, but couldn't dislodge it. It might have been trying to roar, but it had always been silent, and that held true now.

The shower curtain started to sizzle and melt into the creature's fur. Now she knew, from the way it bucked and writhed under the hot plastic, that she had caused it pain. She allowed herself a fleeting smile.

Pain wouldn't kill it, though. And while it flailed in the doorway, Stu and Howard were blocked from entering, but she would have to contend with them as well.

She picked up the shower curtain rod. She still wasn't convinced it was strong enough to do any damage, but she had already been as close as she wanted to be to the thing. She held it in both hands and leaned toward the beast, driving the rod full force into its face, hoping to hit an eye underneath the shower curtain.

At the last second the animal's head reared up and knocked the rod away before it landed. She tried again, but the wolf opened its huge maw and caught it. The end of the rod collapsed like balsa wood under its bite, and it jerked its head, whipping the weak pole from her grasp.

Its strength was indescribable. The other curtain rod, heavier but short, still waited on the bed.

But suddenly her confidence in it as a weapon flagged, along with her confidence in herself. She had intended to survive this. For a time—especially when she discovered that the wolf could feel pain—she thought she had.

It looked like she was wrong.

THIRTY-EIGHT

Sam outpaced Sheriff Beckett before they had gone ten yards from the dais. He could hear the lawman coming along behind, his duty belt jangling with every step, but he kept his eyes front, threading through the confused and still frightened mall customers like a NASCAR racer slipping through the openings into first place.

By the time he reached the west parking lot entrance, word had spread to the sheriff's deputies and security personnel guarding it. They had left their posts and were heading into the lot, their steps tentative, since they were charged with securing the doors.

A couple of them turned around when Sam burst through. Seeing the sheriff close behind him, they froze as if waiting for instructions. Sam heard Beckett grunt something as he neared them, and they let him pass.

He found the other security people, and one sheriff's officer who had responded more immediately, out past most of the ranks of cars parked in the lot. They were huddled behind the last line of cars, guns in their hands. One officer lay bleeding from a vicious stomach wound. Bitter smelling gun smoke hung in the air.

On the other side, where they must have come out of the woods, were their opponents. At least a dozen spirits stood there, flashing and sputtering like lightbulbs on a faulty circuit. They were the usual types: soldiers, Native Americans, and settlers or ranch workers of different eras. A couple of animals, a bobcat and a black bear, stood among them. The humans were male, except for one woman in a long dress and apron, a bonnet tied under her chin. All the human spirits carried weapons of some kind.

The woman led Sam with a long-barreled flintlock rifle. He threw himself to the ground behind a BMW just as the muzzle erupted in smoke and fire. The sports car's windshield shattered.

"You loaded with rock salt?" he asked the sheriff's officer—the only other person on the scene so far with a shotgun.

"That's what the sheriff ordered."

"Good. Regular bullets won't help against these things."

The mall security people had handguns, no doubt loaded with those useless regular bullets. One of them rose up over the hood of a car and fired a shot. *Wasting lead*, Sam thought. At best it might give the attackers pause, keep them back away from the mall while Beckett and his reinforcements came.

Sam followed suit, showing his head and shoulders above the BMW just long enough to fire a blast of rock salt at the spirits. When he dropped back down, the deputy took a turn.

Beckett and the others jogged up and took positions of their own behind the parked cars. Beckett went straight to the wounded officer, a Navajo man with a powerful build. "Benally!" he said anxiously. "You hang on, buddy, we'll get a medic right out here."

"I've already called for paramedics," the deputy next to Sam reported. "They won't come over here until the situation's under control."

"Then we'll have to get Benally to them," Beckett said. "Can he be moved?"

"Don't . . . don't worry about me . . ." Benally managed. "Just take out those sons of bitches."

"Don't worry about that," Beckett said, his face grim. "That's the whole idea."

A couple of the spirit attackers fired shots at once. In spite of the fact that they had no cover, they kept advancing, perhaps counting on their near invulnerability to conventional weapons to protect them. So far it had worked. Soon they'd be able to reach over the cars and pick off the defenders one by one.

At Beckett's command, the sheriff's officers, all armed with shotguns, rose and fired, then ducked again. Bullets chunked into the cars or spewed window glass, but the spirits' weapons were old and not made to shoot through steel. Sam waited until the cops were down and the return volley over, then risked another shot. The attackers' ranks had thinned—the bear, the woman, and four of the men were gone. But more seemed to be materializing behind them, in the woods, a kind of shadow army becoming flesh as he watched.

"Sheriff!" he called when he ducked back to safety. "We have a bigger problem than we thought!" He jerked a thumb over the BMW.

Beckett rose up to look, then dropped down again. "Appears as if you're right, Sam."

"You have more officers on the way?"

"Six more," Beckett said. "All carrying shotguns with rock salt shells. And if I didn't say it before, thanks for that little piece of advice."

"But there are still people watching the other sides of the building, right?"

"Our people are on that," one of the mall security guards said. She was a woman with an athletic build and short red hair. "I wish we knew about the rock salt ahead of time, though."

"I tried to tell Carla," Beckett said. He winced, as if he hadn't meant to reveal even that much, but then must have figured he'd already stepped in it. "But she didn't want you folks toting shotguns. Worried about how it'd look to the customers, I guess."

They could have made dumdum bullets like Baird had, Sam knew, but that was a time-consuming process, carving each one individually in a vise. Even if Beckett had tipped off Carla about that, her people wouldn't have had time to make very many.

Sam took another look at the new force gathering at the tree line. It looked like thirty or more of the spirit people and animals. *Better to look bad than be slaughtered*, he thought. He almost said it out loud, but decided that Jim Beckett and Carla Krug were going to have enough trouble once this was all over—if they lived through it—without him adding to it.

He fired a round, almost without aiming. There were enough spirits out there that he could hardly miss.

Two whining bullets slammed the BMW as he was ducking back behind it. Whoever owned that car was going to be very unhappy.

But maybe alive, Sam thought. *If we can hold this line*.

"Let's go," Dean said, shoving the EMF reader into his pocket and breaking into a sprint.

Passing the red SUV, he saw a body in the driveway, a man whose chest had been torn open. Entrails had been tugged from it and spread around, huge pink worms trailing on the snow. Closer to the house was another man in similar condition. Whatever had been happening here was seriously bad news.

The front door was locked. Already panting from the dead run, Dean backed up a step and aimed a hard, sharp kick just below the knob. "Oww!" he complained. The door was solid, heavy wood. He gave it one more shot, without success.

"Window!" he called to Baird, who had almost caught up. Most of the glass was already smashed out of it. Dean dashed to the window, put his hands on the frame and vaulted over it. His ankle, already hurting from the two kicks into the unmovable door, nearly buckled on landing, but he ignored the shooting pain and ran deeper into the house. From upstairs he could hear the sounds of a ferocious struggle. "Ma'am?" he called. "I'm here to help you!"

Only the crashing and thumping answered him. He hit the stairs at a run, aware that Baird was behind him, crawling with some difficulty through the broken window.

Before he reached the top of the stairs, he knew at least part of what was going on. Two men started toward him, spirit men, blinking between material and not. He recognized them—mostly by their wounds, gaping and familiar—as the men whose bodies he had passed outside. He was surprised they could have risen so fast, since most of the spirits he'd seen in town looked like those of people who had died during the nineteenth century.

This close to the witch's presumed burial ground, though, inside Witch's Canyon and maybe right on the site of her cabin, who knew how much power she still wielded?

Something was going on behind the spirit men, but he couldn't tell what. It involved a lot of thrashing and banging, and he thought he saw what looked like a dog's bushy tail, but then the men blocked his view again, both with empty hands grabbing for him, like they wanted to do to him barehanded what something had done to them.

Dean whipped the shotgun up and fired twice in rapid succession. The echo of the weapon in the narrow staircase rang in his ears, and the smoke stung his nostrils. When he blinked it away from his eyes, the two men were gone.

"Ma'am?" he said. The screaming voice he'd heard had definitely been female, and he thought he heard it again just as he pulled the trigger, shouting curses that would have impressed Dad.

The thrashing had quieted somewhat, although it hadn't stopped. "Ma'am!" he shouted again, louder. "I'm coming up!"

"Come on ahead," a woman called back. "Just be careful! It's not dead, but I think it's hurt!"

It? Dean pumped another shell into the chamber and climbed the remaining stairs more cautiously. Behind him, Baird called out, "What the hell's going on up there, Dean?"

"I'll find out and let you know," Dean promised.

At the top of the stairs he saw a woman standing inside a bedroom. In the doorway, a furry, bloody lump was covered in plastic, twitching and clawing at her. It was a canine of some kind, like a big German shepherd, with black markings on a coat of silver. A terrible stink of burned hair and plastic and God knew what else filled the hallway.

"It's a wolf," she said, and Dean realized it was Juliet Monroe, whom he and Sam had met at the Grand Canyon rim their first night in the area. Her dark curls were everywhere, and blood flecked her face and her sweat-drenched, tattered clothes, but she didn't appear to have suffered any major injuries.

"Juliet? It's me. Dean."

It took her a moment to place him. He couldn't help being upset by that. *She's been through a trauma*, he thought. *And it's not over yet.* "We met at the Canyon."

"Dean. Right, I'm sorry. This has been—this has been a strange few days. You wouldn't believe it."

"You might be surprised."

The big animal on the floor in front of her twitched again, trying to rise. Dean couldn't be certain through the half-melted plastic sheeting stuck to it, but it might have vanished for a split second.

"That's a wolf," he said, her words just sinking in. "But not a real one."

"I don't think so."

The spirit animal shook its big shaggy head and tried to snap at Juliet. "What did you do to it?"

"I set it on fire," she said. "Then I hit it with this." She showed him a metal rod about four feet long, with arrow points on the ends. One of them was crusted with blood and tufts of fur.

"Is that iron?" he asked.

"I think so. Wrought iron."

"Iron's a powerful weapon against magical creatures," he said. "So is fire. If you had salted it, you probably could have destroyed it altogether."

"Magical creatures?" She lowered the rod again and blinked at him. "And you're some kind of expert on that? How did you happen to come by here, anyway?"

"Let me finish this thing off first, then I'll tell you all about it," Dean said. "We have one other thing to take care of, which we need to do fast. Are you really attached to your ground floor?"

"What?"

He didn't answer, just shoved the muzzle of his shotgun under the plastic sheet, pressing it against the big wolf's flank. "This is gonna be loud," he said.

Juliet turned away, plugging her ears.

Dean squeezed the trigger.

The gun roared, flame spitting rock salt into the animal. It reared and bucked once, then vanished. All that remained was the melted plastic sheeting. Even the blood disappeared from the floor, the walls, and Juliet's clothing.

"It's all gone," Dean said. "Now, about that floor . . ."

THIRTY-NINE

The parking lot had become a war zone. Most of the cars in the back row were trashed, their windows and lights blown out, fenders knocked off, tires flattened, bodies riddled with holes. Spent shell casings littered the ground behind them, where the sheriff's officers, security guards, and Sam sought shelter.

At the forest's edge, the scene stayed relatively pristine, because the spirit army's soldiers just disappeared when they were destroyed, taking with them every sign of their existence.

Three of the defenders were wounded now, and Sam had begun to think that Benally wouldn't pull through. At a crouch, he skittered over beside Beckett. "We need to get Benally to the paramedics," he said. "He's looking bad."

"I know," Beckett said. "But they've really got us pinned down. If we lift him—"

"I know," Sam echoed. "I'll take the chance, if there's someone who can help me."

"I will, sir." It was the redheaded security guard. "I'll take his feet if you take his shoulders. I think we should keep him as flat as we can."

"Agreed," Sam said. He turned back to the sheriff. "You guys be okay without us for a few?"

"Get Benally some help," Beckett said. "We'll be just fine."

A bullet tore into the vehicle they were hiding behind, spraying window glass over them, as if to put the lie to Beckett's words. Sam thought the bullet was more right than Beckett was. The attackers kept coming, more all the time, and had started moving to flank the line of parked cars.

Dean, I hope you're there, he thought for about the hundredth time.

"Come on," he said to the security guard. He crab-walked over to Benally, and she went with him. "We're going to get you some medical help, Benally," he said. Benally blinked a couple of times but didn't answer. He hadn't spoken for a while.

Sam squatted behind the officer and shoved his hands beneath him, lifting him by the underarms. The guard grabbed his ankles. Together, they managed to lift the heavy officer several inches off the ground. Carrying him while hunched low themselves was harder than if they'd been able to stand up, putting enormous strain on their backs. But standing would have meant being shot.

Sam gave a grunt and started walking backward,

still at a crouch to keep his head below the protective wall of vehicles. Even so, a bullet whistled past him, a near miss, fired between two trucks. He almost dropped Benally, then firmed up his grip. "I can go faster," the security guard said.

"Okay," Sam said. He was heading backward blindly, not sure how much faster he could go. But he was willing to try.

Benally had the upper torso of a bodybuilder, and Sam realized that he was doing the lion's share of the hauling. He didn't object, but he hoped he'd be able to walk upright again once the task was done.

Sam saw that more uniformed security guards had taken up stations at the door to the mall, keeping people from wandering out into the battlefield. So rather than carrying the wounded man through the mall, they took him around the corner to the south side, where ambulances waited at the loading docks. Paramedics rushed to help, relieving them of their burden and setting to work immediately on Benally.

Sam stretched to work the kinks out of his back. Fully extended, he was far taller than the redheaded guard, who topped out at less than five and a half feet. She popped her back with a loud crack and gave him a bashful grin. "Thanks for helping," he said.

"No problem," she replied. She was about to say something else, but then her face took on a serious demeanor as she listened to her earpiece. Although she had been flushed from the exertion, the color drained from her face. "It's Ms. Krug," she said. "She and the mayor are cornered in her office."

Sam didn't wait for more details. So far the trouble had largely confined itself to outside the mall, with that one initial exception. He had hoped it would stay that way. Dad always impressed upon his sons the necessity of keeping the things they hunted secret. To do otherwise, to publicize them, would terrify the general public. And it would turn the world's accepted knowledge on its head, for no useful purpose. It might even strengthen the bad things, some of which fed off people's beliefs and fears.

If they had gotten inside the mall, while most of the law officers and security guards were outside . . . then it was up to him to deal with them.

He'd left his bag of weapons back at the cars, intending to go straight back after delivering Benally. He had tucked his sawed-off into a deep inside jacket pocket and had a couple of extra rock salt shells on him, but that was all.

The redheaded guard had less than that, though— just the Beretta she'd been issued that morning.

Sam took off at a run without waiting for further elaboration. The guards at the exit were focused on keeping people out, but one saw him coming and opened a door for him. He sprinted through, reversing his previous course, and took the stairs three at a time.

People still milled around the mall, although the sounds of happy, expectant shoppers had been replaced by those of virtual prisoners complaining about being locked in. Smoking was forbidden inside the building, but apparently that rule wasn't being enforced, and Sam raced through pockets of cigarette smoke. As he did, he heard arguments that threatened to turn into outright brawls. These people had to be let out soon or the bloodshed would be strictly human on human.

At the hallway that led past the restrooms and security office and down to Carla's, he encountered the first of the spirit attackers, a rawboned woman with the imprint of hands bruising her throat and her head cocked at an unnatural angle. As she turned to face Sam, he saw that her left eye had been poked out, dangling against her cheek by a thread of ocular nerve.

Violent death was never pretty. This unfortunate woman's, though, had been exceedingly ugly and unpleasant. Her mouth opened, jaw shuddering, as if she wanted to say something to him. Her remaining eye was mournful, but her hands were already clutching at him, eager to reenact her demise.

From behind her, Sam could hear anxious shouts and loud thumps that he guessed came from Carla and Mayor Milner. He hated to waste one of his shells on this single spirit. He knew she was beyond pain, so although part of him flinched away from causing her any more than she'd already suffered, he made a dash past her. She lunged at him as he went by, and he snapped a kick at her knee while she was off balance. She flashed bright black light at him, phased out momentarily, and collapsed on the hallway floor.

By the time she fell, he was shoving through the

door to the receptionist's office. It was crowded with
the dead, some of whom were beating on the door to
the inner office, beyond which Sam could hear the
voices of the mayor and the shopping center manager. The now familiar stink of death permeated the
small space.

Sam raised his shotgun, knowing that at this range
he could destroy several of them. But as his finger
tightened on the trigger, another materialized right
beside him, a burly, bearded guy who could have
played the blacksmith in any western movie ever
made. The spirit man caught the barrel of Sam's gun
and wrenched it from his hands before Sam even reg-
istered his appearance.

The guy grinned—an oddly redundant expression,
because a jagged cut across his throat already smiled
redly—and hurled the shotgun out the open front
door, into the hall. Sam tried to snag it from the air,
but the toss was too high and fast.

The spirit folk turned away from the inner door,
fixated on this new and suddenly unarmed oppo-
nent. Sam counted nine of them. A couple held guns,
some had knives or other edged weapons, while a
few, like the woman in the hall, were empty-handed.
The blacksmith spirit, brandishing a rusty straight
razor, stepped between Sam and the open doorway.

This is not going well, Sam thought.

One of the knife-wielders, a young man barely
out of his teens, if that, sliced the air toward him,
mouth dropping open in silent fury. Sam dodged the
attack but came within range of another spirit man,

who clubbed the side of his head with two huge fists. Sam saw stars, stumbled, and caught himself on the receptionist's desk before he fell. The moment gave his opponents time to swarm over him, though, and they pummeled him with fists and feet. A knife blade caught his left shoulder, cutting through jacket and flesh.

Sam caught the wrist of the woman who had cut him, bending it back until she dropped the weapon. He scooped it up, remembering the grizzly that had been destroyed with its own spear. She tried to back away but he pushed through hands that tried to restrain him and sank it into her chest.

She flickered and disappeared. He had hoped to hang onto the knife, but it vanished at the same instant. He would have remembered that if he hadn't been taking punishment from a dozen sources at once. A gunshot went off, barely missing him and passing through two of his opponents without injuring them.

To get a moment's respite, he worked his way toward the front of the reception desk, where a rolling chair was tucked into the knee well. Another blade of some kind jabbed into his ribs but he writhed away before it could sink dangerously deep. He flailed out with his fists, battering the spirit people back far enough to let him make his move. Kicking the chair away, he ducked into the knee well.

There, he allowed himself one quick breath, relishing the brief moment when the fists of the long-dead didn't batter him. He knew he'd have to put a quick end to this. Their blows were starting to weaken him, and though he'd avoided any mortal wounds so far, there was no telling how long that would hold.

To give himself room to work, he pressed his hands and shoulders into the knee well of the wooden desk and pushed off with his feet, standing suddenly and raising the heavy desk as he did. He spun it around to knock away the nearest of the spirits, then threw it with every ounce of strength he could muster.

It didn't hurt any of those it hit, but it did knock a few down and pinned one against the far wall.

Mostly, what it did was give him a little space. He reached into his pocket, yanked out a spare rock salt shell, and tore it open. Gripping the primer end, he swung his hand in a wide, fast arc. Rock salt sprayed everywhere. The dead screamed soundlessly as it hit them, and the room filled with their freakish fluttering glows as they vanished.

When it was over, there were only three left, including the blacksmith with the razor. Sam reached for another shell but the blacksmith caught his right hand before he could pull it from his pocket. With his left hand, Sam caught the blacksmith's left—the one holding the razor. Both men struggled, and for a second Sam worried that the blacksmith would prove too strong. But he managed to turn the razor's rusted blade toward the man, and then jerked his head forward, butting into their locked hands and driving the blade into the blacksmith's chest.

The man released him and fell back, clutching at his fresh wound. The razor sailed from his hand. Sam grabbed it up, sliced it through the next nearest spirit—accomplishing nothing that he could determine—and kept it moving, slicing it across the blacksmith's throat on a line similar to the one that had caused his first death.

The other two, a Native American woman and a Hispanic man who held the only remaining firearm in the room, backed away from him. The woman clutched a crude stone knife that would do her no good at that range, but Sam got the sense that the man just wanted enough distance to aim and fire his rifle.

He still had a shell in his pocket, though. Before the man could level the weapon at him, Sam tore into it and scattered its contents at the two spirit people. They reacted as the others had.

After the light show, the room was empty.

Breathing heavily, Sam tapped on the inner office door. "It's all clear," he said.

Someone on the inside was turning the knob when the dead woman from the hallway appeared in the outer doorway, holding Sam's shotgun. She aimed it and pulled the trigger.

FORTY

"Ross always called it the 'dead zone,'" Juliet said. She was leading Dean and Baird to a section of her backyard. "Because nothing would ever grow there."

It all looked like snow to Dean. She seemed to realize the same thing, because she stopped and shoved a mass of curls away from her face. "It's right around here," she said. "It's just bare earth, no grass or anything. Not even weeds would come up there, and they're unstoppable here after the summer rains."

She, Dean, and Baird all held shovels hastily gathered from the barn. "Guess we shovel some snow first," he said. He dug his tool's blade under the snow and tossed aside a little of it. More fell into the gap he had made. "Thing's not a very good snow shovel, though."

"There's one of those in the barn, too," Juliet said. "Do you want me to—"

"Never mind. We just have to move enough to locate this dead zone. From your description, it sounds like the witch's burial site to me."

"The previous owners pointed it out to us but said they couldn't explain it, either," Juliet said. "They showed us the outline of an old cabin's foundation here—you can still see some of the stones when they're not covered in snow." She pointed toward one side of her house. "The cabin would have been about there, just beside the current house. This would have been—what?—forty feet away."

"Far enough for a grave site, I guess. If you weren't too picky." Dean dragged his shovel across the ground, pushing snow away. He could see the bare dirt beneath it now, right where she'd said it was. It didn't even look like healthy dirt. No insects had made holes in it, no worms had aerated it, in more than a hundred years.

"Gotta be the place," he said. "Let's dig." He shoved the blade almost straight down into the dirt, pressing it deeper with his foot.

As he did, a vulture with huge black wings and a knobby pink head swooped toward him from nowhere, talons out. He ducked and it whistled just over his head, then flapped away with great wing beats.

"Ugly-ass buzzard almost parted my hair," he said, turning out the earth he had dug up. His shotgun was close at hand; he didn't have any illusions that the vulture would be the witch's last defender.

Nor were his expectations wrong.

The three of them had been digging for several minutes when four arrows *thwipped* toward them. Dean released his shovel—an arrow quavering in its wooden handle—and dove for the shotgun. He rolled into a prone firing position, located the attackers and fired twice. When the smoke cleared and the sound of the shots faded, the four were gone. Dean rose, scanned for any more spirit attackers, and reached for his shovel again.

Harmon Baird fell across the dead zone. "I'm hit," he said, his voice strained. He turned so Dean could see the arrow jutting from his left thigh. "It's just a flesh wound."

"Flesh wound my ass," Dean said. He handed the shotgun to Juliet and went to the old man's side. Baird was trembling, his eyes filling with tears. Dean turned his leg, looking at both sides. The arrow hadn't passed all the way through. He grabbed the arrow's shaft, right where it met the man's leg. "This is gonna hurt," he warned. Pressing down on Baird's thigh, he tugged the arrow free, back out the way it had gone in.

Baird shrieked and clawed at his leg. Dean kept one hand there, pressing down on the wound until Baird stopped writhing. "Keep pressure on it," Dean said. "We'll get you patched up as soon as we can, but right now we've got to finish this."

He and Juliet returned to digging while Baird stood watch—*sat* watch, rather—with Dean's shotgun across his lap.

"The witch's spirits must be busy somewhere else," Dean said as they worked. "I thought we'd have a lot more trouble than this."

"Maybe she was counting on the wolf defeating us," Juliet replied.

"Wolf couldn't even take you," Dean said with a smile. "It—"

His shovel *chunked* against something hard. "I think we're there."

"Not a minute too soon for me," Juliet said.

"You got her?" Baird asked.

"I think so." Dean threw more dirt out of the hole, and scraped his shovel across the hard surface. "It's wood."

"At least they buried her in a coffin," Juliet said. "From what you told me I half expected they'd just throw her into a hole."

"She may have been a nasty old witch, but she was still the ranch owner's mother," Dean speculated. "If he'd hated her that much, he never would have brought her out from back East, much less built a special place for her."

"I thought that was because he didn't want her around."

"He probably didn't. But it also helped keep her out of trouble, by eliminating most of her contact with other people. Isolating her here probably didn't do much for the fact that she was bug-nut crazy, but it kept her from exposing her craziness to everyone around."

"I suppose that's true," Juliet said. "That's why

Ross liked the place, too. Our refuge from the world, he said."

"Sometimes getting away from the world is a great idea."

"You bet it is!" Baird called. He had both hands pressed so hard against his wounded thigh that the back of the upper hand was almost white. "Startin' to be sorry I ever left my place."

"You," Dean said, "have been a lifesaver. In more ways than you'll ever know."

He and Juliet had cleared the top of the coffin, which was in remarkably pristine shape for such an old box. *Protected by her magic*, Dean thought. He could hardly remember being so anxious for something to be over.

"Okay," he said to Juliet. He drew Dad's journal from a coat pocket. "I'm going to be reading her a bedtime story—a counterspell that should negate her spell once and for all." With his other hand he drew out a metal flask, a box of matches, and the bag of salt. "You need to open that box, then pour this salt on her bones. Then dump this flask on her—it's gasoline. Light a match, toss it on, and stand back, because even though there's not a lot here, it's going to go up fast."

He'd been intending for Baird to do that part, but the old man was out of the picture now as far as any demanding physical activity went.

"Got it," she said. "Open, salt, gas, match."

"I already know you've got a little human torch in you," he added with a grin.

"Maybe just a tad."

He located the counterspell and started to read out loud. "'Witch's spell, so long since cast, I'm here to tell, your time is past.'" He caught Juliet's eye. *Go,* he mouthed.

Juliet squinted, bit down on her lower lip, and grabbed the coffin's lid in both hands, reaching awkwardly into the hole they had dug. She pulled, but it wouldn't give.

"'Witch's spell, that's ruled the night,'" Dean continued, "'hear my knell, which brings the light.'"

Juliet gave a mighty yank, and the coffin swung open.

She screamed, and Dean looked up from the book.

A cloud of smoke and dust, glowing as if from some inward fire, billowed up out of the coffin.

Damn it, he thought, *she wasn't done after all.*

And his shotgun was all the way across the grave, on the lap of Harmon Baird, whose eyes had never been so wide in his life.

As the trio watched, the cloud coalesced into a feminine form, seemingly made of luminous sulfuric dust and smoke. She was a crone, an ancient, wizened woman, hunched and twisted with rage and hatred. Her clothing was barely more than rags, and it blew in a cold wind that erupted from beneath, from her grave. The wind buffeted her stringy hair. It carried a foul ozone smell, like electricity passing through burned flesh.

The apparition reached taloned hands toward Dean, who kept reading as fast as he could. The wind tried

to tear the pages from his grasp, and he had to hold on
with both hands, fighting to keep his feet.

"'Witch's spell, of evil unknown,'" he shouted,
"'cannot repel salt 'pon your bone!'"

He nodded to Juliet, who stood back away from
the grave. *Afraid to get anywhere near that freakin'
witch*, Dean thought. *I don't blame her.*

But he couldn't hang onto the book and get the salt.
He wasn't sure he could even take a step—if he tried,
the hurricane-force wind might blow him away.

Come on, Juliet! Salt the bitch!

The icy wind blew into his mouth when he opened
it to read again, distorting his cheeks. Fine dust stung
his eyes, his skin.

And the witch's claws were almost on him now.
Would she be able to snatch the book away from
him? Kill him with a touch?

The shotgun roared, and the witch let out a scream
that almost made Dean's ear bleed, a scream like a
jet engine just inches from his head.

On the other side of the grave, Baird had found
his feet and his courage. "You like that, Miz Marbrough?" he asked. "'Cause I got more of it!"

The witch whirled away from Dean and rushed at
Baird. Her unearthly wind caught his clothes, flut-
tering them like laundry on the line in a tornado.
"Juliet!" Dean called. "The salt!"

Juliet heard him, awareness snapping into her eyes,
and she braved the wind and the miasmic cloud that
still issued from the grave. She dumped the bag of
salt. Some of it blew away, but enough fell in.

The witch shrieked again.

"'Witch's spell!'" Dean shouted. The wind tore at his clothes, his hair, trying to drive him away from the grave. Other people might have fallen, but he locked his knees, kept his feet planted and leaned into it. He wasn't going to let the witch win, because he was a Winchester, and the Winchesters were made to fight battles like this. "The gas, Juliet! 'So late interned!'"

Juliet turned the flask over. Wind whipped some of the liquid up instead of letting it fall, but more pushed through, into the coffin.

The witch had reached Harmon Baird and batted away the shotgun like it was a twig. Baird's eyes were windows showing the mortal terror in his soul, but he swiped at her with his hands, trying to hold her off. At least, that was what Dean thought at first.

Then, as he spoke the last lines of the counterspell, he realized the truth—Baird was holding onto the witch, preventing her from attacking him or Juliet directly. He wasn't flailing at her. His hands jerked and spasmed because she did, writhing with the pain of the salt on her skeleton.

Juliet struck a match, and the wind blew it out. Hands shaking, she opened the box again. Matches spewed from it. She caught one.

"'Now all's well; your bones be burned!'" Dean screamed against the pounding gusts.

As he spoke the spell's final words, Juliet dropped the match.

Nothing happened.

Dean almost had time to formulate a curse in his mind, but before it had fully formed, the cold grave wind turned hot, flame blasting from below as if the wind had turned into propane. The flame enveloped Elizabeth Claire Marbrough, or her disembodied spirit, and she screamed once more, in mortal agony. Juliet fell on her butt in the snow, singed but alive.

Baird had already fallen. His hands were still hooked into claws, his eyes staring at the sky. Trails of blood ran from his mouth, nose, and ears.

"Harmon," Juliet said. "Is he—"

"He shouldn't have touched her," Dean said, taking her hand and helping her to her feet. "It was too much for him."

"But he stopped her—"

"That's right." Dean couldn't feel guilt—the old man had known he might not survive this adventure, but he'd wanted to stop what he called the forty-year at any price. Still, not feeling guilt brought some guilt of its own. "If he hadn't hung onto her, she might have reached me or you. Either of which would have stopped us cold. She'd still be here—and out of her grave, which looks like it was magically sealed against her escape. And her forces would still be overrunning Cedar Wells, and you and I . . . well, we'd be where Harmon is."

Tears trickled down her cheeks as she regarded the dead man. Blood had already stopped pulsing from the arrow wound in his leg. The skin of his face and hands was red and chafed, as if he'd been caught in a blizzard.

"I don't . . . really know what to say, Dean. I mean . . . thank you sounds so lame. So insufficient."

"Thank him," Dean said. "This is what I do. He's the one who volunteered."

The flames inside the grave had died to a steady crackle. Black smoke rose from the box, where the day's gentle breeze—a natural breeze—caught and dispersed it. Dean reached in with the shovel and flipped the coffin shut, then started tossing dirt down onto it. "Help me bury her again?" he asked. "I need to get back out to the road. My brother'll have no idea where the hell we are."

"Our position was being overrun," Jim Beckett explained. "Some of those with guns had us pinned down from the woods, but then more of them came at us from the flanks, with arrows and spears and swords and clubs and what have you. We were shooting so fast we could hardly touch our guns to reload, they were so hot. I thought we were done for."

"And then they vanished?" Sam asked. He knew the answer before he spoke.

He and Dean were sitting at a corner table in the Wagon Wheel Café with Beckett and Juliet Monroe. The Winchester brothers would hit the road in the morning—there seemed to be something strange going on in the Northwest, and they wanted to check it out—but the lawman wanted to buy them a meal before they left. Juliet had taken a room at the motel since she didn't want to spend the night in her house, so Dean had invited her along.

The restaurant was almost empty. It seemed most people in Cedar Wells were sticking pretty close to home, even though the threat had passed.

Maybe, Sam thought, because *the threat has passed. They're just glad to be safe with their families.*

The same went for him.

"That's right," Beckett answered, "they vanished. One second we were surrounded, and I was thinking how much it would stink to die in such a freaky way. The next, they were gone, and we were pointing our guns at empty air."

"What about you, Sam?" Juliet asked. "Where were you?"

"I had just knocked on Carla Krug's door to tell her and the mayor that the coast was clear. Mayor Milner was starting to open the door when one of them fired my own shotgun at me. Of course, it was just rock salt." He shared a conspiratorial grin. "Milner screamed like a girl when it hit the door, though. I told them that she couldn't kill us with my gun—she had to kill the way she'd been killed, which was strangulation. But he locked the door again and wouldn't come out. I didn't want to have to strangle her, especially since I knew the rock salt would sting like hell, and could really hurt me at close range, but I was headed for her when she disappeared."

"Milner wouldn't open the door until I told him it was okay," Beckett added. "Even though Carla was begging him to by then."

"Did you come up with some kind of story to tell the people at the mall?" Dean asked.

"Donald and I worked one up," Beckett said. "But by the time we got out to tell it, there was already a story going around. Armed robbers, trying to get the mall's opening day take."

"That doesn't make sense on so many levels," Sam said. He cut into his steak. Medium rare, still the slightest bit of pink in the middle. "But I guess it doesn't need to."

"People had convinced themselves of it," Beckett said. "They were explaining it to me, like I'm not the sheriff or something. Like I wasn't in the middle of it."

"Better than them knowing the truth," Dean said. "Even though it'd be nice if we could tell them about Baird's sacrifice."

"You said he didn't even really like the town," Juliet said. "Maybe he'd be just as happy without them turning him into some kind of hero."

"Maybe." Dean lifted his bottle of beer off the table, held it up. "To Harmon Baird, anyway."

Sam tipped his bottle against Dean's. Beckett raised his iced tea, Juliet her white wine, and they all clinked together. "To Harmon Baird."

Sam wasn't surprised that Dean would let Baird have all the credit. Baird and Juliet, really—he had stressed her role, and her almost impossible courage, from the beginning. Dean was an amazing guy, Sam knew, with skills and abilities most people would never even imagine, and smarts Dean himself wouldn't credit, even though he relied on them all the time. And yet, at times like this, he was so humble, so unassuming, that he seemed almost unaware of the importance of his own contributions.

At other times, of course, that humility vanished. Knowing and accepting both Deans, he guessed, was what being brothers was all about. *Maybe I wouldn't want to be Dean*, he thought. *But I'm sure glad I have him around.*

"What about you, Juliet?" he asked, largely to take his mind off his big brother before he choked himself up. *That would be embarrassing as hell*, he knew, *and Dean would never let me forget it.* "You going to tell prospective buyers there's a witch buried on your property?"

Juliet took a swallow of wine and put the glass down. "Forget about prospective buyers," she said, chuckling. "I fought for that place. I'll never sell it now."

"You're staying in town?" Beckett asked.

"If the town will have me. I don't think I want to be quite as isolated as Elizabeth Marbrough was, but—"

"I know the town would be happy to have you around, ma'am," Beckett said. "As would I."

Sam caught Dean's eye. Dean's shrug was barely noticeable: a slight shifting of the shoulders, a minute pressing together of the lips. His eyes lit up with a secret smile.

Dean had been thinking about asking Juliet out, Sam knew. He'd been around his brother long enough to read those signs loud and clear. They only had the one night left in town, but Dean could work fast when he had to. And her motel room was only three doors down from theirs, after all.

With the shrug, Dean told him that it didn't matter. There would be other women, maybe even other beautiful young widows. *Let the sheriff have this one*, Dean's smile had said.

"We should . . . call it a night," Sam said, scooting his chair back.

Dean caught his meaning and nodded his agreement. "Yeah, that's right. We've got to get an early start in the morning."

"We can get the tab," Sam offered. Just to be polite; Sheriff Beckett had already told them it was his treat. That was just as well, since he didn't really want to commit credit card fraud while buying a meal for an officer of the law.

"No, it's mine," Beckett said. He and Juliet both rose from the table, but without giving any indication that they planned to leave yet.

"If you're sure," Dean said.

"Absolutely. I'll expense it, anyway, and Donald Milner won't dare say a damn thing about it."

Sam and Dean took turns shaking the sheriff's hand and hugging Juliet, then they headed out the front door, into the chill night air. The Impala was parked right in front. When Sam had first told Dean about the firefight in the parking lot, Dean was afraid that his precious car had been caught in the middle.

"She's really pretty," Sam said as he climbed in the passenger seat. "You sure you don't mind letting the sheriff take a crack at her?"

"Everything you said, he's a brave man," Dean replied. "He'll need every bit of courage he can find. That one's a handful, I can tell you that. In the best possible way. She's full of life, and honestly, I think she might be a little too much for me."

Sam regarded his brother. In the dark he was harder to read, but then he leaned forward, cranked the engine and burst into laughter. A Bad Company tape blared. "Anyway," Dean said when he could speak again, "we're leaving town, and I didn't want to break her heart." He pulled into the street and started toward the motel. "Seemed like the right thing to do."

About the Author

Jeff Mariotte has written more than thirty novels, including the supernatural thriller *Missing White Girl* (as Jeffrey J. Mariotte), the original horror epic *The Slab*, and the Stoker Award–nominated teen horror series *Witch Season*, as well as books set in the universes of *Las Vegas*, *Buffy the Vampire Slayer*, *Angel*, *Conan*, *30 Days of Night*, *Charmed*, *Star Trek*, and *Andromeda*. Two of his tie-in novels were nominated for the first annual Scribe Awards presented by the International Association of Media Tie-in Writers. He is also the author of many comic books, including the original western/horror series *Desperadoes*, some of which have been nominated for Stoker and International Horror Guild awards. With his wife, Maryelizabeth Hart, and partner Terry Gilman, he co-owns Mysterious Galaxy, a bookstore specializing in science fiction, fantasy, mystery, and horror. He lives with his family and pets on the Flying M Ranch in the American Southwest, a place filled with books, music, toys, and other products of American pop culture. More information than you would ever want to know about him is at www.jeffmariotte.com.